ENJOY THE DANCE

Heidi Cullinan

Dance with your heart, and love will follow.

Kindergarten teacher Spenser Harris has carved a quiet, stable future out of his tumultuous past, but his world turns upside down the night a homeless teen appears on his doorstep—a boy whose story mirrors the one Spenser has worked so hard to overcome. The decision to shelter Duon is easy. What's tricky is juggling the network of caregivers in Duon's life, especially Tomás Jimenez.

Tomás wouldn't have hesitated to take Duon in, but his plate is already full working three jobs to support his family. Though Spenser's carefully constructed walls are clearly designed to keep the world at bay, Tomás pushes past Spenser's defenses, determined to ensure the man is worthy of his charge. As the two of them grow closer, Tomás dares to dream of a life beyond his responsibilities, and Spenser begins to believe he might finally find a home of his own after all.

But Spenser and Tomás's world is poised to crash around their ears. Duon's grandmother isn't sure she wants him to be raised by a gay man and challenges Spenser's custody. Tomás's undocumented parents could be deported at any time, and all the while the state of Minnesota votes on a constitutional amendment against marriage equality and the US Supreme Court debates whether or not Spenser and Tomás get a happily ever after. All they can do is hold tight to their love, hope for a better future…and remind each other to enjoy the dance.

Heidi Cullinan, POB 425, Ames, Iowa 50010
Copyright © 2016 by Heidi Cullinan
Print ISBN: 978-0-9961203-7-1
Print Edition
Edited by Sasha Knight
Cover by Kanaxa
Proofing by Lillie's Literary Services
Formatting by BB eBooks

First publication 2016
www.heidicullinan.com

For Vonnie

Many thanks to

Katherine DuGarm for her Bryant-Lake Bowl research field trip

Inez Garcia, Pamela Bartual, LaQuette, Laura Adriana, and Dan Cullinan for beta reading

Twitter for all the random help and general support

Ryan Berg for information on the host home program at Avenues

My patrons, especially Erin Sharpe, Sarah M., Sarah Plunkett, Ashley Dugan, Rosie M., Karin Wollina, Pamela Bartual, and Susan Lee. I would be lost without your love and support.

There is pain and sacrifice in everyone's world. That's why, when I was dancing, I had no pain.

—Suzanne Farrell

CHAPTER ONE

October 11, 2012
Minneapolis, Minnesota

ONE COOL OCTOBER day, after a dispiriting seven hours of teaching privileged kindergarten children, Spenser Harris returned to his apartment to discover a teenage boy—battered, bruised, and coiled into a ball—in front of his door.

Spenser had learned to expect any number of unexpected happenings in his neighborhood, but nothing like this. His apartment building was old, but not run-down. It wasn't quaint enough to attract hipsters but not so low-rent it drew a bad element. People of all cultures lived there, and in the evenings a walk to the laundry room was a world tour of food smells. The family across from Spenser was Mexican by heritage, and the older couple who lived at the end of the hall was Ukrainian. A large percentage of the second and third floors were occupied by Somali immigrants, some who had been in Minnesota for a decade or longer, some who had arrived recently. The family who lived above him was in the latter category, and they argued loudly in a language Spenser didn't understand. The neighborhood had its off-color aspects, yes, but nothing to worry about. A drunk had taken up the habit of sleeping in the vestibule last winter when he couldn't make it all the way home, but he'd simply snored and sometimes vomited. Loud music from cars on the street was a common complaint. But it had never been unsafe, not for the residents or the people living around it.

It hadn't brought him a young man clutching a half-full black garbage bag, bleeding and trembling in the dim, flickering light of the hall.

A boy. He's only a boy.

He was Black, and so at first Spenser assumed he was from a family upstairs, but a closer inspection revealed Spenser hadn't seen anyone like him in the building before. He was dressed like a thrift-store music video, whereas Spenser's new-to-Minnesota Somali neighbors and their friends favored conservative clothes. Spenser couldn't begin to guess who the boy was or why he was here. But when his eyes accustomed to the dim light and saw the extent of the bruises on the young man's face and hands, the blood from his cuts dripping onto the floor, all thoughts of where he'd come from ceased.

Crouching, Spenser stayed several feet away, not wanting to frighten him. "Hey there. Can I help you?"

The boy startled despite Spenser's gentle approach,

and when he lifted his head, Spenser's gut twisted as he got a full view of the damage to his face. One eye was completely swollen shut, and the other was a slit. His upper lip was split, rendering the boy's words barely legible as he spoke. "Waiting for Tomás."

Spenser was fairly sure Tomás was the younger man in the Jimenez family across the hall, the one Spenser's age, not the older man with streaks of silver in his hair who always smiled and wished Spenser good morning with a heavy Spanish accent. "He usually doesn't get home until after eight. Are his parents not in?"

The boy's gaze flickered warily in the direction of the apartment. "Parents? He don't live alone?"

Speaking the *p* made the boy's lip bleed, and Spenser put down his satchel, fishing for a package of tissues. He pulled one out and passed it and the packet to the young man. "Yes. Tomás lives with his parents. I think his sister and her children live there too, at least some of the time." He frowned as the boy bled faster than the tissues could sop it up. "I think you need to be seen by a doctor."

The young man shrank into the door. "No hospital."

Spenser didn't push the issue. Yet. "Will you wait for Tomás inside my apartment with me, at least?"

The boy still seemed unsure, but he also looked exhausted. He surveyed Spenser critically with his good eye, clearly trying to get a read.

Still crouched, Spenser moved a step closer and held out his hand. "Spenser Harris. Pleased to meet you."

"Duon Graves." He accepted Spenser's handshake with a weak, battered grip. "You let me in, I'll bleed on your floor."

"I don't care about that." Spenser rose, tugging gently on Duon. "Come on. Up you go."

"Why you so chill about somebody bleeding out, blocking your door? Might be a gangbanger. Might steal all your stuff."

Spenser's lock was a bitch to open on a good day, and it was significantly more of a struggle with an armful of bleeding teen. "Honey, I'm a teacher. I don't have any *stuff* to steal."

Duon tried to laugh, but the effort made him cough and wince in pain.

The lock cried uncle, and Spenser pushed open the door, leaving the keys in place as he ushered Duon inside and settled him at a chair at the table. His injuries were more alarming in the light, and Spenser debated calling 911 then and there. Instead, he rolled up his sleeves and washed his hands briskly at the sink. "Can I get you something to drink?"

"I'm good." Duon coughed again, glancing around the apartment. "You keep a nice place. Neat and tidy. Homey."

The *homey* comment stroked something inside Spenser. He smiled as he pulled the first-aid kit from the top of the freezer, setting it aside as he filled a bowl with warm water and removed the paper towels from their holder beneath the cabinet, then carried the whole business to the table. "I do what I can."

"You live by yourself? No roommate, no live-in girlfriend?" Duon narrowed his good eye at Spenser, then ventured, "Boyfriend?"

Spenser faltered as he removed a pair of gloves from the small box inside the kit. "I live alone. Do you have a latex allergy?"

Duon's mouth thinned as he watched Spenser struggle with the gloves. "No. I don't have AIDS either."

"Gloves are standard first-aid universal precautions, and you have open wounds." Spenser surveyed the battle-ridden landscape of the boy before him. He decided to begin with his hands, though they were less injured. He wanted to let Duon warm up to the idea of being touched by a stranger, in case it made him nervous.

Spenser kept up get-to-know-you chatter as he coached Duon patiently through cleaning up first one arm, then the other. "I teach at St. Anthony's Catholic School. Kindergarten. My third year teaching full-time."

"You just out of college? Look older."

Spenser snorted as he dabbed antiseptic over a particularly ugly bruise Duon couldn't reach, gently holding his patient's arm in place as he winced. "I'm twenty-eight." He eyed Duon's left cheek as he dipped a towel into the water. "I'm going to clean your face. Is that all right?"

Duon nodded, a tight jerk of his head. He winced and focused on a point across the room as Spenser carefully cleaned his face. "You gay, right?"

Spenser paused. His gut instinct was to refuse to answer, but something about the dogged way Duon went after it made his panic falter. "Would it be a problem if I were?"

Duon stared back, unflinching. "Would it be if *I* were?"

Ah. Spenser resumed his ministrations. "Of course it wouldn't matter."

"Well, I am."

Spenser only hesitated long enough to draw a steadying breath. "Me too."

Duon flinched as Spenser began to clean his more swollen eye. "You should date Tomás. He's gay too. Never has a boyfriend, but I know he wants one."

Spenser fought a blush. He *had* noticed Tomás was handsome, and yes, he'd entertained fantasies about asking him out. But that was all the further he'd allowed himself to consider the matter. "He works a lot. I don't think he has time to date."

"Some good man should force him to *make* time."

Spenser opened his mouth to answer, then bit his lip as his gentle pats inspired a cut below Duon's eye to begin bleeding again. "You need stitches, Duon."

"I'll get those butterfly things the boxers wear. I'll be fine."

Spenser decided it was time he pressed for some real answers. He wanted to ask about how Duon got his injuries, but on instinct he adopted a more casual approach. "So. You know Tomás well?"

"Yeah. He teaches dance at the studio where I go."

"Tomás teaches dance?"

Duon smiled enough to nearly reopen his lip. "Thinking about him in tights? A dance belt?"

Spenser was now. He made a production of peeling off a new towel, dampening it, and wringing it out. "I don't know him well. I've only met him in the hall a few times."

"He teaches modern dance. He's pretty good, but everyone who works there is. The guy who owns the studio used to be a big-time dancer. Laurence Parker."

Spenser had heard of him, which was saying something. "Sounds like a great place to take dance."

"Laurie gave me a scholarship. If I help around the studio, I get lessons. I can't go all the time, though. Grandma says it's too girly, and if I go too much, she gets mad."

The mention of his grandmother made Duon's face cloud. Spenser pressed on carefully. "Do you live with your grandparents?"

"Just my grandma. Grandpa died a few years ago. Mom's in prison until I'm thirty." He smiled, a thin, grim gesture made more menacing by his bleeding lip.

"Mandatory minimums."

Spenser dropped his paper towel in the water, hiding the shaking of his hands in a production of wringing it out as he schooled his reaction. He cleared his throat. "Is your grandmother good to you?"

He shrugged, looked away. "She tries, but she busy. She don't like that I'm gay. Says it's gonna get me beat up. And that it's against God."

Duon stopped talking, shuttering as if he realized he'd said too much. It told Spenser everything he needed to know, and it broke his heart, even as it stirred old ghosts. Leave it to Spenser to have a younger version of himself stop by unannounced.

Of course, Spenser had never shown up on anyone's doorstep bloody. "Who beat you up, Duon? Did they follow you here?"

Duon's laugh was short and sad, full of heaviness. "No. Nobody following me anywhere."

"So it was someone at home who did this."

Duon stiffened, his less-swollen eye welling with tears.

Spenser gentled him with a touch on his biceps. "It's all right. They can't hurt you now."

It wasn't his words, Spenser knew, but his tone that broke through. It wasn't simply six-year-olds who responded to it. Spenser's adoptive mother had said he could lure the devil himself to confession by asking him if he wanted to sit and talk. Everyone wanted to tell Spenser their stories.

Duon included.

"My cousins. Caught me with a guy. Beat on us both. They done it before, but never this bad. I think they would have killed Bobby, except he's older and big. He whaled on them as good as he got, then ran as soon as he could. Took me a little longer to get away."

So nice of Bobby to leave you with the people beating you down. Spenser didn't respond, though, only waited patiently as Duon gathered himself enough to continue.

"I tried to clean up, but nobody would let me into a store all beat up. Wanted to sneak into the bathroom at home, change clothes, and make it not look so bad. But Gran caught me. Asked what happened. She was all upset, and I thought maybe she was on my side, so I told her the truth." He huffed, a defeated, flat sound. "Big mistake. She called my cousins out, and they told her a bunch of lies. Made it all my fault somehow, like I was some big whore. Said I did this all the time, that I was having sex with older men for drugs. She didn't listen when I told her they was lying. Didn't matter to her."

He pointed to the cut on his cheek. "She knocked me into the coffee table, she slapped me so hard. Told me to get my ass out if I was gonna do drugs and be a disgusting pervert." His countenance hardened, though Spenser could still see the wounded boy beneath. "I ain't doing none of that, but I ain't gonna sit there and let them say shit about me, either. I'm done. I grabbed my social security card and the stuff I needed and got out. Gonna get a job and forget them, forever."

Spenser glanced at the garbage bag Duon had brought in and placed beside him on the chair. "Are you sure your grandmother isn't searching for you? Maybe she was upset in the moment, but she'd calm if someone helped explain?"

"Not if some white dude like you was doing the talking." Duon rubbed his leg self-consciously, staring off into space. "She tired. She got all of us dumped on her. There's nobody else around to take care of us, with my aunt working and everybody else a hot mess or gone. I'm better on my own. Was hoping I could crash with Tomás for the night, until I could figure something out. Didn't know about his parents. Thought he lived alone or something. Wasn't thinking." He coughed and winced, the glaze of tears thickening. "Almost went to Ed and Laurie's, but it's their anniversary. They don't need this shit. But it's no big deal. I'll find something."

Tucking his fury into the corner where he would deal with it later, Spenser focused his mental energy on the boy before him. "Did you get anything to eat today, Duon?"

Duon nodded gingerly. He'd begun to appear dull, the fight leaching out of him. "Lunch at school."

"I haven't eaten dinner yet. I'll make extra for you, and we can eat while we wait for Tomás. Why don't you lie down on the couch and rest until it's ready? But maybe you'd like a shower first. Do you have clean clothes in your bag? Or do you need to borrow some?"

Duon tucked his garbage bag self-consciously under his chair and made no further comment.

Spenser pressed the issue gently. "I can lend you a T-shirt and some sweatpants and a pair of thick, warm socks."

Duon's gaze cut to Spenser, the swollen eye cracking open, weighing the man before him as fully as possible.

Spenser held still under the assessment. "We can call someone else, if you want, or wait for Tomás. I can set us up some chairs in the hallway."

Duon smiled around his split lip. "Dude, I know you ain't gonna hurt me." Duon touched his wounded cheek with his fingers. "I can hold it shut with clear tape, if you got some. Done it before."

"Sure. I'll put it on the table so you can use it after your shower."

Spenser helped Duon to his feet and led him to the small bath off the living room. Laid out a towel, a washcloth, a change of clothes. Noted how Duon's gaze lingered on the socks, which were indeed thick and cozy-looking. Spenser put a large glass of water on the tank of the toilet too, after he showed Duon how to work the old-fashioned taps.

"Take your time, okay?" He gestured to the old-fashioned lock. "The door locks. Just turn this knob here."

Duon kept his gaze on Spenser as he clutched the

towel. "Thanks."

"No trouble at all." Spenser waved goodbye, shut the door, and went to the kitchen.

He stood at the sink, rigid, barely breathing until he heard the shower running. Then he let out a breath and went to the table, crouching beside Duon's garbage bag.

It was the smell that got him. Not a stench, not an odor, only a smell. The kind Spenser had caught on a few of the children when he was a student teacher in a public school in Minneapolis. The smell and the memories it brought had made him take a lower-paying job at a private school in hopes it meant he wouldn't encounter the scent again. Now here it was, blooming out of a plastic bag, taking Spenser to places he'd never wanted to return. The smell of unwashed things marinating on a dirty floor. Of a body sweating a little more than it should, of nervousness and fear. Of clothes aired in the out-of-doors on the body of a boy who didn't want to go home.

Or maybe his discomfort had nothing to do with any of those things. Maybe it came from something else, and Spenser's murky memories filled in the rest. Memories involving hastily packing a black garbage bag of his own.

Holding the edges of Duon's garbage bag tight in his fists, Spenser wept quietly for about three minutes. He made silent vows, hatched plans, and outlined stratagems for what he would do if, in fact, Duon was right and his grandmother didn't want him, if there was nowhere else for him to go. If Tomás didn't turn out to be the savior Duon was hoping he would be.

If Duon turned out to be exactly like Spenser after all.

After shutting the bag and tucking it under the chair where Duon had left it, Spenser blew his nose, dried his eyes, and busied himself with making dinner. But the smell of the bag lingered, as did the memory of Duon's too-sharp, weary gaze as the bathroom door closed between them.

WHILE HIS BOSS got ready to go on his first-anniversary dinner date with his husband, Tomás Jimenez argued with his mother on the phone as he dry-mopped the dance floor, sprayed down the mirrored walls, and disinfected the barre of the Dayton's Bluff Parker Dance Studio. "No, I don't need a new sweater, Mama."

"But they're on sale. Only two dollars. In a nice blue. It would bring out your eyes."

"I don't need a sweater. Save the money, okay?"

"You would look handsome in this, and I want you to have it." She sighed. "I'm going to buy it. You'll wear it to church. If you ever go again, God save your soul."

Tomás rolled his eyes but scuttled his frustration, because he knew from experience it wouldn't do him any good. "Mama, I need to go. I'm still at work. I need to finish up."

"I left your plate in the oven. When will you be home?"

"As soon as I finish up here, which will happen a lot faster if I get off the phone."

"Don't be rude." He heard a rustle of hangers in the background as she sifted through racks of clothing. "We'll still be out when you get home. When we finish here, we're going to the other thrift store on the east side of St. Paul. The baby needs new clothes. Oh, I meant to tell you this morning, but you left so early. We have the kids tonight."

Wonderful. This meant his sister was still on her fun bender, out partying while he worked himself to death. *Not the time or the right person for that fight.* "Okay. Tell Dad to be careful driving."

"Of course. He's always careful."

"I'll see you at home. And don't buy the sweater."

"I'm buying the sweater. I love you, *mijo.*"

"I love you too."

When Tomás hung up and tucked the phone in his pocket, he saw his employer had come out of the dressing room. Laurie Parker smiled wryly at Tomás. "Your mother, I assume?"

The entire conversation had taken place in Spanish, and his parents were the only people Tomás spoke to in that language, so it was an easy guess. Though the loving exasperation in his voice while addressing his mother probably gave him away more. "Yes. She's buying me a sweater. And making sure I know I have dinner in the oven." He waggled his eyebrows as he gave Laurie a proper once-over. "Looking good, boss. Ed won't know what hit him."

Laurie waved the compliment away, but Tomás knew the flattery was appreciated. "He should be by any minute. He's running late, he said. Has a surprise."

The trepidation in Laurie's voice was endearing. He and his husband kept each other on their toes, and Tomás wasn't ashamed to admit he was jealous. "One year already. Seems like yesterday I met you and you were getting ready to go to Iowa to get married."

Laurie stopped fussing with his tie and leaned on one of the support pillars at the edge of the floor. "I didn't expect everyone to remember, but they had a big banner at Halcyon Center this morning. My mother sent flowers, and Ed's parents gave us a lovely card. Duon left a gift for me too. A ream of paper, with a note explaining that's what we get for a first-year anniversary. I won't tell him I can see the hole exactly where he took it from in the supply cabinet."

Tomás leaned on his mop handle. "When did he stop by? I didn't see him in class tonight, which surprised me."

"I assume it was earlier today, when I was still at Halcyon. I'll have to ask Effie. But you're right, it's odd he wasn't around."

"I'll check on him tomorrow. Make sure everything's okay." Tomás picked up his cleaning supplies and carted them to the closet. He had his mouth open to ask Laurie about the next day's classes when something in the trash caught his eye. "What's this?" He pulled out the flyer, then swore. "Hell, who brought *that* in here?"

Laurie glared at the paper as well. "Someone had taped it to the door when I arrived."

Tomás buried the flyer in the trash once again, but the green-and-blue-on-white image was burned in his mind. *Vote Yes: Marriage Equals One Man, One Woman.* "This is what, the fifth one this week?"

"Yes. I assume someone knows a married gay man owns the studio." Laurie pressed fingertips to his temple. "I'll be so glad when the election is over. I can't run to the store for a gallon of milk without passing a million signs to VOTE YES or VOTE NO on the way. To say nothing of the newspapers, ads, and Facebook posts."

"What happens to your marriage, if it passes?"

"I don't know. I would like to think nothing, but I honestly have no idea." Laurie folded his arms over his abdomen. "I worry about our insurance, if it were to pass. I have Ed on mine, and you know how much health care need he has. If they pass this and for some reason I can't carry him…"

Holy shit, yeah. That would be bad. Tomás squelched the sick feeling in his gut and did his best to appear breezy. "You'll find a way to work it out. And thank God for the health-care law. At least you have a backup."

"I suppose."

Laurie didn't seem reassured, and it was clear this was a heavy concern for him, one that dwelling on it didn't help. Tomás changed the subject. "Where are you going for dinner?"

"La Belle Vie. And thanks to Ed's surprise, we're nearly late for our reservation." On cue, Ed's car pulled up out front, and Laurie relaxed, glancing at Tomás. "Would you mind closing up before you go?"

Tomás waved him away. "I've got this."

He locked the door behind Laurie and finished securing the studio for the night. The building had a security system far more sophisticated than Laurie's other studio because of the neighborhood it was in. While the St. Paul studio was where Laurie's heart was, the classes in Eden Prairie brought in the money that kept this place going. The instructors over there made more money as well, and Laurie had offered Tomás a job there several times. But Tomás liked the students here. They were, by and large, *his* kind of people. Far more nonwhite faces. The Dayton's Bluff studio attracted a wider swath of socioeconomic status too. Some classes were over half students present because of a scholarship. But they all had heart.

No, this was the studio where Tomás wanted to be.

But because he took the pay cut to be here, he had not one job, not two jobs, but *three* jobs, and only enough time between them to shovel food into his face and get a few hours sleep. His coworkers, the ones who didn't know his full story, all scolded him for working so much. Ed and Laurie had been at the front of that line, until Tomás's meltdown last spring when he'd gotten drunk and confessed it all. It was shortly after this discussion when Laurie had expanded Tomás's hours and increased his salary as much as he could, and Tomás didn't let himself be proud about it, simply accepted the extra cash.

Once the studio was locked up for the night and the alarm set, Tomás drove home. He lived in East Midway, in an ancient four-story apartment building overlooking University. He'd lived there since he was eight, before the construction had begun on the Metro Green Line, before the sex shop had closed. When he and his sister were young, his mother insisted on walking them to school because the neighborhood was bad. Now it was partially gentrified, to the point that every year they were nervous the landlord would sell and their rents would go up, or they'd be kicked out entirely because their grim three-bedroom spread would become shiny new condo space.

It was still his familiar shithole for now, and as he turned into his parking lot he saw the even lower-rent building across the alley had a huge VOTE YES sign in the front yard. In the streetlight it practically glowed. Tomás curled his lip at it. He was pretty sure the place was owned by the guy who kept getting sued by the

ACLU for refusing to rent to refugees.

God, sometimes the world made Tomás so tired.

Thinking of the ACLU dragged up the nagging thought that Tomás did need to call the lawyer tomorrow. And his sister, to have it out with her about chasing potential new boyfriends instead of finding a job. Of course, she wouldn't answer when she saw his number. He needed to call Duon too and make sure he was all right. But first he was going into the apartment and eating his plate from the oven in blissful silence. For at least a few minutes nobody was going to need him. Maybe he'd crawl into bed before his parents and the kids came home, and he'd get an almost decent night's worth of sleep for a change.

Except he wasn't halfway down the dimly lit hallway when the door across from his apartment opened. Tomás stood straighter and smiled at the cute white guy who lived across the hall. He was ninety percent sure the guy was gay, because every time Tomás made eye contact, the man blushed like a wallflower hoping someone would ask him to dance.

But today the white guy didn't smile back, and his blush was more of a flush from being stressed. In fact, he seemed upset.

"Tomás?" The man held out his hand. "Hi. I'm your neighbor, but I don't think we've ever been properly introduced. I'm…Spenser. Spenser Harris. I live…here." He gestured awkwardly at his door.

God, but this guy was adorable. Tomás wanted to

wrap the guy up in a blanket, soothe him, then climb into bed alongside him. He held out his hand. "Tomás Jimenez. Nice to meet you." When his flirtatious tone failed to settle Spenser, Tomás became serious too. "Is something wrong?"

Spenser ran a hand through his straight, light-brown hair, which was styled in an artfully messy way Tomás's dark curly hair would never tolerate. "I…don't know how to explain, to be honest. I suppose you could say I had something of a surprise when I came home. Someone was here, in front of my door, some-one who knows you. Hurt. I've done what I can to calm him, but he's asking for you."

Tomás held up his hands. "Hold on. Slow down. *Who* is looking for me? Who's hurt?"

"Duon. Your friend Duon is in my apartment. Sleeping on the couch, waiting for you. His cousins beat him up, and his grandmother kicked him out." He frowned. "Or he ran away. I'm not entirely sure."

Tomás sagged, staring stupidly at Spenser. Worry tangled with weariness and shock, though to his shame, his predominant emotion wasn't an eagerness to help but rather a sense of exhaustion. *I can't take on anymore.* Pushing this thought aside, Tomás drew an unsteady breath and forced himself to stand straight. "It's okay. Thanks for taking care of him. I'll move him over to our place and figure out where to go from here."

Spenser held up a hand. "There's one other prob-lem. It's fine for him to go with you, since he clearly knows you, but he's been badly beaten. And I'm a teacher, which means I'm a mandatory reporter."

Tomás stilled. "Mandatory reporter of what? To whom?"

"Of child abuse, and possibly neglect. The beating was done by his cousins, and it was his grandmother who kicked him out. I don't have a choice. I have to call DHS."

Tomás could only blink at Spenser until disbelief gave way to quiet rage. "Tell me you're kidding."

Spenser stood straighter, jutting out his chin. "This is a serious situation. I can't send Duon home to be hurt again. Maybe it will work out with his grandmother, maybe he's wrong and she's worried for him, not glad he's gone, but if not—"

Goddamned white people. The thought of what this asshole's searching for a savior cookie would do to Duon and possibly Tomás's family made him tremble with rage. "Whatever the hell is wrong with Duon and his family, bringing the Department of Human Services into it isn't going to fix *shit.* I can take care of this, but you can't—"

"You don't get to figure out where to go from here, and neither do I."

Oh Jesus Christ. The sick feeling in Tomás's stomach curdled into full-on dread. White boy wasn't cute at all, not anymore. He was a meddling *monster* determined to wreck everything. "You have no idea what it means, calling in DHS. You have no idea what you'll do to

Duon." *To me.*

"I do, actually." Spenser looked about as weary as Tomás, but he had steel about him as he gestured to the closed door of his apartment. "Why don't you come inside, and we can all work together to get him through this situation?"

Tomás thought fleetingly of his promised dinner waiting in the oven. Of the silence in his apartment, the soft solitude of his bed. Of his parents and his nieces and nephew, who were due to come home any moment. Then he thought about Duon huddled in this stranger's apartment.

Nodding, Tomás gathered his mental forces and followed Spenser inside.

CHAPTER TWO

S PENSER WAS A meddling asshole, but Tomás had to admit he had a cute apartment.

Technically it was the same apartment as the one Tomás lived in, but the difference between the two was more than one less bedroom and a mirror-image floor plan. Only one person lived here, instead of the three members of the Jimenez family. Of course if the kids and sometimes Alisa too were staying with them, as they often were, there were six or seven people in their tiny space.

Additionally, Spenser was neat as a pin. Tomás didn't have to open the cupboards to know everything would be exactly in its place, probably labeled. There was no dirt, no dust. No stains on anything. There were rugs on the floor, and they all matched. The kitchen and the rooms he saw through the doorway had a clear color scheme and a distinct sense of design. It was clear Spenser had put thought into how he laid out his rooms. The table had place mats, a runner, and a bowl of artfully arranged fruit. The place smelled of food too. It wasn't the food Tomas's family ate, but it made him hungry all the same.

When Tomás caught sight of a familiar form, battered and still beneath a knit throw on the living room couch, all thoughts of food and quiet, charming apartments fled. Duon. What in the hell were they going to do about Duon?

Spenser spoke to Tomás, keeping his voice low and his gaze fixed on the boy in the other room. "He fell asleep while I was making dinner. He doesn't have head trauma, I don't think, but he's sleeping so soundly he has me worried. I wonder if I should have checked for a concussion."

Tomás didn't know about concussions either. He thought about texting Ed, then remembered the anniversary dinner. "Do you have Internet? We can look it up."

"My phone." Spenser tapped at a smartphone screen. His furrowed brow eased as he read. "No. I don't think he does. The only thing fitting is slurred speech, but I could tell it was because of his split lip and sore face."

Jesus. Duon was beat that bad?

Spenser rubbed his arms self-consciously in the uncomfortable silence. "Can I get you something to drink? Have you eaten? I made enough chicken and rice to share." He busied himself in the kitchen, pulling plates from a cupboard and moving a kettle from a back burner to the front. "I'm going to make some tea too. Enough for everyone. He might not drink it, but it's nice to hold something hot."

Probably Spenser was nervous, and this puttering was his way of deflecting. He gave Spenser a second to fuss in a cupboard overflowing with boxes of tea, then dragged them gently to the whole reason they were dithering in his kitchen in the first place. "Can you walk me through this? How he got here, what's happened so far?" He wanted to get up the guy's nose about DHS again, but he decided to go gingerly. Spenser hadn't called yet. Maybe he could talk him out of it.

Spenser indicated the still-silent living room. "I came home and found him curled up in front of my door. There was blood all over the hall—not puddles or anything, but…well, I cleaned it up. I took pictures first, though, in case."

In case of what? "You said he was waiting for me?"

"Yes. He almost went somewhere else, to a couple, but he mentioned something about an anniversary."

Ed and Laurie. "So you brought him into your place?"

"I tried to get him to a hospital, but he was adamant about not going. I cleaned him up. Got him to talk to me a little. That's when he told me about his family. Apparently his cousins caught him with another boy and beat them both up. Then, when Duon went home and told his grandmother what had happened, his cousins embellished the tale, painted him in an unfavorable way, and she kicked him out. From what I gather, he has no other place to go. I can't tell how serious his grandmother was about him not coming back, but I got the feeling it was very."

Tomás would bet she was. She'd been a razor's edge from washing her hands of him all year, from the sounds of things. Reports were the grandmother had become the catch-all for her entire family. God, did Tomás know how that went.

Still, bringing in the government wasn't the answer. "About this DHS thing. You can't call them."

"I told you. I don't have a choice. I'm a teacher. I have to report this. I know it's hard, bringing DHS into the picture, but it's important."

God save us from white saviors. "Have you ever dealt with DHS? Do you have any idea how incompetent they are? How disruptive they can be?" When Spenser flattened his lips, Tomás pressed on. "He's only fifteen. They'll put him in foster care. And he's gay. Do you know what happens to LGBT kids in foster care?"

A flicker in Spenser's expression told Tomás he'd stepped in something good there, but all Spenser did was pull his arms tighter to his body. "He's homeless. Do you know how quickly homeless teens are trafficked? Right here in the Twin Cities?"

Oh, Tomás did *not* care for Spenser's accusatory, sanctimonious tone. "We've been watching out for him. Me, Ed and Laurie, and Halcyon Center."

"Yes, he mentioned the center. A woman in particular. Nicky?"

"Vicky. She runs it. Great lady," Tomás added, in case Spenser wanted to cast aspersions on her too.

"So I gather. Apparently they have a shelter he goes to, when it's open and has a space available. But it's closed now."

"It's not a great time for charities. They're always out of money." Vicky was a good idea, though. He didn't know her, but he knew *of* her, that she was a bulldog. *She* would eat this guy as a snack. "We should call Vicky. She'll know exactly what to do."

He expected Spenser to object, but he only blinked in surprise. "You have her contact information? Excellent. I wanted to call her, but Duon didn't know her number."

"I don't have her number personally, no, but I know people who do." Which meant he was going to have to interrupt Ed and Laurie's anniversary after all.

Spenser's shoulders relaxed. "Good. I think it will make this easier, if she helps explain."

The rustle of blankets from the living room drew their attention. Spenser hurried over, and Tomás followed. Spenser's face transformed as he approached Duon, all gentle smiles as he crouched beside the couch. "Hey there. Feeling any better?"

It took everything in Tomás to school his expression as Duon sat up and the extent of his injuries was revealed. His skin had purpled and was swollen all over, and his face looked like someone had taken a hammer to it. The cut below his eye was dangerously close, and the other eye was puffy.

Duon glanced around, disoriented. "I fell asleep?"

"For a good hour." Spenser kept up his soft, soothing tone. It was hypnotic. Tomás almost forgot the guy was an asshole as he listened. "Someone's here to see you, by the way."

Duon's bleary gaze drifted to Tomás. "Tomás. My man. Where you been?"

It was a typical enough greeting, but Tomás couldn't help feeling as if someone had sucked the Duon out of Duon, and someone flat and exhausted had taken his place. Tomás knew better than to let his worry show. "Hey yourself. I was at the studio. Laurie liked your present, but he missed you in class."

"Yeah, well. I was busy."

Spenser put a hand near Duon's leg, but not on it. "I have dinner ready. Why don't you wash up while I set the table?"

Duon obeyed, letting Spenser help him up and herd him toward the bathroom. Once he was out of sight, Spenser dragged Tomás to the kitchen. "Can you get a hold of Vicky? Do you think she'd be willing to come here now?"

He wasn't sure. "Let me make a phone call, and we can try."

"I'll set the table."

He pulled away, but Tomás caught his arm. "Leave DHS out of this. Let us fix this."

Spenser returned Tomás's stare with steel, implying

he could do this all day. "Go make the call."

He twisted his arm free and busied himself with putting plates and glasses on the table, leaving little else for Tomás to do than go into the hall and ring Ed and Laurie so he could get Vicky's number and settle this DHS nonsense once and for all.

Tomás's friends Ed and Laurie, the ones who knew the director of Halcyon Center, came over as soon as they were called. Spenser would have preferred less people involved, but Tomás was angry with him enough over the mandatory-reporter thing, so he decided to roll with it.

He got some food in Duon first, which he was glad for. Tomás ate too, and they were a strange, ad hoc family, which was good. Spenser wanted normal for Duon, as much as he could get.

Once Ed and Laurie arrived, however, everything became chaotic quickly. Laurie was a lithe, handsome man, and his husband was a big, burly ex-football player, both of them extraordinarily concerned for Duon. Of course, Duon became withdrawn and defensive with so much focus on him, and Spenser could do little to deflect it. This meant when Vicky Richards arrived, Duon was so agitated he was edgy and almost hostile, even in his exhaustion.

"Y'all are making a big deal over nothing. I got low and wanted to rest somewhere for the night is all.

Won't make that mistake again."

Vicky met him exasperation for exasperation. "It's time for us to have the conversation you keep trying not to have with me, the one where I tell you we have to find you somewhere safe to be. Somewhere permanent, not simply for the night."

"Yeah, I bet there are people lining up to take me in." Duon's gaze narrowed, and he straightened, his bruises forgotten. "You try to send me to a shelter, I'm gonna run right now."

They argued for a few minutes, until Ed intervened and distracted Duon. Spenser took the opportunity to draw Vicky aside to talk with her. To his chagrin, Tomás followed.

Spenser did his best to ignore him as he spoke quietly with the director. "How well do you know his case?"

"Fringes. I know his family, know the history. He understands I have to report him, though, so he stays away from me whenever something's happened I'd need to tell DHS about. I've had to bring them in a time or two, and he didn't care for it."

Tomás drew back. "*You* report him? You have already? *You're* a mandatory reporter too?"

Vicky gave him an incredulous look. "I'm a licensed social worker and the director of a youth center. Yes, I'm a mandatory reporter."

Spenser decided this was a good time to come clean himself, at least in part. "I'm an educator, and I'm the one who found him. I know it's my duty to report, and I will, but I wanted a chance to talk to more people who knew him and his situation first."

"I have his social worker's number. I'll give it to you." Vicky ran a hand through her hair. "They might revoke custody over this. They've threatened to, but there's never anywhere to put him, so they hem and haw, hoping a situation like this doesn't happen. Except I think Dorothy is ready to surrender it herself. She's a good woman, but she's not particularly understanding about Duon being gay, and she's responsible for six boys from the ages of ten to eighteen. A saint would crack under what she's dealing with. We'd have removed Duon long ago, but he's a Black, gay teenager. The only way he'd be more difficult to place would be if he were transgender too. Except the shelters are full right now. They were sending kids to Albert Lea and Duluth last I checked. We should be open next month at Halcyon, but we're drop-in, not a residence."

Tomás was furious. "You can't send him away."

"*I* won't be doing anything. I don't get to make choices for him."

"And he doesn't get to make choices for himself?"

"When he's fifteen? Not many, no."

Spenser interrupted before the argument could spiral. "What about Avenues? The Host Home program? Do you think they have an opening?"

Vicky paused mid-breath, abruptly thoughtful. "I don't know, actually. They're always full too, but I suppose it won't hurt to ask. We'd need some legal hoops cleared because he's a minor, but we can give it a shot. I'll call Ryan tomorrow."

Tomás's glare had cooled to a mild scowl. "What's Avenues?"

Spenser answered him. "Avenues for Homeless Youth. They're a privately run shelter in Minneapolis, but they also have an LGBT host home program. They pair youth with local families who are an extension of the shelter, essentially."

"But the waitlist is long." Vicky leaned on the kitchen counter. "Who knows? Maybe we'll get lucky."

"Where does he stay tonight?" Tomás paced Spenser's kitchen. "Will DHS take him away? To Albert Lea or wherever the hell they can shove him?"

Laurie joined them, putting one hand on Vicky and the other on Tomás. "Let's all remember we have Duon's best interests at heart." He smiled at Spenser. "Thank you again for helping Duon. Especially since as I understand it, you didn't know him before tonight."

"I'm a teacher." Spenser was going to use that shield as long as he could. "Helping children is what I do."

"Plenty of teachers would have simply called the police." Laurie turned to Vicky. "But yes, where *will* he stay tonight? Who makes that call?"

"His worker, technically." Vicky pursed her lips. "It would be better, though, if we can come up with a solution to suggest."

Tomás nodded at Laurie. "Could he stay with you?"

"For a night or two, yes, if we put an air mattress in the kitchen. We're no good for the long term, unfortunately. Our couch is more of a love seat, and Ed is up half the night, watching infomercials while he ices his neck in the recliner. There's no room for another bedroom or even a bed in the corner. Plus I assume as an out couple we're a harder sell?"

Vicky shook her head. "Not in Minneapolis. The space is more of a concern, most likely. For anything permanent, he'd need a bedroom."

"Yes. We're probably out, then. If I had a few weeks, I could maybe work on my mother, but I think it would be so much culture shock he'd prefer a shelter. Maybe Ed's parents? Except it's such a huge ask. Duon can be wily, and I'm not sure if they're the right parents for him. I'll talk to Ed."

Vicky regarded Tomás. "What about you? He was coming to see you, yes?"

Tomás went wooden, his gaze flickering immediately to Laurie.

Laurie spoke for him. "Tomás is unavailable, unfortunately. But let me put in a call to Oliver. He might know someone I haven't thought of."

They continued to toss names around, all of them unsatisfactory, and eventually Spenser slipped away, going over to Ed and Duon, who were talking quietly on the couch. With a nod from Spenser, Ed excused himself and let Spenser take his place as he headed to the kitchen.

Spenser smiled ruefully at Duon. "Sorry for the circus. I didn't mean for this many people to get involved, but I didn't have much of a choice."

Duon snorted. "Yeah, well."

Spenser studied the clear adhesive tape on Duon's eye, which was almost peeled off. "We need to get you some of those boxer bandages, though I suspect we're going to end up in the hospital whether you want to go there or not. But I wanted to ask you something first." He indicated the kitchen. "They're trying to think of a place for you to stay, to suggest to your social worker. They have a short-term solution, though not a long-term. I had a thought of something else that might work, but I wanted your permission first."

Duon gave him a sidelong glance. "What's your idea?"

"You can stay here for now, until we figure this out. Couch for tonight, blow-up bed in my spare bedroom once I get one, and if you end up needing somewhere to stay for good and you decide my place is okay, we'll get an actual bed." He paused to let the offer ring a moment, then added, "You can think about it for a few minutes. And if you want to ask me questions to make sure you'd like it here, I'm happy to answer."

Duon gave him a focused stare with his good eye. The unspoken question hung heavy between them. It didn't surprise Spenser, though, that Duon didn't ask. You didn't, when you were on his end of this situation.

Spenser answered it anyway. He double-checked the kitchen, then leaned closer to Duon. "I'm helping you because I know how it feels to be where you are. When I was your age, I was in the foster care system."

Duon blinked at him in surprise. "You were?"

Spenser nodded. "I can tell you the story in greater detail later, but I'd appreciate it if you didn't tell the others, because it isn't their business. You know how it is, people making judgments when you don't live with your birth parents."

Duon huffed a bitter laugh, but when his gaze met Spenser's again, it was softer. "Yeah."

"Staying with me is a temporary solution, at least for now. I know you don't know me, and I won't be offended if later you decide living here isn't what you want. But as someone who has been in your situation, it would be my pleasure to offer you somewhere safe to stay while things get sorted out."

Duon didn't smile, but some of the deep tension rolled off his shoulders. "Sure. Thanks, man."

Spenser put his hand on the blanket beside Duon's leg. Then he rose to go to the kitchen to let everyone else know what was going on.

AT FIRST TOMÁS didn't hear what Spenser said, because he was too busy arguing with Vicky, whom he'd already decided he disliked. But when Spenser repeated himself, they stopped talking and regarded him, dumbfounded.

Ed recovered first. "But you don't know Duon. Why would you offer to give him a place to stay? Because you sound as if you're saying he'd be here for more than tonight."

Spenser was right back in what Tomás was beginning to think of as his zone, that space between steel and softness. "I know him well enough to host him for the night at least, and tomorrow we'll talk more to see if it will work for longer."

"But you said you're a teacher." This observation came from Laurie. "You'll have school tomorrow."

"I have sick days coming, and my lesson plans are in place. I can take some time to help him out."

Tomás didn't like this, but he wasn't sure how to object when he didn't have a solution. "What about a doctor? Someone should check him, make sure he's okay."

"Oh, a doctor will be required." Vicky pulled out her phone. "I'll see if the social worker wants to take him or if we can."

While Vicky made her calls, Spenser went with her and confirmed details. Ed sat with Duon, teasing him and distracting him from the situation. Tomás, feeling like a third wheel, hung out with Laurie in the kitchen. "Sorry about your anniversary dinner. But I didn't know what else to do."

Laurie waved a dismissive hand at Tomás's apology. "The evening was a bit of a mess anyway. We fought on the way over because Ed showed up with one of those *VOTE NO: Don't limit our freedom to marry* decals on the side of his car. He was late because he was getting it put on. And he wanted me to get one too."

Tomás could imagine that argument. "Yikes."

"Things got better at dinner, until a man at a table saw Ed kiss my hand and spent the rest of the meal glaring at us as if we were having sex on the table. We'd left the restaurant and were in the parking lot, trying to pretend everything was fine, when you called." Laurie pursed his lips and leaned against the counter. "I've worried something like this would happen with Duon. I wish we'd bought a house instead of expanding the Dayton's Bluff studio. Then we'd have room."

"I wish *we* could take him. My mom would do it in a heartbeat. But Alisa's leaving the kids all the time now, and we already had our brush with multiple government agencies. I can't risk the system getting closer to my parents or the kids than it is."

"How is everything going? You haven't given me an update lately. I don't mean to pry, though."

Bile rose in Tomás's throat just thinking about it. "Not much has changed. Lawyer is still eating our money, doing squat. But nobody's come banging on the door, so at least we have that. The kids are happy to be with us. Loud and messing up my stuff, but happy."

Laurie put a hand on his arm. "I know I say this every time, but I mean it. If there's anything we can do, let us know. I could talk to my godfather, see if he knows a better lawyer."

Tomás was sure Laurie's godfather, the wealthy and locally famous philanthropist Oliver Thompson, knew all kinds of lawyers, none Tomás could afford. "You let me teach dance. That's enough right there."

"I don't *let* you do anything. I'm glad to have you on staff. The kids love you. I'm not surprised Duon came to you for help."

Came to Tomás, but found…this guy. Tomás frowned at the back of Spenser's head as he spoke with Vicky. "I can't believe they're going to let Duon go with a total stranger."

"Well, I know Vicky, have since high school. She's talking to him so much because she wants to erase some of the unknown around him. I'd put money on her stalling while a background check is running. Though if he's a teacher, he's going to pass it." Laurie stared at Spenser too, but he smiled. "I like him."

Tomás couldn't, not when he was the reason DHS was involved. "It's weird, the way he wants to help a kid he doesn't know."

"Isn't helping strangers' kids what he does all day long? I'm just glad he was willing to step up. We would have taken Duon for the night, honestly. For the week, or forever, if there was truly nowhere else. We'd find a way to make the space work. But he didn't come to us.

This feels significant to me. The only choice for any of us is to ride this out. And we will—together."

The social worker arrived, and Tomás heard his parents come home with the kids soon after. He texted his mother frantically, told her to keep the kids quiet. *DHS next door.* She didn't reply, but the children became immediately silent.

When the social worker insisted Duon be seen by medical professionals, Laurie and Ed hugged Duon, thanked Spenser again, and left. Spenser planned to go with Vicky and the social worker to the ER, and it was clear he was about to invite Tomás along, but the terror on Tomás's face inspired him to focus instead on coaxing Duon off the couch.

Here Tomás wanted to step in, to explain to Duon why he couldn't come along, couldn't let him stay at his place, but Duon seemed to be in some kind of shock. So Tomás simply stood by, useless, until they left and there was nothing for him to do but go across the hall to his own apartment.

His father waited for him, pale-faced and sweating, peering over Tomás's shoulder as if he expected one of the four horsemen of the apocalypse to be following. Tomás held up his hands. "It's only me. They're gone."

The relief rolling off José Jimenez was almost visible weight falling to the floor. "Thank God." He crossed himself as he glanced at the door to the bedroom where Renata and the kids were hiding. "What happened? Why are there social workers here? Where were you?"

Tomás began to tell him, but when José saw how upset his son was, he called for his wife, and the two of them plunked him on the couch and made him start over. Tomás told them everything about Duon. About how he wanted to help. How it hurt him to know he couldn't. How he was angry at Spenser for bringing in DHS.

His mother, however, would hear none of that. "But, *mi vida*, he helped the boy. God bless him for his kindness." She wiped tears from her eyes. "I will take them tortillas tomorrow. And beans. And empanadas."

The idea of his mother interacting with Spenser turned Tomás's stomach. Would he report her too? "You can't tell him, Mom. You can't tell Spenser you and Dad are undocumented."

She touched his cheek, her expression sad and a little weary. "I know, *cariño*. I know."

CHAPTER THREE

A T THE HOSPITAL, Duon was closed off, slightly defensive, and clearly scared. Spenser longed more than anything to reassure him, but he couldn't do much, especially since he wasn't allowed into the exam room. The only thing he could do was take Duon's hand on his way by and look him in his uninjured eye as he spoke. "I will be here when you're finished. Everything will be all right."

Duon's response to this had been an imperceptible jerk of the head, and then the nurse wheeled him through the double doors.

Once Duon was gone, Vicky helped Spenser deal with the forms the social worker had left for him to sign. The first one was the background check, which he'd filled out before. The rest of the paperwork was ridiculously simple, considering the outcome would be collecting a child. The most onerous part was providing references, which meant digging through his email to find phone numbers.

Vicky held her hand out for the last piece of paper

with a weary smile. "Thanks. I'll put in a call to Avenues tomorrow also, in case they have an opening." She leveled her gaze at him, studying him carefully. "You know they won't, though. And you know, don't you, that DHS is going to ask you to take him on permanently, if you show so much as the least bit of willingness?"

"I do." Spenser met her gaze easily. "We'll see what happens once Duon and I have a chance to get to know each other better."

She didn't back down. "There's nowhere else. I know Ed and Laurie would have him, but their lives aren't remotely structured for the support Duon's going to need. They don't understand how much extra work a child in Duon's situation requires. And I can't. It sets a terrible precedent, and once I open those floodgates, I'll feel like I have to house every child I can't home into my apartment. But he's a good kid. A handful sometimes, yes, but he's got a heart of gold. He has so much love he wants to give." She ran a hair through her hair, staring grimly at the empty space before her. "The shelters, even if they weren't full, would have structure, but they're not a great place for LGBT kids. I don't blame him for not wanting to go there. *I* don't want him to go there. Avenues is a good idea, but there's no way it isn't full. And it doesn't matter, because what he needs is a home." She blushed. "Sorry, I get carried away."

Spenser smiled, unable to help himself. "It's okay.

It's good to see you passionate about him."

"I love all my kids, but there are some that get under your skin. The ones you lie up at night thinking about, wanting to help. He's one of them for me."

Spenser liked her. A lot. "If Avenues doesn't have an opening, I can apply to be a host home and create a space in the program. They would support him financially and help get him transitioned into adult life when the time came." He hesitated while he chose his words carefully. "I've…worked with them before. I know what to expect."

"Sounds good to me." She stood, holding up the clutch of paper he'd signed. "I'll get this filed. And I'll check up on you tomorrow, okay? You have my card, if you need anything before then."

Vicky left, and Spenser sat in silence, playing with his phone for a few minutes before simply leaning back and soaking in the stillness while he still had it.

When Duon reemerged, the social worker confirmed Spenser had been accepted as an emergency placement and promised to check in the next day with more information. She waved goodbye, answering another phone call as she headed for her car.

The hospital wasn't far from the apartment, but Spenser drove slowly, deliberately taking a leisurely route home. At first Duon stayed silent, keeping his gaze out the window. Spenser let the silence expand until Duon was ready to fill it.

"You said you were in the system."

"Yep. Foster care from when I was eight until I aged out."

"House, or shelter?"

The old flicker of sorrow, hate, and emptiness swelled. "Both. Lots of houses, several shelters."

Duon examined him critically. "Why you a teacher?"

"I always liked kids. Seemed a good job to have, teaching elementary." He was scraping against shadows, and they were far too live for his liking tonight, the demons woken up by Duon's experience. "I have three little sisters. I used to care for them. I was good at it. But people don't want four foster kids. Not often."

"What'd they take you away for?"

This time it was Spenser hiding pain in the bravado of a stiff shrug. "Drugs. Child endangerment."

Duon held out a fist in Spenser's direction. "Same, brother."

Spenser met the bump smoothly and turned a corner, which would let them talk for a few more blocks. "I didn't do well when I aged out of the system. I was carrying too much inside me. Was on track to end up the same as my mom and my oldest sister. But I heard about this shelter for homeless LGBT youth, and they hooked me up with a lesbian couple who adopted me—not legally, but in every other respect. Gave me a home. Helped me get to therapy, to college."

"This why you took in me? Black Widow got red in her ledger and needs to wipe it out?"

Spenser laughed. "Something like that, yeah."

Duon huffed. "I ain't going to no therapy."

Spenser didn't say anything, only smiled.

The apartment building was quiet as they arrived. Spenser let Duon in and got a spare set of sheets from the linen cupboard. "You okay with the couch for tonight? If you decide you want to stay, I'll find you a real bed and put it in my spare room."

Duon accepted the sheets absently. He looked scared and overwrought. They'd given him painkillers at the hospital, but they only dulled the outside. Spenser knew though Duon was exhausted, he wouldn't sleep tonight. Not anything outside of a few fitful hours. Not until dawn.

Spenser put the remote to the TV on the coffee table. "Keep the volume low. Turn on any lights you need, and eat anything you want from the fridge or cupboards."

Once he had Duon situated on the couch, Spenser locked the doors and went to the bathroom to brush his teeth and wash his face. He closed the door to his bedroom, got into his pajamas, and tucked himself into his sheets. Read a book for a few minutes, then shut off his light, pulled up the covers, and tried to sleep.

But he lay awake long into the night, listening to the traffic on the street. To the sound of the television murmuring on low, in concert to the shifts and creaks of the young man watching it on the couch, the young man who wasn't sleeping either.

WHAT TOMÁS WANTED to do the morning after the scene with Duon was go over to Spenser's apartment and make sure Duon was okay. What he had to do, unfortunately, was go to work. At five in the morning.

Tomás didn't mind working at Starbucks. He was an assistant manager, and he was good at both being in charge and making fancy cups of coffee. Sure, he was tired sometimes, but that's what coffee was for, and lucky him, he worked with the stuff all day long. He swore he absorbed some of the caffeine through his skin. He was every employee's favorite assistant manager and every customer's favorite barista. He didn't let the customers or the other baristas know when they drove him crazy. He didn't like his weekend job doing custodial work at a nursing home, but it brought in the crucial extra money that let him go to his third job, the only one he actually wanted: teaching at Laurie's studio.

It was a dance in itself to make sure he got out of Starbucks in time to get to Dayton's Bluff to teach his classes, and another skill entirely to not be so tired he fell asleep in the car on the way over. But he got it all done. It was tight, and each aspect of it had to move the right way, but his life worked. Sort of.

His mom and dad helped. His dad made sure his beater car got him from point A to point B, did deals with his friends if he needed parts or help with labor. His mom kept his uniforms spotless and ironed. "They'll know you take your job seriously when they see your clothes," she always said. She didn't understand his love of dancing, but she made sure his leotard was clean and his tights had no holes. His parents' care and support helped him get through it, and he did all of his jobs without complaint.

His sister didn't help him at all, and when he ran into her when she flitted in and out of their lives, they nearly always butted heads. But the good part of his working so much was that the number of times they crossed paths was epically low. In fact, though she'd been to the apartment regularly lately, he hadn't seen her in over a month.

Though usually Tomás did his jobs with a happy heart, the day after the incident with Duon, he dragged. He hated that Duon had come to him for help and he'd had to say no. He worried about this Spenser guy too. With a few hours of sleep and his mother's breakfast in his belly, he could admit he'd overreacted and judged the guy too harshly.

On his lunch break he'd done some research and now had a better understanding of why he'd narced. Still didn't care for it, but he'd downgraded Spenser from *asshole* to *Dudley Do-Right*. One of his best friends in high school had been a white kid who lived for sneaking out to get high, and when Tomás refused to go, afraid of getting caught and getting his parents in trouble, Sean called him that name. Tomás had finally asked him what the hell it was about, and Sean had explained it was some old cartoon, and Dudley Do-Right was this Canadian Mountie who was dumb as rocks and moral almost to a fault. Tomás had taken umbrage to the name after knowing its origins, but he didn't mind giving it to Spenser now. The guy probably slept with a rule book.

He likely still looked sexy-cute while he did it, damn him.

Tomás also did some digging on whether or not mandatory reporters were required to report on undocumented immigrants. They were not, to his great relief. Tomás wasn't going to go out of his way to tell the guy, but it was good to know if he found out accidentally, it didn't mean the apocalypse had arrived.

He should've gotten Spenser's number, or given his. As it was, the only hope he had in checking up on Duon before he went home that night was the unlikely chance he came to the studio, which he did not. So Tomás was distracted through his three classes too.

Laurie was there for his last one, since they taught it together. Ideally they would have several classrooms in their space, but for now they only had the one, until the building Laurie and Ed had bought next door was renovated and brought up to code. Laurie's office had been built a month ago, along with the staff break area, and this was all the renovating they could afford right now. Laurie came from a wealthy background, and he had a lot saved, but he also had a husband who had a hard time working and a marriage only sort of accepted by the government.

Tomás knew Laurie was squirreling money away

"in case." In case the amendment passed. In case Ed's pain got worse. In case opening a grant-run dance studio in a rougher neighborhood of St. Paul turned out to be a terrible business strategy and bled him dry. They hadn't moved out of their apartment near the studio because it was inexpensive. But at the same time, he hired too many instructors, paid them good wages, and he gave out too many scholarships. His big heart cost him a great deal of money.

It was part of why Tomás was so devoted to him and loved him so much.

Laurie approached him after class, as Tomás hurried into his street clothes. "Have you had any word on Duon? Is he still with Spenser?"

"I'm going to go see them now. Give them both my phone number and all that. Apologize for getting upset last night."

"Would you mind giving them my number too? I should have given it to Duon before. I knew he had Ed's, and I guess I thought that was enough."

"I hadn't given it to him either. Didn't know if it was appropriate to give it to a student."

"In general, probably not. But I think perhaps this is an exceptional case." Laurie mustered up a smile. "Keep me posted, will you?"

Tomás agreed he would, then hurried home. He saw his parents' car in the parking lot, and his sister's. Oh, but this was the worst day in the world for the two of them to have a confrontation. He gripped the steering wheel, focusing quiet anger at Alisa's three-year-old, gleaming green Ford Focus. Then he pulled out his phone and texted his mother.

I'm going to see Duon before I come home.

She answered fairly quickly. *Okay. I'll keep your dinner warm. Alisa is here.*

I saw. Is she sober?

I don't know. She wants to take the babies, but your father is trying to get her to leave them here another night.

Tomás let out a breath, but his frustration with Alisa and the family's situation remained at its usual constant boiling point. Eventually he put his hand over the rosary dangling from his rearview mirror, closed his eyes, and took several deep breaths until he thought he had a chance of leaving his car without first putting his hand through the windshield.

Then he got out, locked it, and went to see Duon.

His belly turned over as he closed in on the door with the number three hanging straight and shiny above the keyhole. Across the hall he could hear his sister arguing with his father, a heated mixture of Spanish and English punctuated with the anguished cries from Sabrina, Jasmin, and Ashton, Tomás's nieces and nephew. Alisa was drunk, for sure, and maybe high too. Two years ago, Tomás would have stormed in to join the battle, determined to talk Alisa into decency and common sense. But he knew better now, knew the best prayer for keeping the kids safe was if he stayed out of it. His role in the family was to make money.

He didn't know what his role was with Duon. He wasn't sure how to have either of the conversations he was about to have, but he knew he needed to have them.

His knock wasn't loud, but it echoed in the hallway. He heard movement on the other side of the door, the sounds of shuffling feet and Spenser's voice. It was a good voice. Soothing. It smoothed some of Tomás's ruffled edges, waking up the part of him that missed flirting with a man. When Spenser opened the door to smile at Tomás, neat and pressed and polite, the flutter of awareness became a low hum. The guy was cute. And he rescued kids. There were definitely worse qualities in a man.

Tomás wished he had a hat so he could take it off and hold it in his hands. "Hi. I'm sorry if I'm interrupting anything, but I wanted to check in on Duon. And apologize to you."

Spenser blinked in surprise before standing aside. "Come on in. Duon's in the shower. But you don't have anything to apologize for." He closed the door behind Tomás. "Can I get you something to drink? Water? Coffee? Tea?"

His first instinct was to say no thanks, but he thought better of it, deciding it would be a good way to distract the guy while he got his confession out. "Sure. Tea is fine. Something decaffeinated, please."

Spenser returned to the cupboard full of tea boxes and tins and studied it a moment. "I have all kinds of tea. An herbal peach, chai rooibos, decaffeinated Lady Grey—"

"*Lady* Grey?"

Spenser waved a blue box with an orange banner at him. "It's Earl Grey but with a little citrus zest."

"Sounds good. I'll try it."

The ritual of making tea was good cover as Tomás got himself together. "I'm sorry for last night, for being upset about you having to report Duon to DHS. I'm glad you're helping Duon. I'm sorry I wasn't able to take him in myself. I'd like to help in other ways, if I can."

Spenser glanced up at him, pausing with one red and one yellow mug in his hands. "It's all right. If it helps, I was nervous about having to make the call. You helped so much, bringing in Vicky. I don't think I would have been allowed to keep him without her."

It was so hard not to plow forward with all his questions, to decide which ones to dole out first. "Is he here for a while then, or is this temporary?"

Spenser went back to fussing, and Tomás couldn't help noticing Spenser was cute when he fussed. "There's going to be a hearing in a few weeks and an investigation into his situation at home. If the grandmother truly does intend to surrender custody, it won't be much of a hearing, more of a formality. We'll see then if he stays here or not. That gives both of us time to make sure this works out." He bit his lip, a brief worrying. "I keep forgetting to put a note on Craigslist for a bed."

"A bed for Duon? I can help you with that." Tomás indicated his apartment with a nod. "My dad can find somebody who has an extra. Does it have to be new?"

"Clean will do. I think I'm going to get him an air mattress in the meantime."

"I can get you one of those too. Do you need it to-night?" When Spenser raised his eyebrows at him, Tomás averted his gaze. "Sorry. I want to help is all."

The kettle whistled, and Spenser poured the water into their mugs. He passed the yellow one to Tomás. "He'll be out of the shower soon. He's been in there for fifteen minutes, but the hot water will run out any second."

This was Tomás's cue to get out any questions he didn't want Duon to hear. He rushed through the ones in his head, trying to triage. "Is he okay? Does he need anything?"

"Clothes. He had a few with him, but they were mostly a random swipe of things from his bedroom floor, and half of it was dance attire, from what I can gather. He's wearing sweats of mine for now, which fit, sort of, but aren't appropriate for school. The social worker said she'd get me some funds to go shopping, but I know better than to count on that. I would have taken him today, but he wasn't in a mental place where leaving the house was a good idea."

"My mom can help. She loves thrifting. She'll bring

him home a whole new wardrobe for twenty bucks."

Spenser gestured to the table, taking his tea to it as he sat. "You live with your parents, yes? But sometimes there are children there too?"

Tomás tossed up a million filters as he formulated his reply. "Yes. My nieces and nephew. We babysit a lot while my sister is…at work."

Spenser cradled his mug in his hands. "Your mother was by earlier. Brought us all kinds of food. I told her thank you, but please thank her again for me. Duon ate everything she gave us like it was his last meal on Earth. I pretended I wasn't hungry so he could eat as much as he wanted."

"I'll tell her. She'll bring more. She loves cooking for people. Loves taking care of people."

"It sounds as if she passed that trait on to her son."

The smile Spenser gave got Tomás in the gut. The whisper inside him wanting to ask the guy out was louder than ever, but it felt wrong to flirt when the focus was supposed to be on Duon. "Can you get me his sizes? I know what kinds of clothes he wears and can tell my mom."

"That would be great. I'll give her some money."

"It's our treat. Please."

Spenser clearly wanted to argue, but the bathroom door opened then, and Duon came into the kitchen. He wore a T-shirt and sweatpants that had to be Spenser's—tight, neat, and pastel grey. He seemed thinner, more petite in his borrowed clothes. His face looked like meat still, his arms full of bruises. His cheek had stitches on it, and it was going to leave a scar.

Duon lingered in the doorway to the kitchen, making himself smaller against the frame. "Yo, Jimenez. Whazzup?"

Tomás fished a grin out of his gut. "I hear you put away my mom's tortillas like a champ."

Duon's face brightened. "Yeah, they were the bomb. Good thing you work so hard, man, or you'd be fat, eating her food every day."

Time to get to why he came, before he lost his nerve. "I'm sorry I wasn't home when you got here. I'm glad Spenser was able to help."

Duon shrugged. "It don't matter."

The response cut, though Tomás knew Duon didn't mean it that way. The phrase was his standard comeback when he was disappointed, his way of erasing heartache. *It don't matter.* Tomás hadn't ever had it directed at him before, and he hated it. But he couldn't explain himself further, so he was stuck with it. And anyway, Duon didn't need his bullshit right now. "We miss you at class. I hope we see you there again soon."

Spenser had withdrawn, letting them chat, but he leaned forward now. "I think the plan is he's going to relax for the rest of this week. We both return to school Monday. Can you get me his schedule for dance?"

Tomás brightened. "Absolutely. I can give him rides home too. I teach every weeknight."

Duon rolled his eyes, but he didn't say anything. Tomás thought maybe he was mad, but he didn't know how to press the issue. When the silence went on a little too long, Duon pushed off from the frame and disappeared into the living room. A few seconds later, a door shut.

Spenser put his hand on Tomás's, closing his fingers gently. "Don't take it personally. He needs a lot of space right now."

Tomás couldn't help but take it personally. "I would have given him a home if I could have. But our family situation is…complicated."

"I don't think he's angry about that. I think he's afraid, more than anything. I'm glad you mentioned dance class. I'm going to make sure he goes, even if he's reluctant about it."

"Why?"

Spenser went quiet. There were stories there, Tomás could tell. He'd assumed this was a quiet kid from the suburbs bent on saving the world, but he wasn't so sure now. Something else was going on, something Spenser wasn't ready to share and Tomás didn't have a right to ask about.

He saw, too, that Spenser had the same whisper of attraction he did. But he had a wall up as well, apparently deciding it was best to tuck his feelings quietly away. Probably because of Duon.

The realization left Tomás sad. And tired. But he didn't dwell on it, simply buried it as he did so many things he wanted in life, so he could focus on the things he had to do instead.

NEITHER THE SOCIAL worker nor Vicky had much to offer Spenser in the way of news about what would happen to Duon the day after his placement. They both said the same thing, that they were exploring options, and in the meantime if Spenser was willing to continue to be an emergency placement, it would be wonderful and much appreciated. The next day, however, Vicky asked Spenser if they could meet at his place while Duon was at the studio.

"I found a shelter with space for him," she said as Spenser made coffee. "It's in Rochester, which is the first downside, and it's a temporary situation only. It's run by Lutheran Social Services. He'd be in a room with four other youth."

Spenser could well imagine what such a room would be like. He masked his shudder with a shake of his head. "I don't mind being a one-child shelter. I don't think this place in Rochester would be good for Duon. He'd run away the second he could."

"They'd take his shoes to prevent him running, but knowing Duon, he'd be one of them it wouldn't stop."

Spenser sipped his tea, but it did nothing to dull the bitterness of his thoughts. Oh, he remembered *those* shelters. Kids at risk for running away had their shoes removed to make it harder for them to achieve their goal. Spenser had endured such an indignity plenty. It had only made him that much more determined to leave. "I wouldn't mind being his guardian until he came of age. There's no need to consider a shelter, unless there's pushback from DHS or the judge."

"The technical legal term would be *suitable other.* Guardianship is possible, but I'd advise you to give it a few months before you consider it. Basically, you'd be home base. A roof over his head, food in his belly. Because you're not a licensed foster parent and he's a minor, there are a few extra hoops to jump through before we can make a suitable other placement official, but I can't imagine it being a problem. I did, though, get a hold of Avenues. They don't have a host home opening, as I suspected, but they're happy to talk to you about joining the program. I gave Ryan your number, which I hope was all right."

It was, of course, perfectly all right with Spenser.

The social worker stopped by again not long after, calling on her way to make sure he'd be home. At first Spenser had thought the tactic was a means to give him a sort of spot test, not giving him time to DHS-approve his apartment, but when the woman arrived, harried and exhausted despite her smile, Spenser decided it was more that she was running around trying to fit too much work into a day already too long. Her name was Tracy, and she was about his age, though when she spoke, especially about what Spenser should expect from the state, she had the old eyes of someone who had seen too much.

"My guess is the judge will approve you as a permanent suitable other at the hearing. It won't happen right away because court is overbooked, and we also need to check in with the family to be sure they want to relinquish custody and to follow up on the assault. Duon says he doesn't want to press charges against his cousins or his grandmother, but the guardian ad litem wants to crosscheck a few things, and we need to make sure the county attorney doesn't want to press charges in his stead. I doubt she will, to be honest." She sifted through her notes, occasionally passing papers to Spenser. "I have to be upfront and tell you there'd be no compensation of any real means for you as a non-relative suitable other. Okay, to be honest, there's *none* for you. After six months you can claim him on your taxes as a dependent. Halcyon will get him some help with books and clothes and so on, but that's about it. As you said, Avenues would help him, but not you. If you were a foster parent, it'd be a different thing."

"What about health insurance?" Spenser couldn't remember what he'd had, if any.

"State of Minnesota will cover him through Medicaid. We can give you the legal ability to sign for him."

Spenser hadn't considered he'd need such permission, but it made sense. The mention of the law, though, led to some darker questions. "If the amendment banning marriage equality passes, will it change anything?"

Tracy paused. "I…don't know. I don't think so? Unless more legislation followed specifically making it not okay for LGBT people to adopt or care for children."

The thought made Spenser queasy. "Let's hope it doesn't pass then, I guess."

She left just before Duon came home.

Tomás had given him a ride, and he came in with Duon, lingering to smile at Spenser and politely ask about his day. "How's it going?"

Spenser replied in kind. "Fine, thank you. And you?"

"Good, good."

Spenser wished Tomás were asking after his life in earnest. Perhaps he was and Spenser was simply too poorly versed in flirting to recognize it. He didn't think so, though. He'd done more hooking up than dating, but the moves of the dance had to be similar. Show interest, check for interest in the other party. If found, proceed to desired outcome.

Sometimes Spenser thought Tomás was interested, but it was only ever a flicker, like now, as their gazes held too long. Just about when Spenser wanted to invent another question to ask, Tomás turned his focus to Duon, and the moment was over.

Tomás hung out with Duon while Spenser finished putting dinner together. While they did the dishes, Spenser got a phone call from the representative from Avenues, and they set up a time to discuss the situation on Saturday.

They met at a restaurant not far from Spenser's apartment building, where the man—Ryan—had a table waiting. Spenser was fairly sure the man was gay. He had all the tells of a gentle otter—beard, glasses, nice, midsized body, kind smile, and a quick cruise as he shook Spenser's hand.

"It's great to meet you. Thanks for your interest in the program and for taking a child into your home."

Though he'd played it coy with the other official representatives so far, with this man Spenser had the urge to come clean. "I'm a graduate, I suppose you could say, of the host home program. Clara Hanssen and Betsy Sanderson took me in when I was nineteen. I owe them everything."

Ryan beamed. "Oh, Clara and Betsy. I was so sad to hear Betsy passed last year. They'd been out of the program as hosts for a few years, but she was a great advocate for us right up until her death. Of course Clara is still involved in fundraising up to her eyeteeth. How wonderful to hear you were in the program and now want to be a host home family. I'm going to talk to you at some point about doing a testimonial for the website. For now, though, let's discuss Duon." He passed Spenser a folder. "You know how the program works from the inside, but I'm going to give you the full spiel about the history and how it works as a host, not a youth."

"Sure." Spenser flipped through the file. "I never

did hear the story, actually."

"Avenues for Homeless Youth has been around in one incarnation or another since 1994, and we're growing all the time, both in scope of the program and in what we address. A number of the young adults we serve aren't aware they're homeless—they're couch-hopping, turning tricks, basically doing any and everything they can to get their needs met. We have a shelter where youth can drop in or live until they're twenty-one, and we're opening a new facility soon in Brooklyn. Of course, with four thousand youth homeless on any given night and ten thousand homeless at some point in each calendar year, there are countless kids we can't serve. The population most at risk and most difficult to safely house in a shelter are the LGBT kids."

Spenser knew that truth well. "Are you part of the foster care system?"

Ryan's kind face faded, and his tone was briefly sharp. "We're decidedly *not* part of it, no. Many of our youth have run away from foster care or have fled at the threat of being placed. There are good people in the system, but there's also a great deal of prejudice. Liberal-minded people are more likely to give donations in the form of money, not time, and few are willing to go through the certification process to be a foster family. There's a predominance of conservative religious families in the program, and as you can imagine, this doesn't mesh well with the LGBT youth population. We select hosts differently, and while we provide support and some financial assistance, we give that directly to the youth, not to the host family. We operate outside the foster care system, though DHS has come to view us as an asset and often works with us as much as they can."

Spenser scanned the papers. "This all looks good to me. I know I'll have a learning curve on parenting a teen, but I'm willing to try. I don't want Duon in a shelter or on the streets."

Ryan nodded. "There are so many dangers for his population. It would shock most people to learn how quickly young adults on the street are trafficked. Especially in the winter when it's cold, it doesn't take much convincing to get a kid into a stranger's apartment, but that warm cup of soup and a bed soon becomes something sinister and terrible. We don't think about slavery being real in the modern age, but it's here, and the youth we serve are the most at risk. It's usually only a matter of hours before they're picked up and disappeared from the face of the world."

Spenser rubbed his cheek, keeping his gaze on the paper to hide how much thinking about trafficked teens upset him. "What are the requirements to be a host in the program?"

"There aren't many. You need to have an open and accepting home, you need to pass a standard background check, and you need to come up with a few references."

"What about his room? He's on my couch for now,

but I'm going to turn my spare room into his bedroom, as soon as I get a bed."

"Either arrangement is fine. A number of our youth in the host home program sleep on couches. The truth of it is, we set the rules. We have a few more boxes to check because Duon is under eighteen, but I'll be frank. DHS is happy to have their caseload lightened, and in my opinion, we do better by our populations than any other organization going. So if you're interested, we're happy to have you."

Spenser didn't hesitate. "I'm interested."

"Then welcome to Avenues, Spenser Harris." Ryan smiled ruefully. "Again."

As Spenser arrived home, he met Tomás in the hallway. Spenser decided to take a small leap. "I was approved for the Avenues program today."

Tomás beamed. "That's great news. Congrats."

Spenser's heart tripped as he braved onward. "You should come over later. Celebrate with us."

Tomás's face fell. "Ah. Sorry, I can't. Work."

Cheeks heating, Spenser nodded. "Sure." Fearing he'd exposed himself, he added, "I won't keep you," and continued on his way.

Was that regret on Tomás's face? Relief? Hesitation? Spenser wasn't sure, and he didn't linger long enough to find out.

CHAPTER FOUR

Tomás might not have been able to give Duon a home, but he devoted as much time as he could to being present in his life. He got him clothes and a phone and a second pair of shoes, gave him rides home from dance classes, and had him over for dinner with his family every Sunday. Sometimes he invited Spenser, but Spenser always declined, and Tomás didn't push the issue. He wondered often if he should, but by the time he got around the complicated moral wrestling of whether or not it was a good idea, what with his family and his too many jobs, and because he couldn't decide if their mutual concern over Duon meant they shouldn't get involved—well, truthfully, long before he laid out that calculus, Spenser tucked himself back into his cocoon, and the moment passed. Eventually Tomás stopped considering overtures toward Spenser at all and focused on Duon.

It was probably good, Tomás decided as October wore on, that he hadn't been able to take Duon in. His schedule had become so tight he basically came home to eat and sleep, which meant caring for Duon would have fallen to his parents, and they had enough on their plate. Alisa took the kids for a few days here and there, but by the end of the month they'd practically moved in again, and Alisa stopped coming by entirely. Tomás didn't ask where she was because the answer would have unquestionably pissed him off. His sister's thoughtlessness bugged him now more than ever. One slip would start the snowball forming that would take his whole family away from him.

Laurie noticed how stressed he was, and one night his boss strong-armed him into going home with him for a late dinner.

"You need to unwind." Laurie put his arm around Tomás's shoulders and herded him to his car. "I have everything prepped at home for a pasta dish, and I sent Ed out for wine, bread, and salad."

Tomás had enjoyed Laurie's cooking before and wasn't going to argue. He texted his mom as they walked to let her know where he was going. When he looked up, they were at Laurie's car. "You've managed to keep from getting your car wrapped with the VOTE NO banner, I see."

Laurie smiled wryly. "Not for much longer. We're going to Duluth this weekend to get it done."

"*Duluth?* Why on earth are you going there?"

"Apparently that's where the next event is. We're meeting friends of one of our friends there for dinner after." Laurie regarded Tomás thoughtfully over the roof of the car. "You should come along with us."

"I work every weekend. Can't do it." He paused, remembering. "Though, wait. There was a schedule mix-up, so I'm not at the nursing home this time. I have to open at Starbucks, but I'm off at eleven."

"We could make it work." Laurie pressed his hands together and tucked them under his chin. "*Please* say you'll come. I love Marcus, and I'm sure his friends will be fine, but…well, I'd love for you to be there, if you think you can spare the time."

He probably couldn't, but he wanted to. Not for Duluth but to get away from everything for a bit. He should take the kids to the movies or do something with Duon, but oh, he'd love to go with Laurie and Ed. The idea of getting out of town and *being* for a few hours was heady. "I'll think about it."

When they got to Laurie's loft, Ed was in the kitchen, puttering around. Another man was there too, and he turned out to be the Marcus Laurie had referenced.

"I hope you don't mind that I invited him." Ed said this casually enough, but he also put his back to his guest and gave Laurie one of those couple-glances that conveyed whole conversations with the widening of an eyeball.

Whatever message he delivered, Laurie received it loud and clear. "Of course not. We certainly have plenty of food. Marcus, so good to see you. Let me introduce you to Tomás."

Marcus was a lawyer at a high-powered firm and also a big old bear, which Tomás didn't mind. But the man was also clearly nursing a great heartbreak. Sifting through their dinner conversation, Tomás learned Marcus had recently ended a long-term relationship after his fiancé had been caught cheating on him.

They discussed more than anything the impending election, both the Presidential race and the looming vote on the amendment. Ed, a recovering Catholic, was angry at the role the church had in trying to get the discriminatory amendment passed. "It's not like they'd have to go marrying anybody. They don't even have to watch me go down the aisle. All I want is some goddamned health insurance and the right to make sure Laurie can make medical and legal decisions for me if I'm unable to make them myself."

"And tax benefits." Marcus leaned back in his chair and grimaced. "There are over a thousand legal advantages you get by being married."

Tomás chased a tomato around his plate with a fork as he withdrew from the conversation, lost to his own reverie. He'd never, not once, considered getting married, which it occurred to him was weird. It wasn't that he didn't want to do it. He hadn't thought he'd be able to, either legally or because he knew his focus should be on his family. Except tonight, watching Ed and Laurie be a couple, he admitted he wanted to have a partner too. The knowledge cut, though. Even if he could find someone who would tolerate his crazy schedule, total strangers might be about to take that right away before he so much as worked up a good daydream about it.

A daydream about Spenser, maybe. They'd stay up late one night, talking about Duon, and one thing would lead to another. They'd start making dinner together, and Spenser would come over when Tomás's mother invited Duon. Sometimes the two of them would take all the kids to the park. All four.

Tomás's heart hitched. *Shit.* He almost wanted that more than a date. Except going to the park with the kids and a date *would* be a great time for Tomás. Seeing someone who cared about his family, who wanted to join it.

Would Spenser want that? Or was this all because he was the gay man who was handy?

Laurie's tense, terse voice brought Tomás back to reality. "I want it to be over. I can't stand hearing about this every single day."

Ed shook his head. "But that's just it, Laur. If they pass the amendment, it'll never end. We don't know yet how hard it would hit us."

"It's going to remain an issue for another decade at least." Marcus sipped his wine. "If the amendment passes, it could get overturned by the Supreme Court. The DOMA case is already underway. More lawsuits will come. As soon as there's a circuit split on a marriage equality ruling, they'll have to weigh in on the whole mess. If we don't get marriage equality then, people will keep finding ways to challenge the court until it changes enough to get it through. Though every day this drags on, more people join our side. Look at Iowa. They had their ruling in 2009, and they have yet to make any real headway to overturn it, despite effort."

"They voted out those judges who made that decision," Laurie pointed out.

"Yes, but only the one time. The next round in November is expected to have a different outcome." Marcus leaned over the table, his earlier sorrow buried under his animation while talking about the law. "Mark my words. It won't be long before we'll see everything change. You two will be married here in Minnesota. Before we're retired, we'll see marriage equality across the whole country."

When Laurie became visibly distressed, Ed deftly steered them to more benign topics, like Marcus's eagerness to visit his family upstate for the upcoming holidays and Laurie's recent improvements and future plans at the studio. As the evening wore on, Ed seemed to wane faster than he should have, and he'd hardly touched his wine. When he disappeared into the bathroom and reappeared with wires bulging beneath his shirt and a TENS unit in his hand, Tomás realized his host must be having one of his bouts of chronic pain from his neck injury. The pain and injury Laurie was always so worried about—which he wouldn't be able to help him with if the people of Minnesota decided to make it illegal for him to call Ed his husband.

Tomás excused himself shortly after, wanting to give the couple their space, and when Laurie walked him out, he formally agreed to go with them to Duluth that weekend.

When they picked him up from Starbucks on Saturday, Laurie, Ed, and Marcus were already piled in Laurie's car, ready for the adventure. It was a cold and windy day, but this didn't slow the festivities, and Tomás decided festival was exactly the right word to describe watching the volunteer crew apply decals to cars. There were upwards of fifty vehicles waiting their turn and three times that number of people milling around, chatting and sipping coffee and cocoa. In the middle of it all was Richard, the man who'd started the whole project. Ed eagerly explained the story to Tomás while Laurie oversaw the decal being put onto his car.

"Richard came home from an LGBT fundraiser all psyched to do his part, and he started by putting his VOTE NO sign he'd donated fifty dollars to get in his condo's front yard. Except the condo association wouldn't let him. They said it wasn't about his message but about the sign itself. They don't do signs in yards."

Tomás strongly suspected it had been both the sign and the message. "So how did that lead to car decals?"

"Well, he was pissed. He put the sign in his living room window, but it wasn't the same as something in his yard. Then it occurred to him if he made his *car* into a sign, they couldn't do anything about it. You and me, we'd have hung signs in the back window or something. Not this guy—he works for a car dealership. He designed a decal, got a local company to make him a set, and he parked his car in the drive. Then he took a picture and put it on Facebook—and *everybody* wanted one. That led to him making more, and more, until now it's a viral campaign with pop-up parties all over the city. They've done fundraisers and held rallies at universities. Because you can't stop people from driving, and you can't regulate what they put on their cars."

It really was an ingenious idea, and Richard looked plenty proud, wearing a bright blue T-shirt under an open blue puffy parka and an orange fleece headband over his ears. His cheeks were bright with cold, but he never stopped smiling. When Ed passed by him on his way back to Laurie with two styrofoam cups of hot chocolate, Richard waved.

Laurie was huddled beside Marcus and his friends from Logan, the small town where they'd all grown up and where Arthur and Paul still lived. Laurie looked entirely out of place beside the three burly bears, but he appeared relaxed and charmed despite himself. "I thought there'd be protesters. I mean, this can't be terribly welcoming country up here."

"Nah. It'd be too much confrontation." This comment came from Arthur, Marcus's shorter, red-haired, and more boisterous friend. Arthur gestured vaguely to the environs surrounding the parking lot. "They'll save it for when people go home. Pick them off one by one. It's the bigot way."

Paul, lingering at Arthur's elbow, nodded in agreement. "I'd get a decal, but my family would have kittens."

Arthur grunted. "I'm tempted to buy you one for that reason alone."

Laurie did his raised-by-a-socialite routine where he drew polite conversation out of Arthur and Paul. They told him about their hometown of Logan, about their jobs at the local lumbermill, about the cabin they shared and hoped to lure Marcus into sharing with them when he moved back home.

Soon it was time for Laurie's car to receive its decal, and all conversation stopped as the six of them watched Richard and his team apply the wrap to each side of the vehicle. Ed squeezed his husband's hand, checking him for signs of second thoughts. Though Laurie did seem nervous, he kept his chin high. When the decal was finished, he shook Richard's hand and thanked him for spearheading the activism, then wrote him a check for the decal.

They chatted idly on the way back to the Cities, and Tomás tuned some of it out, enjoying the space to simply exist without demands. As they approached the Cities, however Ed raised his voice and addressed the car with a grin and a wicked look in his eye. "Let's take a drive around town."

Laurie raised his eyebrows. "Where do you want to go?"

"Everywhere. Maybe drive real slow past houses

with VOTE YES signs."

That was exactly what they ended up doing. For two hours they canvassed the Twin Cities in Laurie's newly wrapped car, broadcasting their opinion on the upcoming vote everywhere they went. The four of them made a contest of coming up with more and more conservative neighborhoods to drive through, and to Ed's delight, Laurie sniggered when a particularly WASPy woman in Anoka pursed her lips at their car.

"Let's go dancing," Laurie suggested as they finally meandered to St. Paul.

Marcus frowned. "Where do you want to go? It's Sunday night. Nothing's open."

Ed waggled his eyebrows. "Well, as it happens, I know a guy."

They went to the Dayton's Bluff studio, giggling like schoolboys as they unlocked the door and turned on the lights. Ed, Laurie, and Tomás put on their dancing shoes, and they fished out a pair from the lost-and-found that fit Marcus. Laurie put music on the stereo, and the four of them partnered up, laughing as they spun around the floor to the rhumba, samba, and then, for Ed and Laurie, a tango.

Marcus wasn't much of a dancer, but Tomás taught him as best he could on the fly, and the guy was a pretty quick study. "Where'd you learn all this?" Marcus asked when they were finished and sitting on the warm-up bench sipping bottled water. "Were you a child prodigy like Laurie?"

Tomás laughed and wiped water away from his mouth. "Not even close. I took lessons when my family could afford them. Mostly I taught myself, watching videos and practicing in a mirror."

"Ed told me about the trouble with your parents because he was hoping I might have ideas on how to help you. Has your lawyer gotten anywhere with their application for naturalization?"

Tomás swallowed the bitter bile that rose at the mention of their lawyer and at the thought of having his laundry aired, even for a benevolent reason. "Nowhere. All he's done is take my damn money."

"I don't specialize in immigration law, but I have a good friend who does. He might not be able to do it pro bono, but he could do it for administration costs."

The offer caught Tomás so off-guard tears formed in his eyes. "You don't have to do that."

"I don't mind. You're a friend of Ed's, so that's enough for me. Plus this same guy knows Laurie's godfather. We can call in a favor at both ends. It's no trouble. Happy to help."

Tomás ducked his head to hide his tears, but they were evident in the thickness of his voice. "Thank you." He drew a ragged breath, let it out. "Thank you."

Marcus gripped his shoulder, squeezing it gently. "Not a problem."

Tomás did cry on the way home, so hard he had to sit in the parking lot for a minute and pull himself together before he could go inside. Once he was in bed, he lay awake listening to his mother urge the children to go to sleep, soothing the youngest from a nightmare.

He wanted the amendment to fail, yes. He wanted to find someone to marry him, yes—Spenser, or someone he had yet to meet. But he hoped his friends wouldn't hold it against him to know if he had to pick between marriage equality and a law promising he wouldn't come home one day to find out his parents had been raided and taken to Mexico…well, it wouldn't be a choice.

Like Marcus said. Family first. Except Tomás didn't share Marcus's optimism about people's willingness to give him, or his parents, any protection at all.

THE FIRST FEW weeks with Duon went exactly as Spenser expected. Duon was quiet, freakishly obedient, and polite to the point of being ridiculous. But while he rinsed every plate and always hung up his towel, he also spent half the night awake raiding the fridge, sometimes eating all but the jars of condiments. Once he ate those too. Sometimes Spenser heard him crying in his room. But if he asked him what was wrong, Duon wiped his emotions away and said only, "It's cool, man. It's all cool."

His responses were far, far too close to home, and they dredged up old ghosts.

Spenser's time in foster care hadn't been particularly traumatic, but it hadn't been pleasant, either. His first home was in an Eden Prairie subdivision, the house so nice and so large it felt like a palace. The neighbor children were mean though, and they'd teamed up with his foster brothers to pick on him. Though he hadn't felt attachment to the family, it hurt when they chose to resolve the issue by sending *him* away, not the older boys. He'd learned to school his emotions, but it hadn't mattered. He was a legal adult before he found a home.

He wanted more than anything to be that safe space for Duon.

Because he knew it would be good for both of them, Spenser focused on routine, the coping mechanism that had always gotten him by. He woke at six. He worked out for three miles on the elliptical. He showered, ate breakfast, then nudged Duon through his own morning routine enough to get him ready for school. Nearly every day Duon went to the studio, sometimes driven by Spenser, sometimes Tomás. While Duon was there, Spenser ran errands, did laundry, and fixed dinner, so that when Tomás brought Duon home, the apartment was homey and welcoming. They discussed their respective days while they ate and did the dishes, and then they sat at the kitchen table and did homework. If they had time, they watched TV or played a game of cards. Sometimes Tomás joined them, but usually he was busy with his family, or he had to go to bed early because he had to get to Starbucks at four thirty in the morning. Sometimes Vicky or Laurie or Ed stopped by to check on Duon. But the routine was there, a gentle scaffolding to hold them all in place. It seemed to help Duon become accustomed to his new environment. It definitely helped Spenser.

School, as always, kept him more occupied than he wanted to be. It was his third year at St. Anthony, so he knew what the fall festival and Christmas pageant would require from staff. This year, however, they had an added chore, and it was particularly uncomfortable for Spenser.

While a majority of the staff was either Lutheran or nondenominational, St. Anthony's principal, Dr. Brett Harvey, was a strict and conservative Roman Catholic. He required the staff to not only participate in morning prayer in the school chapel, but to also know the Catechism and endure pop quizzes on its minutiae whenever he met them in the hallway. But this fall, in the months running up to the election, Harvey put out calls for volunteers to canvas local neighborhoods, distributing literature devoted to the passage of Amendment 1, the amendment seeking to ban same-sex marriage in the state of Minnesota.

Spenser wasn't out at work, and he had no intention of changing that, but his closet made moments such as this incredibly awkward. He kept his coworkers at a polite distance, attending group gatherings but never seeking out one-on-one friendships. Letting his guard down felt too risky. School was work, and he didn't want it complicated by anything personal. His decision felt wise as he watched colleagues he'd counted as friends take up the cause to "protect marriage" with a zeal that pierced Spenser's heart. His teaching partner, who he'd nearly come out to several times, had a *Vote Yes* bumper sticker on her car.

The all-staff activities lately had focused around lobbying efforts to pass Amendment 1, and since Harvey had a public chart in the teacher's lounge keeping track of who had canvassed and who had not, Spenser eventually had to "participate," in that he accepted the clipboard full of flyers, chose a liberal neighborhood far from the school, and dumped the notices in his trash can as soon as he was home. Caring for Duon provided some relief from these demands, as a child in need took precedence, thankfully, over canvassing for hate, but Harvey didn't stop watching Spenser like a hawk. There was no reason for him to know Spenser's orientation, but Spenser still felt exposed and uneasy every time he walked into the school.

Happily, the responsibility of caring for Duon and the intensity of parenting lessons he was learning on the fly and in the field kept Spenser adequately distracted from both Harvey's crusade and the impending amendment itself. As the date of Duon's court hearing came closer—the hearing where they would learn whether or not Duon's grandmother was dropping custody and if Duon could stay with Spenser permanently—Duon became less and less of a perfect child. When the court date was moved at the last minute to November sixth, Duon became more agitated, obsessed with not going to school. He invented a million reasons to stay home, none of which Spenser accepted.

"Why don't you want to go to school? Is someone harassing you?"

Duon rolled his eyes. "Come on, man. I just don't want to go. Why do you care?"

"I'm an educator. Of course I care."

This reply, of course, never won him any cool points. More than once Spenser had prodded his charge into complying by stating, calmly but clearly, that a condition of his staying with Spenser was school attendance. While Duon accepted this dictate, he didn't care for it. Spenser suspected he was the first person to ever require Duon go to school.

Tomás became Spenser's ally in the struggle, his cheerleading counterpoint to Spenser's hardline stance. "Come on, D. You know you can do it. You're smarter than all of them."

This never failed to puff up Duon. "Damn right I'm smarter than them. But I don't need to go to prove it."

"Yeah, but why waste it? Get your degree. Light the world on fire."

"I don't want to go to school. I want to focus on dancing. *That's* what I want to light on fire."

It was at this point Spenser appeared with the hammer. "Well, the only way you get to go to dance is to go to school first."

This tag-team approach worked for a long time.

Every day through the rest of October, Spenser drove Duon to school, getting him there almost an hour early. Duon hated this, especially because Spenser arranged for Duon to wait in the office and do any missing work during that time. After school Duon always went to the studio, sometimes driven by Spenser, sometimes by Tomás, sometimes by Ed or Laurie, and the promise of going there at the end of the day was usually enough to get Duon through even the greatest morning resistance.

But on Election Day, the day of the rescheduled hearing, Duon woke up surly and obstinate, insisting he wasn't going to go. Spenser was nervous too—this would be the day when he either became a parent or watched the boy he'd come to feel strongly for be removed from his hands. But avoiding it wouldn't solve any problems.

"Duon, I need you to go to the hearing. I'm open to bribes to get you there. I'll take you anywhere you want to eat tonight, if you go."

No response.

"We'll go shopping."

Not even a glance up.

As Spenser racked his brain, he saw Duon's dance clothes stacked neatly in a pile on top of the laundry basket. "If you go to the hearing, I'll come with you to your dance class. I'll *join* your dance class."

It had been a Hail Mary, this bribe, but it was the one that got Duon to not only look up but smile. "For real? You'll be in my dance class?"

Spenser seized the lure with both hands. "Yes. Absolutely. I'm not going to have time to buy a leotard, but I will attend and I will dance." His nerves bubbled out of their box. "Even if everyone laughs at me."

"Nobody's gonna laugh. And it's modern dance. You just gotta wear loose clothes."

Spenser marched to his room, grabbed workout clothes and shoes, and deposited them in a bag. "Done. Get your backpack. If we leave in the next thirty seconds, we have time for Egg McMuffins on the way."

They had their Egg McMuffins, but Duon barely got to eat his because he talked a mile a minute about all the things he was going to teach Spenser in dance class. None of it made any sense to him, but Spenser didn't care. He was only glad to have gotten his charge out the door. He had time to wiggle out of actually dancing later.

The hearing was quick and far more banal than Spenser could have imagined. Spenser had anticipated the grandmother would attend, but the guardian ad litem said she'd surrendered custody voluntarily. It wasn't quite as big of a deal, Spenser supposed, than if it had been Duon's mother. He didn't understand how the law worked, but he couldn't help thinking this was rather a perfunctory, unfeeling way to give a child away.

In other words, the system hadn't changed.

The judge asked a few questions of the social workers and the guardian ad litem about Spenser and Duon, confirmed this was what Duon wanted, and basically that was it. She said she was pleased to see someone had stepped up to take on Duon, and with the gentle tap of her gavel, she made Spenser a parent.

Duon didn't have much reaction in the courtroom, and Spenser didn't prod him for one. As Spenser drove him across town to deposit him at school, however, Duon bounced higher on the seat as he explained how amazing dance class was going to be together. Spenser nodded absently, mostly dizzy with the realization of what he had so casually been handed, hoping he was up to the task.

But once he was at school, it dawned on him he had some news to share. So he pulled out his phone. Also, it dawned on him he should let them know they should expect another person for dance class. So he texted.

Hi, Tomás. This is Spenser. I wanted to let you know I was officially named a suitable other placement for Duon today. Also, it's a long story, but I only got Duon to the hearing by promising I'd join his dance class tonight. I hope that's okay. I'll obviously pay whatever fees I need to, but I thought I should let someone at the studio know. Let me know if you need anything else from me before we get there. Thanks.

He sent similar texts to Vicky, Laurie, and Ed, minus the information about dance class. Soon his students began arriving, and Spenser was able to think no more on being a new parent and whether or not he had bitten off more than he could chew with his rash promise of attending dance class. Not until his lunch break when he checked his phone and saw he had a missed call, voicemail, and text from Tomás. Spenser read the text while he spread his lunch across his desk. There were several texts, in fact.

So glad to hear about the hearing! As for class, that's not a problem at all. We'll be glad to have you. Do you have loose clothes and soft shoes? The shoes will be the most important part.

What size are you? You might be able to borrow a pair of mine.

I'm a nine.

Oh, but you'll need thinner socks.

Hey, I called but couldn't get you. I'll bring some stuff with me in case.

Oh, and you don't have to pay anything. This one's on me.

Amused, Spenser listened to the voicemail too, which was basically the same information delivered with more enthusiasm. There was a sparkle to Tomás's voice he'd never heard before. Like Duon, dance was where Tomás's passion lay.

It wasn't Spenser's. In fact, he frankly hated to dance. He'd been keenly aware every time he went clubbing that some people had natural rhythm and some people did not. He was one of the latter.

Sometimes he wondered if his failure at dance was the reason he never dated. Hookups only wanted a bed, but dates always seemed to involve a dance floor, which meant whatever charm Spenser had managed up until that part of the evening evaporated in five minutes of awkward gesticulations. So now he only hooked up, never dated, and never danced, full stop. Not even at weddings.

But he had made a bargain with Duon, and though initially he'd planned to weasel out, he decided as a parent now his job was to stick to his word. He could hide under his covers and work through his mortification once he was alone at home.

The bell rang to announce the end of noon recess, and Spenser stopped thinking about dance lessons and how much he didn't want them. Not until the bell rang again, signaling the end of the day, letting him know it was time to pay the piper.

He half-hoped Duon had forgotten, but he had no such luck. Grinning wide enough to split his face, eyes dancing with anticipation, Duon leaped into the car when Spenser approached the high school. "You ready for your lesson, *teach*?"

Spenser gave a defeatist salute, and Duon laughed. He then peppered Spenser with questions—did he know this move or that one, and he was incredulous when every question received a "no, I don't" as the answer. Thankfully, it wasn't far from Duon's school to the studio, so Spenser didn't have to endure this for long. Unfortunately, this also meant it was that much less time until Spenser walked into the boy's locker room, clutching his duffel and wondering what in the hell he'd gotten himself into.

Tomás was in there already, wearing a tight T-shirt and a pair of shorts barely covering his ass and showcasing his…everything. He was a little taller than Spenser and significantly more muscular, though not like Laurie's husband. His muscles were lean but well-defined.

They were also highly distracting.

Tomás hugged Duon and wished him congratulations on his new official home, and then he smiled at Spenser, an eager grin making the sparkle in his eyes that much brighter. "You ready for your dancing lesson?"

"Hell yes, he is," Duon answered for him, tossing his arm around Spenser's shoulders.

Spenser disentangled himself gently from his charge. "I'm fairly sure I'm about to make a fool of myself, but I made Duon a promise, and I intend to keep it."

"Don't worry. We'll go easy on you." Tomás winked, and Spenser blushed.

He tried to hide in the back, but both Duon and Tomás insisted he be up front. Duon wanted this because *he* was in the front, Tomás because he pointed out he could see his instruction from there. There were twelve other students, all of them teenagers, most of them male, exactly one of them white—Spenser. Until Laurie came out of his office to lean on the doorway and watch, Spenser was the only one melanin-challenged in the whole studio.

And yes, he understood dancing ability wasn't correlated to race—the owner of the studio being exhibit

A—but he couldn't help feeling like everyone else present had come with not only a crib sheet but the teacher's edition to the lesson Tomás was giving. They didn't laugh at him when he screwed up *every single step*, but that was almost worse. And the more badly he performed, the more nervous he became, until he left the floor, red-faced, making a great show of drinking from the fountain on the side of the room until he could get his mortification under control.

This was worse than his failed dates in college. This was a goddamned nightmare.

He wanted to call it quits, but when he saw Duon watching him, smiling and motioning impatiently for him to come back to the dance, he knew he couldn't. Spenser was almost wooden now as he endured the lesson, no longer trying to keep up, only doing his best to get to the end of this class so he could never, ever offer to do something so awful again.

But when it was over, Tomás and Duon ganged up on him, telling him what a good job he'd done. Spenser couldn't handle it any longer. "Are you insane? I was awful."

Tomás held up his hands. "Whoa, *whoa*. You weren't awful. And you had a pretty big disadvantage, because we've been working on this routine for months now."

Spenser wasn't having any of this. His face was red, with exertion, with embarrassment, and with decades-old shame. "I've never been able to dance. And it turns out when you don't try for ten years, you get worse."

Duon and Tomás exchanged a look. Then Duon scuttled toward the locker room. When Spenser attempted to follow, Tomás caught him gently by the elbow and led him to the floor. "Oh no. You, Mr. Harris, are getting another dancing lesson."

Spenser broke free of the grip and backed away. "No, thank you."

Tomás did a fancy step and blocked him. When Spenser went the other direction, Tomás blocked him again. And again. When Spenser sighed in frustration, Tomás winked at him. "See? You're a natural. You're dancing right now."

It had been a long day, the next day would be longer if the amendment passed, and Spenser didn't need this. "I don't care if I can dance or not. I want to go home."

"I can't let you go, not when you're this frustrated. I'd be a terrible teacher if I allowed you to leave."

Oh, this was a low blow, because of course he was right. Spenser went for blunt. "I'm tired."

But Tomás wasn't having it. "Fifteen minutes. Give me fifteen minutes."

"Take an hour." This came from Laurie, who stood at the door to the studio with Duon, who now wore loose sweats and a winter jacket. "I owe a young man some ice cream, and the next class got cancelled because Susan's sick." He waved at Spenser. "Knock 'em dead, tiger."

And just like that, Spenser had landed himself in the middle of an hour-long private lesson.

With Tomás.

CHAPTER FIVE

I T WAS CLEAR to Spenser there was no way out of this situation but through it.

He threw up his hands and faced Tomás. "Fine. Go ahead and teach me. But when you find out it's hopeless, I want you to remember I told you so."

"You're not hopeless. Nobody's hopeless." Tomás went to the stereo and flipped through to some pop music. "That's the first rule of dancing. Believe you can." When Spenser rolled his eyes, Tomás wagged a finger at him. "Say it, Spenser. Say, 'I can dance.' Out loud, right now."

To think it was *Duon* getting the ice cream. "Fine. I can dance." When Tomás gave him a stern look, Spenser schooled himself and repeated the phrase with the best fake enthusiasm he could muster. "I can dance."

It came out dripping with sarcasm too, and Tomás laughed. "Nice start. All right. Let's give you some moves to back up your statement."

Tomás was a good teacher. He walked Spenser through a few basic steps, some of them things he'd covered in class, taking the time now to go through them more slowly. He corrected Spenser's form, explained how if he moved his foot this way and held his arm that way it would be easier, and it was. Soon Spenser had only mild loathing for dancing.

But sometimes he'd catch sight of their audience, the students who had lingered to watch the show, and he'd falter. Or he'd see himself in the mirror and remember he was a terrible dancer, and then he would be. After several rounds of this, Tomás paused the music, turned to their audience, and made shooing motions. "Okay, time to go home. We'll see you guys next week."

They complained, but they left, and once they did, Tomás locked the door and shut the blinds. Now it was only the two of them in the studio. When Tomás turned the music on again, he also switched to something with a little more pulse. "You've loosened up some, but you're still in your own way. Your greatest obstacle to dancing is that you don't think you can dance. And you'll never get anywhere if you don't get rid of those negative thoughts."

"But I don't *care* if I get anywhere," Spenser pointed out. "I only did this for Duon. He's not even here anymore."

"You should dance for you. And you *should* dance, Spenser. You're bursting to. Five times now you've nearly let go, then remembered yourself and buttoned down. It's killing me. It's killing *you*."

Spenser gave him a long glare. "*That* is the most overly dramatic thing I've heard anyone say this month. And I teach kindergarten."

"I don't care whether you believe me or not. But I'll tell you one thing. You're going to let go and enjoy yourself before you leave this dance floor."

This was a nightmare. "You don't get it. *I don't enjoy this.* I never have. I never will."

"You will tonight."

Spenser meant to say no. He intended to insist, to turn on his heel and march—no, *flounce* off the dance floor. Yet he did none of this. He simply stood there, awkward and miserable, waiting for Tomás to do the impossible, to teach Spenser to dance.

"Put your hands on my shoulders." Tomás's hips were already undulating, his body moving with some kind of compulsion to the sound of the music, as if it were wired under his skin. When Spenser obeyed him, Tomás smiled and put his hands on Spenser's hips. "There you go. All right. I want you to relax. Don't try to dance. Simply stand there and allow me to move your body. Surrender your muscles so I can show you what they can do."

Spenser surrendered for three seconds, then went rigid as ridiculousness set in. "I can't."

"You can. You just did. But then you got afraid. Why are you afraid, sweetheart? Who said you couldn't dance?"

Spenser's laugh was short and bitter. "Everyone."

"Someone is telling you right now that you can. Shut your eyes. There you go. Shut them, and stop thinking. Listen to the music. Listen to the sound of my voice. Let it seep into your skin."

It helped, shutting his eyes. But each time he began to relax, panic set in, and Spenser's eyes would fly open. After the third time, he apologized before Tomás could scold him. "I'm not trying to react this way. I can't help it."

Tomás winked at him. "Don't worry, *I* can help you."

He released Spenser, and for a moment Spenser thought he was free. But Tomás only reached into a basket on a shelf near the stereo and came out with a bandana, which he rolled into a flat strip and applied to Spenser's eyes.

"It's clean," he said when Spenser balked.

It wasn't the potential dirtiness of the blindfold freaking him out. "I can't see." Obviously that was the point, but Spenser was nothing but constant panic now. He didn't know why. "Tomás, I don't want to do this."

"I know, honey. Except you want to do it as much as you don't. We only have ten more minutes. Then I won't push you anymore. I promise."

It was scary to dance with a blindfold, though all he was doing was standing still with his hands on Tomás's shoulders, allowing him to move his hips in time to the beat. But there was magic in having his sight taken away, because this time when Spenser let go, he couldn't open his eyes and make it stop. This time, once the beat got its hooks in him, it stayed there. Even when he panicked.

His self-consciousness floundered for a new target. "I must look ridiculous."

"You look beautiful," Tomás said, and kept him dancing.

Spenser didn't enjoy what he was doing, but he didn't hate it either. It felt like grinding gears that hurt to turn yet wanted to anyway. It reminded him of the time when he'd gone with his aunt in Wisconsin to the House on the Rock, the one nice family outing he remembered. They'd walked out to the farthest reaches of the Infinity Room, the bridge suspended over the forest. He'd stared down through the plexiglass and felt his stomach flip over in terror while his mind reveled in the thrill that they were doing this incredibly stupid thing and getting away with it.

Dancing felt similar, but with the roles reversed. His mind was full of warnings of his imminent death, but his body, free and happy with Tomás's touch, said *shut up and let me have this*. It was so much more than simply letting go. It was being this close to Tomás. He was handsome in his dancing getup, but he was something else entirely to touch. To brush against. To feel those muscles working under his hands. To smell his sweat, his deodorant, his uniquely Tomás scent.

To dance with. *Awkward Spenser Harris is dancing with*

a hot guy, and the world isn't burning down around his ears.

Yet.

"There you go. Don't stop, Spenser. Keep dancing."

Was Tomás still moving Spenser's hips? Were these moves he made all by himself? Did he look ridiculous? Spenser didn't know, but when Tomás drew them together, ground their hips in a circle, Spenser's brain stopped whispering he was an idiot and flipped over, as if it had thrown a switch. It stopped telling him he was awful and pointed out that Tomás looked, smelled, and felt amazing. Noticed this man was handsome and wore his muscles well—muscles holding Spenser close, keeping him tight to Tomás's body. Remarked that Tomás's sharp, enticing scent was something Spenser should shut up and pay attention to.

Whispered that maybe this was leading somewhere interesting, and Spenser should find out what was at the end of this road.

When he felt Tomás's stubble on his cheek, Spenser startled, but he didn't stop dancing. He turned into the touch, and when the motion made their skin brush together a second time, a pulse began in the center of him and radiated out, shutting down all thoughts and directives except *let him touch you again* and *keep dancing.*

"There you go." Tomás's breath was on Spenser's cheek. His voice was low and gruff, his body so close it was practically merged with Spenser's. "Relax and enjoy it. You're dancing, sweetheart. You're dancing, and you're good at it."

Spenser felt drugged. Drugged and high and lost, and he didn't want to be found. Older, sleepier parts of him woke, and he turned his head, seeking…*more*. More touch. More smell.

Taste. He wondered how Tomás would taste.

He leaned closer, breathless as Tomás's lips grazed the corner of his mouth, his hot breath against Spenser's skin. Spenser met Tomás's mouth, parting his lips for a kiss.

The bell above the door sounded, a discordant jangling cascade of notes clashing with the song, and shattered the moment. Tomás stepped out of their embrace, and Spenser staggered back blindly as he pushed up the blindfold.

Laurie and Duon stood in the doorway, regarding them with wide eyes.

Spenser glanced away, and Tomás cleared his throat as he hurried to shut off the music. "Just an exercise. You know the old trick. Blindfolding a student to get them to let go of their self-consciousness."

"He was sure letting go all right," Duon drawled, and Laurie shushed him with a quiet chuckle.

Spenser ignored them all, hurrying to the locker room. He blushed the entire time he changed, angry with himself, embarrassed, and…sad. It was the latter that hung on, carving out an emptiness inside him. Or maybe it illuminated something that had been with him all along.

Whatever it was, Spenser didn't let himself dwell on it. He packed it away with his clothes into his duffel, along with all the other silly, unhelpful emotions dancing with Tomás had woken up.

SPENSER WASTED NO time bugging out of the studio with Duon, making noise about homework and laundry, avoiding further eye contact with Tomás the entire time. Tomás, still dizzy and disoriented as he acknowledged he'd practically made out with the man during a dance lesson, was barely able to muster up a "See you later" as they disappeared.

As soon as they were gone, Laurie rounded on Tomás with a gleam in his eye. "So. You and Spenser?"

Tomás tried to throw up a denial, but he could still feel the scrape of Spenser's jaw on his cheek, their bodies pressed together in a way that told him exactly what their dance would have led to if they hadn't been interrupted. He sighed. "I don't know. I mean, he's cute as hell. But it would never work."

"Sure it would. He's a wonderful man. Great with kids. The kindergarten teacher who rescued Duon. And from the looks of things, a promising dance partner."

Yeah, there certainly was that. "I never have time to date, and he has Duon to think about. Plus I have my family."

"He's into you. It was obvious as anything tonight. And you like him too." Laurie nudged him playfully in the arm. "Think about it, is all I'm saying."

Tomás noted the *I voted* sticker on Laurie's lapel. Election Day. He'd voted absentee weeks ago, and he hadn't kept track of the days enough to realize the big moment had finally arrived. The election was a good distraction, though, from thinking about dating Spenser. "Are you guys going to stay up and watch the election returns?"

"We're going to the Minnesota for All Families headquarters. They're having a watch party there." Laurie slung his duffel over his shoulder. "Why don't you come with us?"

Tomás began to give an automatic denial, then stopped. "Maybe I will."

Laurie hooked his arm through Tomás's. "I'm going to kidnap you now, before you change your mind and remember an obligation."

They drove over separately, but they both listened to election coverage on the radio as they drove, and they compared notes as they made their way from the parking lot to the building. "It's a good sign that the amendment is failing," Tomás said. "Not by much, but hopefully it starts failing by a lot as more returns come in. Obama's doing okay too."

Laurie shook his head. "It's too early to know anything on any outcome. I'm not getting excited yet."

The room teemed with people. For most of the evening the campaign had been busy making last-minute phone calls and arranging rides to polling stations, but now everyone was gathered in an auditorium, talking in low voices as the returns were broadcast on a projector at the foot of the stage. Ed waited for them near the back, talking with Marcus and an older woman with a buzz cut, a bright-orange VOTE NO shirt, and a worried expression. Ed excused himself and joined them as they settled into their seats, but after a quick rehash of the same non-news Tomás and Laurie had shared in the parking lot, they didn't say much. Ed made small talk with a middle-aged straight couple to his left and a pair of young gay men in the row in front of them who were excited because they'd just voted for the first time. Laurie remained quiet, his gaze fixed on the screen showing the returns as they came in.

Tomás checked his phone for texts, but he didn't have any. On impulse, he opened the chat window with Spenser from earlier and tapped out a message. *I hope you enjoyed your lesson. You did great.*

It was about as bold as he dared to be, and he worried whether it had been the right thing to say or the right tone as soon as he hit send. But a few minutes later, a reply came.

Thank you. It was more fun than I thought it would be.

Tomás tried to tamp down the ridiculous thrill he got at those words, but he didn't do very well. *I hope you come again. You can, you know. Anytime. Group or private lesson. My treat.*

He bit his lip and held his breath, sure *that* would be a text too far, but the next reply made him grin.

Maybe I will.

Tomás didn't want the conversation to end. Partly because he wanted to flirt with Spenser, partly because the watch *party* was anything but. He texted Spenser again.

I'm at an amendment watch party with Laurie and Ed. I think it'd be more relaxing to walk across the Mississippi River when it was only partially frozen.

This reply was almost immediate. *I had the radio on, but I could tell it was making Duon nervous, so I turned it off.*

Well, nothing is happening. You're not missing anything.

Will you tell me if there's any news?

Of course I will. Do you mind if it comes in late?

I won't be able to sleep until I know.

Okay. I'll tell you, then. Whenever it comes through.

Their conversation was more subdued from that point on. Every hour or so Tomás would give him an update, letting him know there was no change. Eventually Duon went to bed and Spenser put the radio back on, but they still texted occasionally, mostly venting their frustration at no definitive outcome.

Tomás hadn't meant to get so invested in the vote, but after being in Duluth, seeing everyone so excited, he hadn't been able to disengage his heart. He hoped for the best, but he didn't know what would happen if the amendment vote didn't go their way. He didn't know what would happen for his rights—or his parents'—if Obama lost and Romney won. He didn't know what would happen either if the amendment *did* go their way. All he knew was he couldn't stop his hope. He hoped so hard his chest hurt, each breath an unbearable tightness against his ribs.

When New England was called for Obama, the room cheered, and Tomás and Spenser shared a joyful bevy of texts. As both Florida and Pennsylvania went for him too, the cheers grew louder. Tomás clapped along, but he couldn't stop staring at the return numbers for the amendment. They were ahead, but not by much.

At eleven, Ohio went to Obama, and the Presidential election was declared over to another round of riotous cheers. Laurie, Ed, Tomás, and everyone around them exchanged hugs and shouts of joy, and Tomás sent Spenser a picture of them all grinning and making the thumbs-up sign. But at midnight, Amendment 1 still hadn't been called. All signs indicated it wouldn't pass, but it was too close to know for sure.

Ed began to rub his neck more and more, and when he took the last of the narcotics in the pill pouch he kept in his pocket, Laurie declared they were going home for the night. Tomás stayed another hour, but there were few people left, and he realized nice as they were, none of them were the people he wanted to celebrate or console himself with.

I'm coming home, he texted Spenser.

I'll still be up when you get here. Stop by, if you want.

Tomás wanted to, but he wasn't sure if it was a good idea or not. If he went over, after all the flirting, after their dance, he'd be starting something. With Duon's official legal caretaker. With his neighbor. What if it didn't go well? What if it went too well?

What if they got so close he had to explain his family—and Spenser reacted badly? What if it got in the way of his relationship with Duon?

What if this amendment passed and wrecked all their lives?

He listened to Minnesota Public Radio all the way home, and he drove slowly, prolonging the decision he was about to make. Once he was at the parking lot, he sat in his car, avoiding going inside while he dithered over whether or not it was a good idea to go through this door with Spenser. Admitted the real reason he was nervous to start things with Spenser—with anyone.

What if he fell for someone…and the lawyers couldn't help his parents? What if his parents had to go back to Mexico and Tomás's heart was torn in half because no matter what he did he'd have to leave someone behind?

Better not stop by. Better go home and tell him you were too tired. Better to disappoint you both now than break everyone's heart later.

As he put his hand on the keys to turn off the car, an announcement came through the radio.

"It's official. They're calling it. Amendment 1 to the Minnesota State Constitution has failed. The marriage ban has not passed."

Tomás froze.

He stared unseeing at the dashboard, sure he had to have misheard, but as he listened they kept saying it over and over again, trotting out pundits from the national radio, not local, explaining how it had come about, what counties had given it the final push, and what was expected now that the measure had failed to pass.

Failed to pass. The amendment had failed to pass. There would be no discrimination in the Minnesota constitution. Because the people had said no.

They'd said no.

"It's the first time in US history voters have defeated an amendment banning same-sex marriage," the announcer went on. "This is one for the history books. Because if this kind of support carries over, and all signs point that it will, it means Minnesota could easily be looking at full marriage equality within the next year. And with this kind of referendum from a Midwestern state, the tide of public opinion truly has turned on the issue of same-sex marriage."

Tomás let out his breath. He breathed in again, breathed out. Turned off the engine and let the silence of the car ring in his ears.

He was out of the car before the first tears ran down his cheek, but this time he didn't try to stop them from falling. He felt drunk, giddy, like this had all been some kind of a dream, one he didn't want to wake up from. He stumbled up the stairs to the door, pulled it open, and hurried down the hall to apartment three.

Spenser had the door open before he could knock. He held it wide, and they stared at each other, unspeaking, tears streaking their faces. In the kitchen, MPR chattered on, but in the doorway Tomás and Spenser stood frozen.

The amendment failed.

Hope lived.

Tomás didn't know who moved first. Maybe they moved together, a continuation of their shared, strange, mad dream, the one that had started on the dance floor hours ago. The hope fueled by touch, propelled by the promise of the vote.

Whatever the source, all Tomás knew was one minute he stared at Spenser and the next Spenser's face was in his hands, their lips meeting in a kiss more benediction than explosion of passion. A soft press of flesh, a gentle point of contact, but it was enough to finish lighting the spark between them. The flame kindled by their dance flickered and swelled as their lips moved against one another, driven by the wonderful giddiness of possibility.

The kiss ended as quickly as it began. Spenser drew away first, but he caught Tomás's hand, squeezed it. Tomás squeezed back. They stared at one another, the moment heavy with potential as they weighed the decision before them. Tomás saw the hope in Spenser's face, but he also noted the hesitation. The fear.

If we open this door, what happens next?

Tomás didn't know. Except as he stood there, the kiss still burning his lips, he acknowledged the door was already open. The only thing left was to go through.

He stepped forward and kissed Spenser again, another tentative meeting of lips. Then, with a reluctant stroke of Spenser's cheek, he withdrew. "Good night, Spenser."

"Good night, Tomás." Spenser's reply was soft as he held the door, not closing it until Tomás had opened his own. Even then he did so slowly, watching Tomás until the barrier closed between them.

No one was awake as Tomás entered his apartment. It smelled of beans and spice, of fresh tortillas. Of home, of safety, of love. He ate the plate of food his mother had put in the oven by the light of the saint candle his mother kept burning on the kitchen counter, then crept to his room, undressed, and crawled under the covers. Lying on his back, he stared at the ceiling, letting everything sink in.

Marriage equality was going to happen. It had already started. Obama had been elected for a second term, with promises of passing the DREAM act and more.

Spenser Harris had kissed him, tender and sweet like a fairy tale.

With his father's snores drifting through the wall, his belly gurgling with his mother's food, and Spenser's soft lips and quietly eager gaze lingering in his memory, Tomás shut his eyes, tears leaking out as his face split into a grin he couldn't stop.

CHAPTER SIX

EVERYONE WARNED SPENSER about the honeymoon period.

Everyone warned him: Ryan, Vicky, Duon's caseworker, other people in the host home support group. For several months, they said, Duon would be on his best behavior, and things would for the most part be fine. Eventually, however, Duon's subconscious would decide to accept he was truly in a safe place, and the things he'd been avoiding processing for years would rise to the surface, one by one or possibly even all at once. They told Spenser to be ready and to not set things up too lax and easy in these opening days to make his job harder later.

Since Spenser was still unpacking his own shit and felt his parenting on his best day was akin to putting an elephant in flippers, the thought of his job becoming more difficult made him want to curl into a ball. Also, if what Duon was throwing at him now was part of the *honeymoon* performance, Spenser quaked in fear of the day his foster son brought the curtain down.

To start, unless Spenser pulled him out of it, Duon never left his room. He had a laptop issued by the school, and he used it as a television, stereo system, and phone booth. He watched random nonsense on YouTube that would never in a million years make it onto so much as local access cable, and yet Duon was glued to it. He loved watching people yell over each other as they played video games or pulled jump scares on each other in a public park. He hooted in laughter over three-minute rants about toilet paper delivered in slurred slang broken up by jarring edit cuts. He listened to music via free streaming services, but the songs were nothing Spenser had ever heard before.

Duon Skyped, too, with an endless stream of people. Spenser asked who they were, and he swore each time it was a different name. He wondered if he should police this, but when he listened at the door, all he heard was Duon laughing and goofing off with whoever was on the other end of the video chat, trash-talking celebrities or mutual friends. Sometimes he waxed on about his plans once he was eighteen. Apparently Duon was going to go to New York City. Or Los Angeles. Or Vegas. Or Chicago. At first Spenser worried Duon was about to run away. But then he noticed Duon made these plans with *everyone* he spoke to online. They were dreams and fantasies. The same kind Spenser had fabricated for himself as he lay in his bunk in the shelter.

Someday I'm going to get out of here, and it's going to be okay.

This recognition, or at least his projection, made Spenser hesitant to rope in Duon's Internet use. Part of him felt he should be monitoring it, but a greater swell of his soul suggested butting in would break Duon's bubble of safety and dreams. Lurking over his shoulder seemed the quickest way to getting himself shut out entirely.

He wanted to get Tomás's opinion on the issue, but he barely saw the man after their election night kiss. According to Duon, Tomás had shortened his hours at the studio and added a temporary job through the holidays, which amazingly was his *fourth job.* When Tomás saw Spenser in the hallway he smiled, maybe even lingered. But then he was off again to another job or to catch a few hours sleep before he went to work once more.

Spenser tried not to take Tomás's absence personally, but it was difficult. He'd gone to bed election night scolding himself that the kiss meant nothing. It was simply high spirits during a miraculous moment, like that sailor kissing the nurse on V-J Day. Downplaying the incident had been an effort to guard his heart should the kiss *not* lead to something more, but when his pessimistic predictions began to look like accurate assessments, Spenser's feelings were bruised nonetheless.

Focusing on parenting Duon was a good distraction, and so Spenser threw himself into being the best substitute parent he could be. He read every book on parenting adoptive and foster children he could find, and listened to online webinars. He bookmarked several sites discussing trauma in foster children, learning quickly those lessons were best doled out in small batches as they tended to scrape too close to his own experience. It wasn't comforting to see his and his sisters' stories laid out so matter-of-factly, especially when he read things that said, essentially, the deck was stacked against them no matter what. The information on reactive attachment disorder left him sleepless for a whole night. Because by God if the two forms weren't Spenser and his sister Kaylee, two halves of the same dark coin.

Spenser didn't *mean* to be unsociable. He wanted friends as much as anybody. It was hard for him, is all. He didn't know how to trust people. They always said things but didn't mean them. They told him they were so glad he'd come to live with them, then sent him away two months later. They'd tell him if he was a good boy, everything would be fine, and he'd literally do nothing, would be practically furniture, and he'd still come downstairs one morning to see his social worker at the table, his foster mother dabbing at tears, and he'd know he was going to be packing another garbage bag. People told you they loved you, but they lied. How was Spenser supposed to trust anyone when they acted like that?

According to the article he read, it was his mother's

fault, and as usual, hearing her blamed roused complicated emotions in Spenser. *She* had loved him, he was fairly certain. His memories of her were blotchy and hazy, but he remembered hugs. Often she was crying, but she hugged him, a lot. She was always especially loving when she came back late and Spenser had been babysitting. He got so nervous, because he was still small at six, and the babies were heavy and difficult to manage, but when she came home, even if she was drunk or high, she'd always, *always* told him she was proud of him. Always hugged him and kissed him. Then they'd snuggled together on her bed, and in the warm darkness, all of them together, it had been worth every moment of his terror.

Intellectually he knew now it had been horribly wrong of his mother, putting such a burden on him at his age. He wasn't sure when he'd begun caring for his younger siblings, but he couldn't remember a single babysitter, couldn't remember *not* caring for his sisters. He understood her behavior was neglect and abuse. He also had enough sense to not diagnose himself by reading a single article on the Internet.

Kaylee, though.

If Spenser had RAD as a child, it was the inhibited form, meaning he couldn't attach to his caregivers. Kaylee, in contrast, could have been the case study for the disinhibited form. She had *always* gone to *anyone.* When Spenser got too busy with the babies and couldn't give her enough attention, she'd roam the halls of their apartment building, looking for someone to play with. They were the only kids in the building, and it wasn't a great neighborhood. Who had she talked to? What had they said or done to her?

Had Spenser's failure to watch her been the reason she'd failed so many placements? He'd heard some of her story while he'd been at his aunt's place in Wisconsin. He'd hidden on the stairs, listening to his aunt and uncle talk about Spenser's mother and her children. They'd called Spenser creepy and robotic, but they'd called Kaylee a little tramp. Apparently she'd wandered in and out of neighborhood houses at every placement until she was ten, and then she'd run around with boys and been "inappropriate." Spenser had been old enough to understand the gist of their insults but had not been worldly enough to process what they were saying. All he knew was he would be as appropriate as he could be, the best boy in the world, and he wouldn't go back to the shelter.

Of course, it hadn't mattered. He'd gone to a shelter anyway. And Kaylee…Kaylee was long gone by the time he was old enough to look for her. She was lost, and Gina and Hannah had been absorbed by another family, one that didn't want him around.

Spenser wasn't going to let Duon be shut out. Spenser *had* attached to caregivers: Clara and Betsy. True, he didn't call Clara as much as he should. But he did love them, and he'd wept like a baby at Betsy's funeral. They'd loved him too. Clara still regarded him as her son. Even if he got distracted and didn't return her calls, eventually she'd appear on his doorstep and kidnap him for brunch on a random Sunday morning.

Spenser could be Clara and Betsy both. He still knew a pang, though, whenever he heard the Jimenez family through their door, his heart pierced by Tomás's low rumble in Spanish. It was foolish to let himself dream he wouldn't *have* to be both, that someone like Tomás could be his other half, but unfortunately this self-scolding didn't stop him from wishing for such a reality.

Having a second parent would have made many things easier, and not simply the logistics of a second pair of hands. Sometimes Spenser straight up didn't know what to do with Duon. When he picked Duon up from school, he witnessed garish, provocative displays with friends, full of swearing, big hand gestures, and bravado that didn't fit at all with the gentle, playful young man who helped Spenser with the dishes. This was preferable, however, to when he collected a sullen, hunched Duon who refused to speak more than a handful of mumbled words between the school and the Dayton's Bluff studio.

Was there something Spenser was missing? Some article on parenting he hadn't yet read?

Should he get over his broken heart and ask Tomás for help, because a platonic second parent was better than none?

Possibly, but he never did. He continued doing the

best he could, worrying always he'd done the wrong thing or hadn't been supportive enough.

Two weeks before Christmas, on a miserable, sleeting afternoon, Spenser went to Halcyon to turn in a form. There was nowhere to park nearby, and he ended up trudging three blocks through slush. His only saving grace was that, as a native Minnesotan, he always carried a pair of boots in his car, so though he was wet and shivering when he arrived at the neighborhood center, his feet were fine. As he opened the door to the building, he caught sight of an elderly Black woman coming up the sidewalk. Slightly stooped, she walked with a cane, but she moved with an elegance that caught Spenser's attention. She was smartly dressed, in a red wool peacoat buttoned primly, white gloves, and a neat felt hat. She had boots on too, red to match her coat.

Though damp with the same weather making Spenser shiver, she was stoic about it. As she moved toward the door Spenser held for her, she smiled at him. "Thank you."

"Not a problem." Spenser waited patiently until she was through, then hurried around her to open the next set of doors on the other side of the vestibule.

This time, as she walked past him, she chuckled. "Aren't we a gentleman. Thank you again, young man."

They ended up walking down the same hallway, though Spenser moved faster. He was already seated in the chair outside Vicky's office, waiting for her to finish with whoever was in the room with her, when the woman he'd held the door for made her way around the corner, heading toward him. When she stopped in front of Vicky's office as well, however, he hopped up out of his chair and offered it to her.

"Thank you very much." She sighed in relief as she lowered herself into the chair, then leaned on her cane as she regarded Spenser. "Since we keep running into each other, we might as well introduce ourselves. I'm Sandra Stevenson."

Spenser straightened and held out his hand, then hesitated because she hadn't extended hers. "Spenser Harris."

She accepted his hand with much more grace than he'd offered it. Her hands were thin and weathered, but her grip was strong. "What brings you to Halcyon on a night like this?"

He waved the manila envelope in his other hand. "I need to turn in a form." After a pause, he cleared his throat. "You?"

Her voice was warm and bright, but slightly tremulous with age. "I'm volunteering to help organize the donations of Santa presents. Do it every year. Have done since 1982."

"Santa presents?"

"Somebody's got to help be an elf. Santa's got a lot on his mind this time of year." She shifted in her chair and leaned on her cane as she continued. "My church and a few others in the neighborhood gather gifts for children and families that can't afford to spend money on presents, then we help wrap, sort, and distribute them. With my arthritis, I'm not much good at the wrapping anymore, but I'm pretty good at bossing people around."

A memory floated to the surface, reminding Spenser of the Christmas when he was a freshman in high school. He'd recently moved to a new shelter and was feeling pretty miserable. He'd blocked out thoughts of what would come on Christmas morning, because he knew the answer would be nothing. And yet when he'd woken up, there at the foot of his bed had been a package. A handmade hat, scarf, mittens, a leather-bound journal, and a fancy pen. He'd worn the winter gear until it fell apart, except for the scarf, which he still had at home, and he'd filled the journal with all his jumbled thoughts and feelings. "I think I might have been the recipient of one of your deliveries, once upon a time."

"Well that's lovely. You should come by and help us get the presents ready this year. We meet Saturday morning at ten, right here at Halcyon."

Spenser's first instinct was to say he was busy, but then he thought about the way Sandra had shuffled up the sidewalk in the sleet, because her task was more important than the inconvenience of the weather. He also thought about the article on reactive attachment disorder, telling him to be more social. "I think I can make it work. Can I bring…?" He hesitated, unsure of how to refer to Duon. "Can I bring the young man staying with me?"

She laughed. "So long as he's not so young you ruin Santa for him."

"I think we're safe there." Spenser glanced around the empty hallway, seeing through a window that the sleet was now full-blown snow. "Do you have a ride home? It's looking nasty outside."

Sandra waved a hand at him. "I'll be fine. I don't live far, but Vicky will bully me into getting a ride from her if it's too bad. Thank you kindly for the offer."

The door to Vicky's office opened, and Vicky herself stuck her head out. "Oh, hi, Spenser." Her smile became a beam as she saw Sandra. "Mrs. Stevenson. I'd give you a lecture for coming on a night like this, but I know you'd tan my hide, so I'll hustle you inside so we can get things set up and get you home."

She rose, waving her cane as she winked. "You best behave, because I brought my stick with me. Don't think I can't whup you, just because I'm ninety." She nodded at Spenser. "Besides, I got us two more volunteers while I sat here. I'm working, girl."

"I don't doubt it." Vicky grinned at Spenser. "You and Duon are coming to the Santa present setup? I think that's a wonderful idea."

Blushing, though he wasn't sure why, Spenser handed her the envelope in his hand. "I'm going to let you two have your meeting. It was nice to see you, Vicky, and to meet you, Mrs. Stevenson."

"Likewise, Mr. Harris. I will see you and your boy Saturday."

Spenser worried Duon wouldn't want to go, but in fact he got excited. "I got those presents when I was little. Do we get to go shopping for them too?"

"I think we're just wrapping them." Spenser felt a swell of pride at Duon's excitement over the activity. "But I could get us a couple Santa hats, if you want."

"Hell *yes* we're wearing Santa hats."

They stopped by Walgreens to get some on their way to the center on Saturday, and they were the hit of the gift-wrapping event, Duon with his expansive gestures and comic antics, Spenser with his patience with volunteers who needed help figuring out where they were meant to go. True to her word, Sandra kept them all in line, telling them how to tag the gifts and criticizing them when they didn't wrap properly. "Santa doesn't have sloppy elves," she said over and over. "These presents are going to be the bright spot of a child's morning. Treat them with the respect they deserve."

It was clear Sandra did more than take this gift wrapping seriously. She knew where every present belonged, knew each child and what they wanted most on Christmas morning. There were two hundred and fifty gifts wrapped by the time they broke for lunch, and Sandra had supervised every single one. She knew where all the gifts were going, and why it was important each household got the bundle they were assigned. The level of knowledge of the community Sandra had to possess boggled Spenser's mind and humbled him.

When he was packing up to leave, Sandra approached Spenser. "Young man, I'm going to give you some advice about that boy of yours. You going to listen?"

Spenser nodded earnestly. "Yes, ma'am."

"I know Duon and his family. I know they've had some tough times, and I'm sure what he's gone through has your heart aching. But don't you go softening the ground too much for him. You've given him a home, and that's more than most would do. It's the base he needs, and that will take him a long way in life. But remember, the rest has to be his."

Spenser frowned. "I don't understand what you mean."

"He has to walk his path the same way you walked yours. I see how you look at him, like you want to take away all the pain, but you can't do that. You have to let him find his own way. If you try to live his life for him, you won't do him any favors." She patted his hand. "That's the hardest lesson, sweetheart. Sometimes we have to love people enough to watch them fall."

She shuffled away from him then, leaving Spenser to stare after her, trying to digest what she'd said. He thought about it all the way home, as he lay in bed staring sleeplessly at the ceiling.

Sometimes we have to love people enough to watch them fall.

Spenser didn't know how he was supposed to do

that. He didn't want Duon to fall, not even an inch. He wanted to wrap him in a blanket and keep him safe from the world. He didn't want him to know any more pain. He wanted, more than anything else in the world, to give Duon the experiences he hadn't had as a child. A safe space. A loving parent. A permanent home. He didn't want Duon to grow up and read articles on disorders and see himself in them. He didn't want Duon to be afraid to date, to resort to hookups or fall for the first loser who looked his way.

He didn't want Duon to turn out like him. He'd fallen, and no one had cared. No one had so much as noticed. It hadn't taught him anything *but* pain.

Duon wasn't going to fall, not while he lived with Spenser. It was going to be perfect.

Perfect.

ALISA DIDN'T COME home for Christmas.

It was what Tomás expected, but that didn't stop it from upsetting him. It was all he could think about every time the family sat down to a meal or planned activities for the holiday. What drove him nuts, though, was that they bought presents for her, as if she'd arrive any minute. Tomás couldn't decide what would be worse, the presents remaining unclaimed under the tree, or her showing up and everyone acting as if nothing was wrong.

His mother noticed his foul mood and tried to talk

him out of it one night as she fed him a late dinner. "It's not a bad thing to hope for the best, Tomás."

"There's no best of anything where she's concerned anymore." He stabbed his fork into his enchilada, cutting viciously. "She's abandoned the kids. She's left us all holding the bag. I'm not welcoming her anywhere."

"She's your sister, *mijo*. She's having a difficult time."

Oh, *that* did it. Tomás glared at her. "*She's* having a difficult time. God, I didn't realize that's what we were supposed to do when times were tough, fuck over our families and run off with—"

Her slap against his cheek wasn't hard, but the surprise arrested him as she shook a finger in his face. "You will not use the name of our Lord in vain or such language in my house." She gentled as she went on, but not much. "Alisa is my daughter. Your sister. The mother of the children asleep in that room. You will treat her with respect."

"But she doesn't have to treat any of *us* with respect? Mama, I've given up my *life* to cover for her mistakes. We all have."

Renata sighed and sat beside Tomás, still holding his hand. "You are a good boy. Your sister has treated you poorly, and I have told her this. But you need to understand—if I tell her that too much, she doesn't start behaving. She leaves. Why do you think she left this time?"

"I don't know. I assumed her boyfriend offered her a trip somewhere more exciting than Minnesota."

"No. She left because your father got angry with her. Told her how much you work. Told her she needed to be a better parent. He spoke from anger and hurt and frustration, and she left in tears." Renata's eyes weren't exactly dry either as she squeezed Tomás's hand. "Alisa has made bad choices, but life has been hard to her. She falls in love too easy, and the men she gives her heart to keep breaking it. She gave into the escape of drinking and drugs, and now she can't stop herself. She is lost, yes. But what should I do? Kick dirt in her face and turn away? She is my child, forever. I must always try to bring her back."

Tomás's anger evaporated, leaving him with tears of his own, enough that swiping his thumb over his eyes couldn't make them stop. "I'm so tired, Mama. So tired. It hurts to know she doesn't care."

She stroked his hair, his ear, the back of his neck. "Let me care in her place, my sweet boy. Let me feed you and wash your clothes and push the anger out of your heart, so you have room for love to come in. Love of the nice man across the hall who blushes when he sees you."

"Spenser has enough going on right now. Me too. Dating isn't a good idea for either of us."

"You need love and affection even more when you're overwhelmed."

"I don't think he likes me. I've flirted here and

there, but he doesn't seem interested." He didn't bring up the kiss on election night, but weirdly it was almost the same thing. He'd smiled every time they ran into each other, thinking maybe they'd start something, but Spenser always had a wall up.

"How do you know, if you don't talk to him? Go visit him. He's a shy boy. You must take the lead. You are both men, but he is…" She waved her hand in the air, searching for the right phrase. "He isn't an aggressive man. He's smaller and shy and has a softness about him. You can be soft too, but you are bold. You are fire, and he is water. Go carefully to him. Share your day. Let Duon stay with us for an evening while the two of you go out and eat at a restaurant. Or he can cook you his hot dishes. Or you can teach him to make tamales. But you should be with him. Get to know him. He wants this as much as you do. I see him look at you, and I know. I feel it in my bones, he is the man for you."

Tomás wouldn't mind a relationship with Spenser or at least exploring one. But at the same time, thinking about asking the man out struck a terror in him he couldn't explain. He fished for excuses. "What if it didn't work? What if we dated and it went bad? Then it would be awkward for me to help with Duon, and that's so much more important."

"That's a silly excuse. Of course you could still help with the boy. But it will work with Spenser. I told you, I know it is right. It's the perfect match, the two of you.

Don't waste it."

"But what about immigration? What if being so close to him and DHS brings immigration here, to you?"

She gave him a long, impatient glare. "If you make one more excuse, I won't give you the empanadas I saved."

He knew she was teasing, but he couldn't laugh. "Mama, what if you're wrong? What if he isn't interested and I have a broken heart on top of everything else?"

Renata drew Tomás down and kissed his forehead. "Then I will simply have to love you harder, until the pain goes away." She tweaked his nose. "And lucky for you, there are *two* empanadas."

CHAPTER SEVEN

A s THE NEW year rolled in, Tomás began working less, and he also appeared more and more in Duon's life—and Spenser's.

When he came to Spenser's apartment, Tomás was full of smiles, and at first it threw Spenser. He couldn't help being wary, though Tomás flirting with him was exactly what he wanted. *You'll wreck it,* he scolded himself. *You'll be cold, and he'll stop.*

But Tomás didn't stop. He kept showing up, ostensibly to hang out with Duon, but whereas before he'd let Spenser slip away and leave the two of them alone, now he always roped Spenser into joining their card game or recaps of their day. He lured Spenser into listening to funny stories about work or his family.

Sometimes the two of them ended up having a conversation on their own. Every now and again when Duon retreated to his room, Tomás lingered and asked Spenser about *his* day. Sometimes they discussed music they had in common. Movies they would like to see. Places in the world they wished to go. Dreams they had and wanted to pursue.

"I want to take my mom to New York City." Tomás revealed this one night, feet up on a chair across from him at Spenser's table as a blizzard raged outside. "I want to save up and buy her tickets to a Broadway show. She loves musicals. Her English is fractured at best, but you should hear her sing along to *Funny Girl* and *Les Misérables.*"

The mental image of Renata singing along to songs from musicals made Spenser grin. "Which show is her favorite?"

"*Wicked,* at the moment. But she loves all of them." Tomás threaded his hands behind his head and stared dreamily at the ceiling. "I have it all worked out. I'd book her a room at The Plaza. I'd have her and Dad go on one of those carriage rides in the park. Send her out to get her hair and nails done, have a pretty dress waiting for her on her bed when she came back. Something *not* from a thrift store. Then I'd take them out to eat in a nice restaurant, somewhere fancy but not so much that she'd feel out of place. Then we'd go to the show."

It sounded wonderful to Spenser. "Have you ever been to New York?"

Tomás shook his head. "Haven't so much as left the state. What about you?"

"I went to Wisconsin once. A small town north of Madison, to visit family. Not for a long time, though."

Tomás sighed. "I always wanted to travel. I still do.

There's so much of the world to see."

"I suppose. It would be all right if I had someone to travel *with*. I wouldn't want to go alone."

"Maybe the three of us could do a day trip sometime. You, me, and Duon." He paused, then rolled his eyes. "Of course, I'd have to have a day off to make it work."

"You work a lot, I noticed. I don't know how you do it. I'd be exhausted doing half of what you do. I feel bad keeping you up talking when you clearly need sleep to fuel everything you do."

He shrugged, lips tipping up in a grin as he winked at Spenser. "But I love being kept up talking. It's one of the best parts of my day."

These kinds of flirtatious glances sent Spenser's heart fluttering and gave him hope, which was dangerous. "You're just being kind."

"Nope. Sometimes the only way I get through the last few hours is knowing I'll be able to sit here and chat at the end of the day. With you."

Spenser felt his blush take over his whole face, his body, a force he couldn't control. That he was used to, but this time the blush made him smile too, as if he were a fruit whose skin had split. Even when he cast his gaze away from Tomás, the feeling bloomed inside him, pushing aside all his warnings.

Tomás likes talking to me.

Tomás likes me.

Tomás nudged him playfully with his foot as he sat

up and put his feet on the floor, scooting closer to Spenser. "Hey. I've been meaning to ask you, but with the holidays and the grades you kept saying were due, I thought I should wait."

Hope rose on a nervous, eager tide inside Spenser. *He's going to ask me out?* "Yes?"

"I wanted to know if I could entice you back to the studio. Give you another dance lesson."

"Oh." Hope crashing to earth, Spenser held up his hands as he hastily built walls around his disappointment. "No thank you."

Tomás leaned forward. "Come on. It'll be great."

Spenser brushed imaginary lint from himself. "It's not something I'm good at."

"Well, that's why it's called a lesson. But nobody expects you to sign up for *So You Think You Can Dance?* or anything. Just come and have a good time. You can't tell me you don't have stress you need to work out of your body."

Yes, but dancing in front of Tomás was only going to generate more. Especially since this was a platonic offer, and Spenser couldn't stop his ridiculous fantasies of Tomás asking him out. "I don't like making a fool of myself in front of other people."

"You're never foolish to me."

The hand on Spenser's leg startled him, making him look up. Tomás was only a handful of inches away. Spenser forgot to guard himself as he met Tomás's gaze, forgot to hold back the truth of how much he loved these conversations. Forgot to hide the part of him that secretly did want to dance, if it was with Tomás.

When Tomás's gaze falling to Spenser's lips, Spenser closed his eyes and held his breath, waiting for the kiss.

But it didn't come. Tomás's cheek brushed his, but his lips never touched his skin as he whispered, "Come to dance class Thursday night, Spenser." When Spenser pulled away, Tomás caught his shoulder, holding him gently in place. "Please."

"All right."

That wasn't what Spenser meant to say. He wanted to call the words back, but Tomás stood, grinning, clearly pleased with himself. "Great. Come at eight. We can have the studio to ourselves again."

Spenser wanted to tell Tomás they could meet here at eight. He could take the dance lesson in his bedroom. But thinking something so bold made him blush and scold himself, and all he could do was nod a little stupidly as Tomás let himself out of the apartment.

When he was gone, Spenser sat alone, dunking his tea bag absently in his nearly spent tea, his emotions banging around helplessly inside him.

TOMÁS COULDN'T WAIT to dance with Spenser.

He'd been working up to asking Spenser out for weeks, but every time he got close, he chickened out.

Despite what his mother said, he couldn't be sure Spenser was into him. But Spenser had seemed different this last time. The longing look he'd given Tomás had undone him, pushed his nerves aside.

Well, almost aside. In his mind, asking Spenser to come to dance class was asking him out. The first step to it, anyway.

His anticipation drove him through his shift at Starbucks and had him humming as he hurried into the studio the next day. Duon, clad in his leotard, sat behind the desk. When Tomás glanced at the clock and raised an eyebrow, Duon held up his hands. "Don't you go lecturing me, man. In-service early-out day. You can check the school website if you don't believe me. Ed picked me up and dropped me off on his way to therapy."

Tomás remembered something about this, vaguely, from going over the schedule of who was picking Duon up when earlier in the week. He wondered if this meant Spenser was free too, and had a flutter imagining he could kidnap the man and have their lesson *now*. But no, he was in a private school, so they likely had a different schedule.

With a sigh, he leaned over the counter. As he did, he caught a glimpse of Duon's feet, which were now pressed so tight to the front of the desk they bent to the side.

Feet sporting pointe shoes.

Duon's whole face flushed in embarrassment as he

flailed desperately for a response. "I was, you know, fooling around."

Nothing about Duon's body posture supported this explanation. His shoulders were rolled forward, his back rounded, blush creeping down his neck.

The worst part was, Tomás couldn't laugh at this incident or pretend it didn't matter. "Whose shoes are they?"

"Sierra's. She let me try them on the other day for fun, and I saw them hanging on the pegs with the others. Thought I'd try again. They fit okay—I'm not breaking them or anything. I just wanted to try some shit. Practice some moves. You know. Make the girls laugh."

These kinds of moments with Duon always felt like dancing with knives. Tomás didn't want to accidentally step on Duon's feelings or cause insult, but he had to solve the issue of Duon using another dancer's shoes without her permission. Especially Sierra's, since her mother was unlikely to approve anyone borrowing her daughter's one-hundred-dollar Gaynor Mindens.

Tomás was still working out how to deal with the situation when Laurie breezed into the studio, shivering under his parka. He smiled when he saw them. "Well hello there. What are the two of you up to?"

Tomás was absolutely happy to toss this grenade to Laurie. "Duon was telling me how he wants to learn pointe. He was practicing in Sierra's shoes."

Duon glared at Tomás for narcing, then reprised

his *it's no big* attitude as he addressed Laurie. "Just for fun, man. I know guys don't get to do it. I wanted to try it once. I'll take them off."

Laurie didn't scold, but he regarded Duon with gravity. "Pointe is a serious discipline. It's true, men don't normally dance it except for comedic effect. But more and more male ballet dancers are learning it." He nodded at Duon's feet, which were still tucked as far out of sight as possible. "If you decide it's more to you than a joke, we can work your ballet training up to where I can teach you some pointe. But you'll need your own shoes. You could more comfortably wear underwear three sizes too small than you could wear someone else's pointe shoes. Plus you'd spend three Sundays cleaning the studio from stem to stern to earn enough money to replace those if you broke them."

Suppressing a flinch, Duon drew a foot onto his lap and began to unlace the shoe. "Sierra didn't say they were expensive."

"Sierra doesn't think about those kinds of things, unfortunately. The saddest part is the shoes don't truly fit her either, but her mother didn't like the idea of her dancing in anything but what someone at a dinner party told her was the best brand."

Duon laid the shoe carefully on the desktop and lifted his other foot onto his opposite leg to undo the other one. "They sure are bitches, these damn shoes. I can't stand up on them even if I hold on to something."

"Like I said, they need to be fitted for you. But you also need a little more training."

Duon cast Laurie and Tomás a sidelong glance. "You ever dance pointe?"

Tomás shook his head, but Laurie nodded. "I *teach* pointe, remember. I danced it in performance as well. Cinderella's stepsisters several times in my youth, and I was Bottom in *Midsummer Night's Dream* in a benefit production last fall."

Duon perked up. "So you got shoes here now? What's it gonna take to get you to dance pointe for me?"

The vulnerability in Duon's tone caught the edge of Tomás's heart.

"I'd dance for you anytime, and I'd be happy to teach you too."

Duon looked like someone had offered him a puppy. Eager, and a bit undone. "You would? For real?" The light in his face dimmed. "But I ain't got the shoes."

"Oh, the shoes come later. For now, we'll work on the basics. So go get ready. Both of you."

Tomás blinked. "Me too?"

"Absolutely. Even if you never teach it, it's good for you to understand all the disciplines." Laurie clapped his hands together. "Go on, both of you. Tights, belts, slippers. I'll meet you on the floor."

It was only Tomás and Duon in the dressing room, as Laurie always arrived wearing his dancing attire and kept his shoes in his office. Duon only had to fish his shoes out of his locker, but he sat on the bench all but bouncing as Tomás hurried into his clothes.

Laurie was already out in the studio when they emerged, standing flat-footed at the stereo in his pointe shoes, frowning at his MP3 player attached to the system. "I want to begin with a demonstration, but I'm trying to think of what I want to dance to. I could do the routine I taught a young lady in Eden Prairie two years ago. She wanted to dance *en pointe* to something modern. Not to brag, but the routine I devised for her has been copied by every single dancer to go to competition since then."

"Yeah, you bragging." Duon waved at the floor as Laurie finished lacing his second shoe. "Go on. Stop talking and dance already."

Tomás was eager to see his instructor dance this routine too. "Show us how it's done, Laurence Parker."

It took Laurie a few minutes to find the song in his digital library, but soon the opening notes filtered through the speakers, and Laurie stepped out onto the floor. "It's simple at first, but pay attention, because it doesn't remain that way. You'll have a temptation to watch my whole body, but notice my feet. They won't be as showy, but they're the reason all of this can happen."

The dance was indeed subdued at first, and then, as if Laurie were sleepily lifting his head, his steps became more and more complicated. It was so different than how he was used to seeing Laurie perform. There was a grace to his movements en pointe, a different kind of fluidity and beauty.

When the song finished and Laurie bowed, Duon and Tomás both clapped loudly in appreciation.

"Beautiful, man." Duon kept shaking his head, rapt with wonder. "*Beautiful.*"

Laurie reached for his towel and bottle of water. "I was so disappointed as a young dancer to learn as a male I'd rarely, if ever, dance en pointe. The only times I've ever done so without my performance being designed to elicit laughter is when I teach young ladies how to master their form."

Tomás was pretty sure Laurie danced en pointe better than anyone he'd ever seen. "Why *don't* men dance en pointe more often?"

Laurie shrugged. "Prejudice. Tradition. Women are supposed to appear delicate and beautiful, so they get the showy moves. Men are present in ballet to be strong. Except, of course, in the Parker studio, where we get to be both." He waved a hand at them. "Come over to the barre, gentlemen, and I'll give you your first lesson, which will be entirely boring."

It was pretty tedious, compared to the demonstration Laurie had given. Roll ups and dorsal stretches at the bar, prances around the room. Laurie explained as they worked that these were the foundations to dancing en pointe, and he wouldn't allow them anywhere near a pair of shoes until they had mastered the basics. Tomás was glad when the lesson was over because his feet were killing him.

Not so Duon. He had an intense look about him at the end of the class, making it clear he was hungry for more. It was all the moments Tomás had seen the young man pine for more dance instruction magnified, focused, and concentrated. He didn't appear to want to dance. His whole being telegraphed, with underscore, that he *needed* to. Needed *this* dance.

When Tomás took Duon home, he talked the whole way, plotting how they could have pointe lessons every week, vowing he'd practice every day. All night long. Indeed, when they arrived at Spenser's apartment, Duon wolfed down his food, blew through his homework, then went to his room calling over his shoulder that he had pointe homework to do.

"Point homework?" Spenser repeated as he brought mugs of tea over for himself and Tomás.

"He's talking about dancing *en pointe*. The toe shoes ballerinas wear so they can…well, stand on their toes."

"Men dance that way too? Huh. I've never seen it." His cheeks stained pink. "But I haven't seen much ballet."

"No, it's not common. But Duon is really into it, so Laurie's teaching him."

Spenser brightened the way he did whenever they discussed Duon. "Oh? Does he need more dance gear? I can take him shopping Saturday. We already put up a stair rail for him to use as a barre. I'm sure I did a terrible job and ate up my rental deposit with my shoddy carpentry, but it makes him so happy."

"You installed a barre for him? You're awesome. But you should have told me. I'd have helped, or my dad would have. If you ever need anything handy done around here, ask him. He lives for that stuff."

"Okay."

The eagerness Tomás had nursed all day returned in a rush. "I'm so excited for tomorrow night. It's going to be great." He wanted to add a suggestion they go out to dinner afterward, or for tea somewhere other than Spenser's table, but he chickened out.

The way Spenser's expression dimmed didn't help. "Oh. The dance lesson. Yes."

Tomás faltered too. "It's still okay, right? You can come?"

Spenser fiddled with the pen Duon had used for his homework. "Yes. Of course."

It wasn't a ringing endorsement, but it wasn't a no. Tomás offered what he hoped was a reassuring smile, not one reflecting the nervousness and doubt he felt. "It's going to be great. You'll see."

Smiling weakly, Spenser sipped at his tea and said nothing more.

Tomás excused himself soon after. He lay in bed a long time, imagining all the ways he could woo Spenser with dance. It would be like the last time, but better. They'd connect. Spenser would let go.

And Tomás would be there to catch him.

CHAPTER EIGHT

W HEN SPENSER WOKE on Thursday morning, he
thought of his impending dance lesson with
Tomás and had a panic attack.

It had been years since he'd had one, and it
shocked him so much that for several minutes he didn't
realize what was going on. He was in the shower to
boot, which meant to collect himself he had to sit on
the edge of the tub with shampoo still in his hair as he
pressed his face into the tile and took deep breaths
until he could put himself together. By the time he was
able to turn the water on and rinse off, he barely had
time to get dressed and zero time to eat anything more
than a granola bar.

He managed to bluff a cheerful mood as he
dropped Duon off at the high school, but his anxiety
returned as soon as he was alone in the car, and he
made himself late as he sat in the teacher's parking lot
at St. Anthony's, putting himself together.

Panic attacks had once been a regular part of his
daily life, but years of therapy and stress management

had made them by and large a thing of his past. He didn't have a prescription for Xanax anymore, it had been so long. He would have guessed it would have been becoming a parent overnight that would bring his old ailment back, but no. He was laying this squarely at the feet of the threat of going dancing.

Obviously he needed to call the lesson off, but once he collected his mail and set up for the morning, the students arrived, so he told himself he'd send his regrets at lunch. Except he'd forgotten he had recess duty, so he wolfed down his food before huddling against the wall outside as the children played. He intended to text during his free period in the afternoon, but his cooperating teacher had a question for him, and he forgot. He had a staff meeting after school as well, so he didn't get home until five.

Which meant it was too late to send a text, because Tomás was teaching already.

Spenser told himself he could give his regrets via message anyway, but every time he pulled out his phone, he felt the shadow of the panic that had followed him all day threaten to rise. At this point he knew he was feeding it, but he was tired and overwhelmed and didn't know how to shut it off.

Tomás hadn't asked him out, which he could have handled. Would have *welcomed*. But he'd asked him for a dancing lesson instead. Why did he have to go and do such a thing? Was this some kind of test? If so, Spenser would fail. He *wanted* this to be step one toward having a relationship with the neighbor he was more and more infatuated with by the day. But if this was how Tomás insisted they start, it was going to be over before it began. He'd make a fool of himself.

As the hour of seven grew closer, Spenser paced his apartment, trying to outrun his anxiety and failing miserably. At six he acknowledged he had to let Tomás know *somehow* that he wouldn't be there for the lesson, so he left his apartment and drove to the studio to give his regrets in person. Except when he arrived, Tomás was teaching a class, which Spenser should have thought of. A class that included Duon, who waved eagerly at Spenser as he spied him.

Spenser waved back, but his hand shook and his smile wavered. Oh God, he was going to have another panic attack, this time with an audience.

He tried to put himself in an out-of-the-way spot, but the waiting area was full. A foam core wall hung from the ceiling, obstructing the view of the instruction area, but the few available chairs were occupied by parents and children. Others leaned against the solid wall by the windows or sat on the floor, crowding into every last inch of space. There were seats on the *other* side of the wall—on the long bench placed so people could observe the active dance class. This of course was the last place Spenser wanted to be, so he did his best to hunker by the door, wishing more than any-thing he could go back out of it and apologize to Tomás later. When it became clear his panic wasn't going to subside, he fumbled with his coat with full intent to return to his car.

"Spenser?" Laurie stepped into the space between Spenser and the door, regarding him with concern. "Are you all right?"

God, no, he wasn't anything close to all right. He could barely look Laurie in the eye. "I should be going."

But he couldn't make his legs work. Laurie put a hand on his arm, a light, gentle touch. "Let's go into my office."

Spenser didn't want to go anywhere, but he let Laurie lead him. He felt dizzy and foolish and ready to throw up. "I'm not feeling well is all." It wasn't a lie.

Laurie helped him into a chair, a padded, stuffed thing that looked like it was a good place to read a book or take a nap, curled up. "Do you need me to call someone for you?" When Spenser stared at him blankly, he went on. "Sweetheart, it's all right. Just breathe for me, okay?"

Spenser didn't know what to say, how to get out of this situation, what to say to make it end. He began to babble. "Tomás wanted me to come by for a dance lesson at seven. But I can't. I can't dance with him."

"Because you're sick? You could have called and left a message."

"I can't dance with him because thinking about dancing *makes* me sick."

A little late it occurred to him perhaps that wasn't

the thing to say to a professional dancer who owned his own studio, but if Laurie was offended, he hid it well. He regarded Spenser carefully before altering his line of questioning. "I'm sorry to hear that. Would it be all right for me to ask why? Or would you prefer I invented an excuse for you for Tomás and urged him to keep from bothering you about it in the future?"

The offer was tailor-made for Spenser to get out of this situation, so it was a mystery why he didn't take Laurie up on it. He slumped in the chair. "I'm no good at dancing. I never have been." He shut his eyes briefly on a long blink. "But I'm attracted to Tomás and couldn't bring myself to tell him no when he coaxed me into coming by for another dance lesson. Which is ridiculous. He's probably not interested in me that way."

"I'm fairly certain he is. But tell me more about why you hate dancing. Why is it a nightmare?"

Spenser considered how to best edit his past. "I moved around a lot when I was young. I've never made friends easily, but in middle and high school things were especially grim, and being gay didn't help. I wanted to go to dances, but when I did, even dancing with girls wasn't pleasant. I was self-conscious about my body, aware I didn't have as nice of clothes as the other kids, that I was different from them in every way. When I was older and went to gay bars, though, the differences were still there. I was still self-conscious too, and trying to dance with other men was, disappointingly, as bad as those high school dances." He sighed. "I've developed a kind of phobia around the issue, I think. It's never been a problem until now, though I admit this is true largely because I avoided it. I thought I could override it with common sense, but that technique doesn't seem to be working."

Laurie didn't reply right away, and Spenser appreciated the chance to recover from his confession. When Laurie finally did speak, his tone was careful, gentle. "Do you *want* to dance? I'm asking sincerely."

Spenser didn't know how to unpack the question, so he leapt onto the tail end of it. "I can't dance. I mean, I danced the one night with Tomás, but I was terrified the whole time."

"Surely you've danced by yourself. In the kitchen when a good song came on, or in your bedroom as you got yourself ready for something."

"I listen to MPR. And no, I don't dance by myself."

Laurie tapped his finger on his cheek. "So is what you're telling me no, you don't want to dance at all?"

Spenser was starting to get a headache. "Obviously I would like to dance. Everyone would. What I'm trying to tell you is I *can't*."

Laurie's smile was enigmatic, making Spenser feel both comforted and nervous at once. "Ah. I see. All right, I have a few questions for you. First: Spenser, do you trust me? That I have your best interests at heart, and I'd never do anything to hurt or embarrass you?"

Spenser blushed. "Yes, I trust you. Why?"

"You teach kindergarten, yes? Does your school allow guest classroom speakers?"

"Yes, we have to fill out a few forms is all."

"Good. I want to come to your classroom and do a dance demonstration for your students. With them."

Spenser frowned. "Why? I mean—that would be lovely, thank you. The students would love it. So would my principal, in fact. But why are you telling me you want to do this?"

"Because once we're done here, I'm going to go talk to Tomás. I'm going to send you home and give him your regrets for this lesson tonight. And if you decide you're willing to take dancing lessons, *I* will be your instructor." Spenser's jaw fell open, but Laurie only rose and patted Spenser's shoulder. "Not now, though. First I'm going to come to your class. Then we'll see what happens."

Laurie ushered Spenser out of his office, sending him out of the studio and to his car, bearing Laurie's business card and a promise he would be at St. Anthony as soon as Spenser told him it was acceptable to come by. He also reiterated his promise to speak to Tomás.

Spenser went home calmer but still agitated. Mostly he felt confused and uneasy, not entirely understanding what had happened, or why, or what he should do in response. He felt a deep, hollow ache, thinking he'd killed his relationship with Tomás before it started, even if it was for the best. He moved listlessly around the apartment, until shortly after seven, Duon returned home.

Tomás was with him.

Embarrassed at his behavior, Spenser tried to stay out of the way and hoped Tomás would leave him alone, but Tomás found him in the living room and came to sit beside him on the sofa. "Hey there."

Spenser gave him a weak smile and rubbed his arms self-consciously. "Sorry about the lesson. I…wasn't feeling well."

"No worries." Tomás's tone was gentle, soothing.

He sat close to Spenser, but he also tilted in so he made the couch cushion cave toward him, inviting Spenser to tip into him. Spenser noted Duon had gone straight to his room. "Is Duon okay?"

"He's fine." Tomás rested his hand on Spenser's thigh. "I'm sorry if I was pushy about the lesson. I didn't mean to upset you."

Spenser's cheeks heated. "It's my fault. I have some kind of complex about dancing, I guess. I'm sorry."

"You don't need to apologize. I do." His grin was sheepish. "I'll be honest—that was all a cover. I'd meant to ask you out, but I got nervous and asked you to let me give you another dance lesson instead, because it felt safer."

Embarrassment faded as waves of tenderness, hope, and desire took its place. Spenser glanced sidelong at Tomás. "You could have asked me out. *That* would have been safer."

"I know that now." He held Spenser's hand, laced their fingers together. Leaned closer. "So."

Spenser leaned in too.

The kiss was slow and sweet, their lips coming together on the softest of sighs as they backed into the sofa, hands sliding over shoulders. Spenser's skin felt charged with electricity, sending jolts along his nerve endings every time Tomás brushed his fingers along it. Spenser couldn't help thinking this was the kind of kiss he'd dreamed of in high school, from the kind of boy he'd wished he knew how to talk to. Tomás was a solid, safe space, and Spenser sank into him, forgetting his shame over the abandoned lesson. Steeped himself in the dizzy wonder of Tomás's slick, wet mouth, his teasing tongue. His strong, gentle hands.

The promise of what kisses would come next time. Because this was absolutely a kiss that whispered of a next time.

"Saturday night," Tomás whispered when they came up for air. "Go out with me Saturday night."

Spenser ran fingers down Tomás's cheek, ducking his head because his grin was so wide. "Saturday night it is."

ALL DAY LONG on Friday, Tomás obsessed about where to take Spenser on their date.

"Go to a bookstore," Duon suggested the next evening on the way home from the studio. "The man loves his books. If we go to the mall, I gotta get ready to put in at least an hour at Barnes & Noble. Don't get me started on *used* bookstores. You'd think every aisle was a possible path to a big pile of money."

Tomás wasn't sure a bookstore was fancy enough, but he liked the mall idea. "I could take him to the Mall of America. Unless that's too cheesy."

"The man would stand in the rain beside a row of stinking garbage cans if he knew you'd be standing with him." Duon put his feet up on the dash and slumped lower in his seat. "He's gonna tell you it's fine, whatever you say."

Tomás scoured potential date sites across the Twin Cities, trying to find the perfect venue. Restaurants. Art shows. Bars. Ice skating. IMAX at the zoo. He asked for advice from everyone—Laurie, Ed, one of the other Starbucks assistant managers. He had a million ideas, but none of them made him think this was it, he'd found the right opening date.

On Saturday morning as he got ready for work, he asked his mom. Which meant he had to first explain he had a date in the first place.

She gasped and beamed, looking across the room at the door and Spenser's apartment. "Oh, *mijo*, how *wonderful.* You must take him somewhere special."

"That's just it, Mom. I don't know where the special place is."

"Somewhere *romantic.* Somewhere you can show him what a wonderful partner you could be."

This didn't help, either. So, out of ideas, Tomás cried uncle and knocked on Spenser's door. "Where would you like to go tonight?"

Spenser didn't hesitate. "I was thinking Bryant-Lake Bowl could be nice."

Tomás blinked. "The what?"

"Bryant-Lake Bowl. It's in Lyn-Lake. It's a restaurant, bowling alley, and theater built into one space."

Bowling. But Spenser seemed excited about it. "Do we need a reservation?"

"No. I could see what was playing at the theater, though. Unless it's something really popular, I doubt we'll need to buy our tickets in advance. We went all the time while I was in college." He paused, enthusiasm waning as he bit his lip. "But maybe this isn't your kind of thing. We can do something else."

Spenser was the kind of thing Tomás was interested in, and if he had to wear stupid shoes to be with him, so be it. "Bryant-Lake Bowl sounds great."

Once alone, though, Tomás doubted whether or not agreeing to go bowling was such a good idea. He'd gone only a handful of times, once in elementary school for a party, and then for a short unit in middle school for PE class. He'd been okay for the class, but somehow he doubted the skill had remained dormant inside him.

What made him nervous was his perception of bowling alleys was that they were for white people. Older white people, usually men, wearing ugly shirts and shitty shoes, laughing loudly and patting each other on the back between chugging pints of beer. Blue-collar guys, but *white* blue-collar guys. White, straight, blue-collar guys in organized gangs.

Gosh, what could possibly go wrong there?

There wasn't much to be done about it now, though, so he took a shower, tamed his hair, put on his nicest jeans and the blue sweater his mom had bought him, and declared himself ready. Before he was allowed to leave the apartment, however, his mother fussed and picked at him and gave him lectures on how he should behave with his date. Tomás endured it without complaint because he knew plenty of Latino gay men whose parents never gave up on the right girl changing their minds about liking dick. His parents had tried that angle only for a few days, and afterward they were fully on board with Tomás finding a nice man to settle down with instead.

"Open doors for him. He is a man, yes, but he is a sensitive soul, and the gesture will make him feel treasured. Ask him about himself and his hobbies. Let him talk to you, and seem interested."

"I *am* interested, Mama."

"I know, *mijo*." She patted his cheeks, sighed, and pulled him down so she could kiss him on the forehead. "You are a good boy, Tomás. The best boy in the world." Then she took his chin in her hand. "Which is why you will be chaste tonight. Kisses, touches, but nothing more."

Tomás sputtered. "Mama!"

Renata didn't relent. "This is the danger of two men. There is no one to force things to be slow. Take your time and enjoy it. You should both go home full of yearning, dreaming for the next date. The tension is how you make real love. Love that lasts."

"Listen to your mother," José called from the kitchen, where he was finishing up dishes. "She made me wait two months before I could so much as hold her in my arms. And look at us now."

They continued with their lectures and advice for another fifteen minutes, until Tomás was nearly in danger of being late. He was confused, because this wasn't his first date with a man. Why were they behaving this way now?

When Spenser opened the door to his apartment, smiling and smelling subtly of cologne, framed by the doorway and backlit by the light above the table so he looked like a saint, Tomás began to understand why his parents had treated his date with Spenser differently. Because Spenser was different. No one else Tomás had dated was so clean-cut, so polite, so kindhearted he'd take a child he didn't know into his home. No one else could, with one smile, make Tomás vow he would endure *two* bowling alleys full of judgmental, white, straight men if that was what it took to be with Spenser.

The chaste part, he thought as he caught another whiff of Spenser's cologne on the way to the parking lot, would be harder.

Spenser offered to drive, since he knew where the place was, and they chatted all the way into Minneapolis, mostly about Duon. "He's spending the evening with Ed and Laurie. He did well in school this week, so he gets to help out all Sunday afternoon at a dance clinic Laurie is hosting."

Tomás knew a pang of jealousy. *He* wanted to help at the clinic, but he had to work. "I'm glad to hear that about school. I know it's been a struggle. He hasn't asked me for help with homework as much lately, which I'd hoped was a good sign. I was going to ask, but I didn't want to push him. You know how testy he gets when he decides you're too bossy."

"I do indeed. I hope I'm doing all right with him."

"You're doing more than all right. Trust me. I only wish I were able to help out more."

"You're with him plenty. I don't know how you do it, with all your jobs."

Tomás laughed bitterly. "I don't know how I do it either, most of the time."

"Your mother babysits, yes?"

Oh, they were in dangerous waters. "She watches my nieces and nephew for my sister a lot of the time."

"Your sister is the woman with the long hair with a red streak I see sometimes?"

"Yes. That's Alisa." Time to switch the subject. "Are you from the Cities, or did you move here?" When Spenser became almost wooden, Tomás quickly backtracked. "Sorry. I don't mean to pry."

Spenser smiled, but he looked tired. "It's fine. I don't like to talk about my past much, is all."

"Then let's talk about your present. What do you do when you're not teaching school or taking care of Duon?"

Spenser bit his lip. "Um, not much. Read, I suppose."

"What do you *want* to do?"

Spenser considered this a moment, then shook his head. "I don't know. Sorry, that's not meant to be a cop-out. I truly don't know. Until Duon came into my life, I pretty much went to work, came home, and did things around the house. Watched Netflix."

"But no chill?" When Spenser only regarded him blankly, Tomás tried to recover the joke. "It's, you know. The euphemism for..." He blushed. "Never mind."

"Oh." Spenser blushed too, but he smiled. "Right. It's supposed to be code for *have sex*, but then all the adults used it to mean 'hang out', and now we run around looking insane if we use the phrase to mean watch movies and relax."

"Yeah, a local pastor advertised a Netflix and Chill outing in the church parking lot. The kids had a field day."

They both laughed, but it also made Tomás think about having some *Netflix and chill* with Spenser. He ran his thumb down his jaw as he stared into traffic and let the fantasy play out in his mind for a few seconds. Nothing said they couldn't take their food to go and continue this conversation on Spenser's couch. Or the edge of his bed.

Nothing except, much as he hated to admit it, his mom might be on to something. It wasn't the right move to go straight to the sack with Spenser. The trouble was, Tomás didn't know how to get from where they were to under the sheets. He decided maybe confessing that was the place to start. "I'm going to be upfront with you. I haven't dated tons. So if I suck at date talk, I apologize in advance."

Spenser kept his eyes on the road, not meeting Tomás's gaze. Tomás was ready for him to say he hadn't dated much either, but to his surprise, it wasn't what Spenser said. "When you asked about my past, I was hesitant to talk about it because my past isn't like yours. In fact…" His cheeks stained with embarrassment tinged with shame. "I have quite a lot in common with Duon."

Tomás tried not to let his shock lead to a dumbass reaction, but…well, he had *not* expected to hear that. He glanced between Spenser and the car ahead of them a few times, then surrendered with a heavy sigh. "Damn. I had no idea. I'm sorry. I—" He cut himself off, fairly sure he'd fucked up.

"I work hard to make sure people don't have any idea, so there's nothing to be sorry about. Unless you meant you were sorry I had to go into the system at all, which I'll accept with thanks. When I realized where Duon was headed, knowing what it would be like, I didn't have to think about my choice to be his placement. In a way, it was like being there for myself." He ran a hand through his hair, staring at the dashboard. "I was in the foster system at eight. In hindsight I know it was better than continuing as we were, but at the time it was rough because it meant being separated from my sisters and living with a series of strangers until I was finally so old no one took me in, and I went to shelters instead."

Tomás couldn't begin to imagine. He had so many questions, but he didn't know which were okay to ask. The sisters seemed like a safe subject. "How many sisters do you have?" He hadn't ever seen anyone come visit Spenser. No family of any kind, except occasionally the one lady who was old enough to be Spenser's grandmother but didn't look anything like him.

"Three. Kaylee, Gina, and Hannah. I'm the oldest. They're…oh, I guess Kaylee would be twenty-six now. Gina twenty-four, Hannah twenty-two."

"Why did you get separated from your sisters?"

"It's difficult to keep that many kids together. Plus Kaylee had behavior issues. Gina and Hannah were in the same home and eventually adopted. But not Kaylee. She ran away from everywhere they put her. Then one day she ran and they never caught her. I don't know what ever happened to her." He flinched. "Sorry. I'm not much for date talk either, I guess."

Tomás took a moment to get over the idea of not knowing where his sister was. He wanted to punch her face half the time, yes, but… He gripped the wheel tighter. "Wow. I'm so sorry, Spenser. Are the other two…okay?"

He nodded. "They live in the area, I think. I tried to keep up with them for a while, but their adoptive parents never wanted them to have contact with me, so it became easier to go along with it."

"They what? Can they do that?"

"I think maybe now, no. Maybe they couldn't then? This is one of the things you learn with kids in the system. There are rules and laws and ideals, and then there's what actually happens. I don't think it's malicious on anyone's part. I think the system is simply overwhelmed and underfunded."

That must have been a real comfort to Spenser as a kid. Tomás couldn't imagine being away from his parents at age eight. Though he supposed he was lucky they hadn't been deported and decided to leave him in the states with a foster family. Hell, he could have ended up in a bunk next to Spenser. "Is it bad in the shelters?"

Spenser shrugged, keeping his gaze on the road. "It's not a home, is the best way to put it. You don't have much privacy or security of your things, either, which are precious few to begin with. For queer kids especially it's dangerous because shelters are always strained for resources and staff, and it's rare they make helping you feel accepted for your orientation or sexual identity an important issue. I'd like to think they're better now than they were when I was a teenager, but I wouldn't count on it. Probably depends on which shelter and who sponsors it. The ones I went to were religiously affiliated, and it wasn't the best place to be gay."

Tomás couldn't begin to imagine what it must have been like. He didn't know what to say, either, except to offer another *I'm sorry*, which was phenomenally unhelpful. But it was all he had. "That's awful. I'm so sorry, Spenser."

He shrugged again, and this time Tomás saw through the gesture for what it was: a mask. "I made it through. Now I get to help make sure Duon does too."

They lapsed into silence, and soon they were at Bryant-Lake Bowl. It was a funky neighborhood, and the outside was a little bit hipster but nothing too insufferable. Tons of bicycles, and a long row of benches with ashtrays, though no one was smoking. The inside was a mix of pseudo-retro and legit retro—a peek at his feet revealed generations of flooring in various stages of wear, from several linoleums to a straight-up hardwood floor on the bottom. But it was bright and clean and not too noisy.

Spenser pointed to a poster on the wall. "It's an indie band for the show tonight, at nine. If you want, we can eat, bowl, then hit the show. Or we can eat and chat in the bar while we wait for a show. Or eat and then leave. Lots of options."

Tomás would have happily skipped the bowling, but after their heavy nosedive into serious discussion on the way over, he wondered if maybe a buffer activity wouldn't be bad. "I'm fine with bowling so long as you understand I haven't done it since I was fourteen."

Spenser grinned. "Oh, this will be fun. I'm going to wipe the floor with you."

They scored a lane for an hour and a half later, which gave them plenty of time to sip funky cocktails and chat, though Tomás indulged in some serious people-watching too. While it was mostly white people as he'd predicted, they were not the predominantly middle-aged male assholes of his imagination. In fact, a pride flag hung from the awning outside, and Tomás thought he saw a few other same-sex couples seated at or waiting for tables.

They decided to buy tickets for the show too and sign on for the full Bryant-Lake Bowl experience. The food was much better than Tomás had expected, and the ambiance was fun and nonthreatening. Though it was definitely a hipster place, and there was exactly one other brown guy bowling, it was all so much more fun than Tomás had anticipated.

Except for the part where Spenser kicked his ass at bowling. Like, *kicked* his ass.

"Were you a professional bowler in another life?" Tomás asked after Spenser's fourth strike in a row.

"The shelter I lived in had a bowling alley down the

street that gave us free passes. When I couldn't get a ride to the library, I went bowling."

This reminder that Spenser's childhood had been grim drew a cloud over Tomás's pleasure, but Spenser didn't seem fazed and carried on slamming his ball into the pins with ferocious glee. Normally Tomás was competitive, but he didn't have a chance here, so he did his best to relax and enjoy losing in an epic fashion.

After Spenser finished handing Tomás his ass, they waited in the theater for the show, talking about the dance studio, how Tomás got involved with dance. "They had free classes at the Y, and I begged my mom to let me go. She saved up for me to take more lessons at a studio once she saw how much I loved them, but I could rarely do the shows because I couldn't afford the costumes. When I was in high school, I had jobs and paid for my own, but then I couldn't do as much because I was working. I'm nothing like Laurie, but I do okay, and sometimes I even get to use my Spanish. We have a few families where the parents can't speak English, and I have to translate."

"Are your parents native citizens? I assumed not with their accent and limited English, but…"

Once again, way too close. Tomás did his best to gingerly edge them away. "They were born in Mexico, but my sister and I were born in Arizona."

"What brought you to Minneapolis?"

"Better jobs, better education system. Though my mother regretted it immediately once we hit our first winter."

Spenser looked wistful. "I love how you're so close to them. Your parents are both wonderful."

Tomás couldn't help smiling. "I'm pretty fond of them too."

The music started, and while technically the band wasn't great, Tomás would remember the night for the rest of his life as a magical, perfect time. The music felt exactly right too, in its way. Everything was soft and framed at the edges, rose-colored, and whenever Spenser smiled at him in his shy but eager way, Tomás's chest puffed out.

They held hands on the way to the car, and on the way home too, in fact. As they walked down the hall of the apartment building together, grinning like fools, Tomás's only regret was the evening was coming to an end.

But when he tried to leave Spenser at the door with a soft kiss goodbye, Spenser had none of it. "Come in. Have…some tea with me."

Tomás hesitated. "I want to." He glanced over his shoulder at the door to his family's apartment and thought of his mother's warning about too much kissing. Thought about how it had seemed such an important warning…when he wasn't standing outside Spenser's apartment with Spenser looking utterly kissable.

Utterly fuckable.

Spenser ran a shy but deliciously coy hand down

the front of Tomás's shirt. "Then come in already."

Weak, Tomás went.

Spenser was happier than usual, full of a brightness that was hard to resist. He was still slightly hesitant, deliberate in a way Tomás had begun to understand was his way of guarding himself. But tonight some of those walls were down. He bounced on his heels as he put on water for tea, selecting a pair of mugs, blue and green ones this time.

"What would you say to some peach tea?" he asked, withdrawing a box from the top shelf of his tea cupboard.

Tomás fixed his gaze on Spenser's backside, which was nicely outlined by his jeans as he stood on tiptoe. "Peach sounds nice."

Spenser put the bags in the mugs, turned around, and smiled at Tomás. It was a real smile, projecting an ease and happiness Tomás had absolutely never seen on the man before, and it did him in. He stepped forward, took Spenser into his arms, and dipped his head as he went in for a kiss.

The weight of Spenser made Tomás ache. The sweet, wet press of his mouth sent him spinning. Kissing Spenser felt like dancing in a dream, as if he'd stumbled into somewhere he shouldn't be but could linger without getting caught. He smelled like…linen and pepper. Clean and bright, with a bit of bite. He tasted that way too, but with an echo of the rum and fruit juice he'd had in his cocktail at Bryant-Lake.

He felt like heaven. He felt like home.

When the water began to boil, Spenser paused kissing long enough to turn off the burner—then he pressed Tomás to the kitchen wall and dove in. The insistent ridge of his erection along Tomás's own left him torn between shifting this afterparty to the bedroom and letting himself drown right here in the kitchen, in this perfect moment in Spenser's arms.

A sharp knock sounded on the door, startling them both. A few seconds later a familiar, heavily accented voice rang out. "Hello? Spenser? Tomás? I have something for you."

Tomás shut his eyes, sagging into Spenser as he rested his forehead against the wall. "Oh my God, my mother. I'm so sorry."

Renata knocked again. "Hello, boys?"

After they composed themselves as best they could, Spenser opened the door, bewildered. Renata Jimenez stood in the doorway, smiling innocently and holding up a glass pan with a pair of potholders. "I make empanadas. Cinnamon."

She pushed past them breezily, as if she didn't know exactly what she'd interrupted, and set them on the table. "Very hot. Tomás, come bring ice cream."

Spenser, who had a known weakness for empanadas and had practically begun drooling at the sight and smell of them, snapped out of his food trance. "Oh, I have ice cream, Mrs. Jimenez."

She patted his cheek. "You call me Renata, *cariño*. I

have ice cream. Homemade. You must try." She grabbed Tomás's arm and dragged him from the apartment. "Tomás will bring."

As soon as they were out of earshot, she launched into him in Spanish. "Tomás, you must let there be longing. You cannot have sex tonight. You will ruin everything!"

Tomás sighed, but he didn't roll his eyes because he knew that path led to terrible things. He also tried not to think about how she knew what had been going down in the kitchen before she delivered her food bomb. "Mom, it's fine."

"No. It's not fine." She went to the freezer, pulled out a plastic tub, and slammed it into his hands so she could shake a finger at him. "I know what I'm talking about. Listen to your mother. Be a good boy. *Take your time with Spenser.*"

She scolded him in Spanish all the way across the hall, until they were in the apartment again, at which point she smiled brightly, as if she hadn't been chewing him out for five minutes straight. "Eat, boys," she said in English, then gazed meaningfully at her son. "Eat, and Tomás will come home."

She left them then, knowing full well the damage had been done. But Spenser looked bewildered, not annoyed. In fact he seemed almost amused. "What was that about?"

Tomás didn't know how to varnish this one, so he laid it all out. "She thinks if we have sex too soon, we'll ruin any hope for a relationship. And she likes you." His cheeks heated as he added, "I do too."

"Oh my gosh. That's…that's *so sweet*." He pressed his hands over his mouth as if holding back a prayer. "Oh, Tomás. I'm in love with your mother. Your whole family. I'm so jealous."

Tomás, his throat thick, took Spenser's hand. "In case you missed it, this was her way of welcoming you into it."

They kissed then, a soft meeting of mouths…and then they ate empanadas and ice cream, and drank peach tea. They were almost shy with one another now, barely speaking, smiling at each other then glancing away. Tomás thought several times about trying to resume his seduction, his mother be damned, but he frankly feared how she'd interrupt him the next time.

So they had one last kiss at the door, lingering but almost chaste. He didn't take Spenser into his arms, only held on to his elbow, anchoring himself as he went in for another taste of Spenser. And then another. And another.

Spenser broke the kiss, blinking slowly, letting his breath out on an unsteady sigh. He smiled at Tomás with the same lightness he'd had as they'd entered the apartment. "Can I have another date, Tomás?"

Tomás grinned back at him. "You get as many dates as you want, sweetheart." He ran his knuckles gently down the slope of Spenser's cheek. "As many as you want."

CHAPTER NINE

S PENSER PRACTICALLY FLOATED through the rest of the weekend, caught up in thoughts about Tomás and their Bryant-Lake date. He hummed as he did his chores and made Duon's favorite meal when he came home from the dance clinic on Sunday. Caught himself smiling at odd moments. Obsessively checked his texts. Tomás didn't send too many, as he was either sleeping or working, but each buzz of his phone sent Spenser's spirits a little higher.

Can't wait until this shift is over. How's your Sunday going?

Spenser bit his lip as he replied, but his smile couldn't be stopped. *Good. We're watching a movie.*

Oh yeah? What movie?

Big Hero 6. *Duon's request, but I like it too.*

Wish I could be there watching with you guys.

I do too.

Still thinking about kissing you. Want to do it again as soon as possible.

He did kiss Spenser that night when he was home

from his Starbucks shift. He looked dazed, his eyelids trying to close and force him into sleep, but before Spenser could point out he should go to bed, Tomás cupped Spenser's face and kissed him long and slow and sweet, right there in the doorway.

When he pulled back, he grinned. "Yeah. Gonna sleep *so* much better now."

Spenser slept well too, waking up smiling like he was some kind of fool. He didn't care. At school, he greeted the other teachers and support staff with a cheery "Good morning." He even had goodwill toward Dr. Harvey, who approached him about finalizing the plans for Laurie coming to give his dance demonstration.

"He's clear for whenever he wants to come," Harvey said. "And if he wants to give an all-school assembly, we'd be happy to do that as well."

"I think he wants to keep it a small group." Spenser did his best to end the conversation. "Thank you, Dr. Harvey."

Harvey put a hand on Spenser's shoulder. "I've been meaning to speak with you, Harris. I've noticed you haven't been to any of the rally meetings."

Spenser did his best to blank his expression. The rallies Harvey referred to were an extension of the former pro-amendment forces, a teacher-parent group lobbying lawmakers to resist the push in the legislature to sign full marriage equality into state law. "I hadn't realized they were mandatory."

"Of course they're not *mandatory*. But as a member of our community, I assumed you would be interested in the call for morality."

Spenser wasn't sure if this was a trap, if Harvey had heard a rumor, or even a truth, and wanted to rid himself of one of his resident gays. He resurrected his dismissive smile. "I'll tell Laurie he's clear to come for a demonstration."

Harvey didn't say anything more, but Spenser knew he hadn't heard the last of the issue.

Laurie ended up coming to his class Wednesday of that week, right away in the morning since in the afternoon he had classes. After he changed into his dance clothes, they pushed the desks to the edges of the room, making as large a demonstration space as possible.

"Thank you for coming," Spenser said as they waited for the children to arrive. "The children will absolutely love this."

Laurie winked. "I hope you have at least a little fun too."

The bell rang and the halls and then the room filled with children. As Spenser's students entered, they whispered and pointed at the strange arrangement of the furniture, at the newcomer to the classroom. Many of the children were so overcome they didn't know what to do with themselves and forgot everything about the protocol of putting their things away.

Spenser greeted them all and then prompted them

back into formation. "Hang your coats on your peg, put your lunch pails on top of your cubby, and put your bags inside your bin. Then stand in your place on the yellow line."

A girl in pigtails looked almost overcome with distress. "But, Mr. Harris, our desks are all smooshed together."

"I understand that, Felicity. This is why I told you to stand in your place on the yellow line."

"But we only use the line for recess and lunch and specials," a boy pointed out, dubious.

"Normally this is true. But today we are using it for something else. We have a guest in our room today."

Now the whispers focused on Laurie, who was seated at Spenser's desk on the far side of the room. Bit by bit the students settled down in their places on the line with only a minimum of pushing and shoving and whining. Once the final bell rang, Spenser took attendance and hot lunch count, then addressed his students for the morning greeting.

"Good morning, class."

"Good morning, Mr. Harris," they echoed.

He smiled at them. "It's lovely to see you again. You've noticed something special is happening today. We'll do weather and day of the week after first recess, but first we have a guest in our room." He shifted his body so he could make eye contact with both Laurie and his students. "This is my friend Laurie Parker. Will you say good morning to Mr. Parker?"

They replied in nearly unison singsong. "Good morning, Mr. Parker."

Laurie stood and made a graceful bow. "Good morning. It's lovely to meet you."

Spenser gestured to Laurie. "Mr. Parker is a ballet dancer. He's performed all over the world, and now he has a dance studio in Eden Prairie and another here in St. Paul. Today he's here to dance with us."

There was a susurrus from the students as Laurie moved to the center of the room, but they quieted when he began speaking. "Today I'm going to teach you some dances."

Felicity's hand shot into the air, but she spoke at the same time, too excited to be called on. "I tooked dance class before."

"That's wonderful." Laurie scanned the group. "Has anyone else taken dance class already?" A few hands went up, and he nodded encouragingly. "Excellent. We're going to learn more dancing today, but first I'm going to demonstrate for you, and then we're going to dance together. Would you like that?" They chorused yes, and he smiled. "Let's start with ballet. This is the type of dancing I've done most."

He motioned to Spenser, who was stationed at the stereo. The opening notes of a piano solo drifted through the speakers, slow and easy. The class oohed and ahhed as Laurie began to dance, first in slow, graceful steps, then leaping, twirling, and arcing in a mesmerizing performance. When the song, which wasn't long, ended, he nodded to Spenser, the cue to pause as he addressed the students.

"There are a number of types of ballet. I can dance fast or slow. I can dance to make you feel happy or sad, or to make you laugh. Watch this one." This time when Spenser started the music, the piano was more playful, and Laurie moved almost comically, his facial expressions and gestures indeed making the children giggle.

He bowed when he finished, and then he sat down and changed his shoes. "There are other types of dance, though. The dance I'm about to do now is called jazz. See if you can tell how the movements are different in this one."

The next song opened with a slow saxophone solo before breaking out into something that felt very 1940s, full of swing and fluidity. So were Laurie's movements, radically different now—jerky at times, controlled but freer, more wild. It reminded Spenser of a far more sophisticated version of the dance he'd done with Tomás. He liked it, but it brought back too many uncomfortable memories of how he'd become embarrassed and failed to show up for his lesson, and he was distracted as Laurie led the students in a comparison of the types of movements between the two dances.

"For the next dance," Laurie said, his tone waking Spenser from his trance, "I need the hard floor where you're sitting, because the carpet won't work."

A girl raised her hand high in the air, and Laurie called on her. "Why do you need the hard floor, Mr.

Parker?"

"Because I'm going to give you a tap demonstration, and the taps won't make noise on the carpet." He pulled a pair of black shoes with silver taps out of his bag and showed them to the line of students. Then he brought out his ballet shoe and jazz shoe too, displaying all three for their rapt attention. "The light brown shoe is my ballet slipper. I used it for the first dance. The soft shoe is my jazz shoe. The tap shoe is more rigid. Do you feel the stiff piece inside? That's the soundboard. It's what helps the taps make noise. Do you want me to make some noise for you with my feet?"

Of course the children all insisted they did, so Spenser helped rearrange them in a semicircle on the carpet facing Laurie, who took their place on the yellow line in front of the cubbies. "I'm not quite as good at tap as I am at ballet or jazz. But I do enjoy it. That's the beautiful thing about dancing. You don't have to be the best at it, or even good at it, to enjoy it. All you need to do is move your body and have fun." He winked at Spenser. "When you're ready, Mr. Harris."

Spenser faltered as he fumbled for the play button, knowing that last bit had been a nudge at Spenser more than it had been instruction for kindergarteners. But once the music began to play, he forgot everything, could only watch Laurie dance.

The song was quite fast. It had a lot of piano and a kind of jazzy feel, but it was different than the song

Spenser had danced to with Tomás. This felt like something out of an old movie where the leads…well, tap-danced. And that's what Laurie was doing. Moving back and forth along the yellow line, tapping, spinning, sliding his feet in time to the music. The children became animated, laughing and clapping and getting excited. The tap dance was so much more involved, Laurie making funny faces at the children and at Spenser, a constant stream of motion. Sometimes the music would shift and so would his dance—there was one refrain, only a bar or two, where the music nearly evaporated and Laurie did this sort of pigeon-toed jump—but mostly it was perpetual motion, the click of his taps punctuating every step.

It was a fun, brilliant demonstration, and it made Spenser itch. He didn't realize he was tapping his toe until he looked down and saw it. He watched Laurie tap dance and wished, with a yearning that surprised him, that he could dance like that too. When the dance was over, Spenser was disappointed.

He rose to stop the player, but Laurie shook his head as he removed his tap shoes and put his ballet slippers on again, addressing the class all the while as an ambient song began to play from the stereo.

"You watched me dance three dances. Would *you* like to dance now?" When the children gave him an eager chorus of *yes*, he smiled. "Good. All right, I want everyone to stand up. That's right. Now I want you to make your circle big, so big you can stretch your arms out and not touch your partner. Oops, I see some people need to keep moving on this side. That's better. Please leave a space for me, and one for Mr. Harris."

Spenser snapped to attention. "Oh, I don't—"

"Oh, but you do, Mr. Harris. That's right. Everyone get into place. You hear the music playing? It's soft and pretty, to get us started. I want you to listen to this song. Maybe close your eyes, see if you can hear it better in the dark. Listen to the music and ask your body how it wants to move to the sound. Don't move yet. Listen."

Spenser did the exercise too, from his place in the circle. He hadn't meant to, but when he closed his eyes and listened, he couldn't help it. He imagined himself tap dancing. It didn't make any sense, because it wasn't a tap-dance kind of song. But it was what he saw, what his body longed to do.

"Good. Okay, keep your eyes closed. Raise your hand if your body heard the music and wanted to do something like ballet. Oh, how nice. A lot of hands. How many of you wanted to do jazz? I see. Now, I know Mr. Harris imagined tap dancing, but did anyone else?"

Spenser's eyes flew open, but Laurie paid him no attention. His focus was on the children, some of whom had their hands up.

Laurie nodded. "And how many of you didn't im-agine any of the dances? How many made up your own?"

Some of the students who had their hand up for tap put their hand up again—they were the habitual hand-raisers, and it didn't surprise Spenser. But some of them were indeed free spirits who would have danced to their own style.

Laurie moved out of the circle, tapping students on the shoulder as he went. "If I touch your shoulder, that means it's your turn in the center to dance with me. When the song changes, those of you that I tapped can come out and dance in the middle. Everyone will get a turn, and everyone will dance. No one will laugh at anyone else's dance, unless they're dancing in a way that you can tell they mean to be funny. And if someone laughs at your not-funny dance, it's okay, it means someone else got something different out of your dance than you meant. When you're not dancing in the middle, you can dance in your space, so long as you don't pick up your feet. Oh, I hear the song is about to change. Ready? Let's dance."

This song was faster, still ambient, but there were also words, subtle and in the background. The children who had been chosen to dance with Laurie went eagerly into the middle and began doing exaggerated, terrible copies of things they'd seen Laurie do, or remixes of their own. After thirty seconds, Laurie tapped new dancers and sent the first crew back to their circle positions. In the second group two girls began proudly doing what looked to be actual dance routines, and Laurie praised them for using certain steps properly.

Then he switched the group out again, and again, until all the students had danced.

"Well done, dancers. You're all having a good time, and that's the most important part of dancing. Yes, we want to make sure we do the steps of our routine correctly when we're performing, but sometimes we dance only for fun, like we are today. You can take dance classes at studios like the one I run, but you can also dance for yourself. At home, at recess—whenever you want to feel your emotions with your body." He glanced at the stereo. "Ah, we're about to switch songs. And for this one I need Mr. Harris."

Spenser wanted to object, but Laurie only grabbed his hand and brought him out as a new song began to play. Laurie leaned in close.

"None of your students speak French, do they?"

Spenser shook his head. "No, they don't. But, Laurie, I don't—"

Laurie stepped away, taking up a position across from Spenser. "Mr. Harris," he said to the class, "is going to play follow the leader with me. I'm going to perform a dance step, and then he's going to perform it too. Sometimes he's going to have a hard time. But we don't laugh at people trying. We encourage them and help them do better. Okay. Ready? Let's go."

Laurie held his hands up, did a movement back and forth across the carpet, crossing his feet one in front of the other. When he looked expectantly at Spenser, he put up his hands and did his best to mimic the movement, because it was the only thing possible for him to do in that moment. When Laurie praised him, the children clapped. Then Laurie did a similar but slightly different movement in the other direction, and ended with a turn.

Spenser copied him—mostly. Then he did it again when Laurie did another step, and another. He became so absorbed in watching and trying to copy he forgot to be nervous, and after a while he began to legitimately have a bit of fun. They were easy steps, but they were satisfying to do. When Laurie caught him smiling, he let it turn rueful in anticipation of an *I told you so*.

Laurie said nothing of the sort, only stood beside Spenser, body still moving to the beat. "Now we're going to do one together. This is called the step-ball-change. A very easy step. Yes, like that, Mr. Harris. And now we'll add a box step. Well done. Now we'll repeat the steps and end with another step-ball-change and a turn."

They kept dancing, and all the while a male singer belted out a tenor line in French. Spenser had no idea what the words meant, except he seemed to be telling someone named Emily to dance in a sexy French accent. It helped, in a strange way, that he couldn't understand the words. It fit with what he was doing, feeling his way through the dance to an unfamiliar song in a language he didn't understand. Sometimes, yes, he completely messed up the dance step. But those became almost his favorite parts because his students encouraged him then. "You can do it, Mr. Harris!"

In fact, most of the time, Mr. Harris *was* doing it. Spenser was dancing.

When the song ended, the students clapped, and so did Laurie, beaming at him. "Well done. And did *you* have fun, Mr. Harris?"

Spenser grinned back. "I did."

The bell rang for recess, and Spenser herded the students to the yellow line after they got their coats. The aide came to take the children outside, and as they departed, Laurie leaned in and spoke quietly to Spenser.

"That's lesson one in your dance instruction. I think you did quite well." He patted Spenser on the shoulder, gathered his things, and walked out of the classroom with a wink.

Spenser stood in the empty space, heart pounding, his body still bubbling with the energy dancing with Laurie had spurred. Acting before he could second-guess himself, he fished his phone from his desk drawer and texted Tomás.

I danced. With Laurie, in front of all my kids.

Tomás's reply came immediately. *That's great! Did you have fun? Were you nervous?*

Yes, I had fun. I was nervous, but it was good.

Do you want to do it again?

Why did that question make Spenser flutter so? He let out a breath in a huff, pushing out the fear. *I do.*

Will you dance with me someday?

This time the flutter wasn't fear. *Yes. I will.*

TOMÁS WANTED ANOTHER date with Spenser, but first he had to have an evening or part of an afternoon free to romance the man.

It didn't help that he'd added taking dance lessons to his list of things he had to do. Laurie didn't give Tomás and Duon pointe instruction each night, but they were expected to practice every day before closing, once the students had gone home. They didn't have on pointe shoes yet, but they did several of what Laurie named key pointe exercises. And while it wasn't high on Tomás's list of thing to do, learning pointe, it was absolutely Duon's top priority, and it was clear he expected them to learn together. So that's what Tomás did.

"We have it easier than the girls," Duon boasted one night as they did an exercise at the barre. "I watched the beginning pointe class the other day, and they were all whining about how much their ankles hurt. Mine feel fine." He raised his voice in a pointed way. "Would be nice to put some shoes on and do these exercises for real."

Laurie, seated behind the receptionist desk, didn't look up as he replied. "You are indeed doing the exercises for real. You're creating muscle memory and mapping brain patterns of what it feels like to hold your body in these positions. If you put on pointe shoes before you're ready, you will learn bad habits, perform poorly, and injure yourself."

"That white chick who started last week boasted

about how she got on pointe shoes her first damn lesson at her old studio."

"Yes. And that's why she's not in *my* pointe class, because she's unwilling to go back to pre-pointe and learn her basics."

Tomás sighed. "If you think you're going to get through this intro period faster by complaining, you're not half as smart as I thought you were."

Duon rolled his eyes. "I know that. I'm bored with this stuff is all. If I gotta stand here and do this for an hour, he's gonna be miserable along with me."

Laurie rose then and came over to the barre. "And he *is* going to be miserable with you tonight, because I'm sending Tomás out with Ed, who will be here soon." When Tomás turned to him in surprise, Laurie gave him a pointed look. "Marcus is in town, and he's going to talk to you about that legal matter."

"He is? Right now?" Nerves threatened to bowl Tomás over. "I've got to change." He remembered he was Duon's ride and opened his mouth.

Laurie shooed him away. "I'll take Duon home. Possibly via Dairy Queen if he can keep the complaints to a minimum. You go on." He touched Tomás's arm briefly. "And good luck."

Ed was indeed waiting outside the studio when Tomás finished getting dressed, and he drove him straight to an old-school steak house on West Seventh. "I've been coming here since forever. My whole life, whenever my parents wanted to celebrate, they took the family here. Normally my sister and I would fight and fidget when we went out to eat, but at Mancini's we were too busy feeling rich to pick at each other." He grinned sheepishly. "Obviously since meeting Laurie I've been to a hell of a lot fancier. But I still have a soft spot for the old place."

Tomás had never been to Mancini's, and he was mostly concerned about what Marcus had to say. "Is your friend meeting us there? Is he bringing the lawyer?"

"It's just Marcus for now, and yeah, he's meeting us there. He was in town to get the last of his things. He's moving to Logan permanently."

"Good God, why?"

"His father passed away unexpectedly of a heart attack shortly after the holidays. And his mother isn't doing well either. Alzheimer's, I think." He nodded at a pickup truck at the edge of the parking lot, the topper on and flatbed filled to the gills. "I think that's him."

They parked and got out of the car, and it was indeed Marcus who met them on the other side of the pickup. Tomás shook his hand, and Ed gave him a hug. Then Ed nodded at the overflowing vehicle. "So. This is it, huh?"

Marcus nodded. "Sold or donated all the furniture, which helped me out. Not sure where I'm going to put all this, though. Arthur's cabin doesn't have much in the way of storage." He smiled politely at Tomás. "Let's go inside."

The hostess led them to a seating area near the bar. Tomás lingered at his chair, taking in the space around them. "Wow. This isn't retro-revival. It's the real deal, uninterested in the passage of time."

"It's my favorite time capsule." Ed sighed as he sat in a vinyl booth with super-slick varnished wood edges. Marcus sat too as a waiter appeared, smiling as he gave them the specials before depositing a fragrant basket of bread on the table between them. Ed placed his order while Marcus finished perusing the menu. Once they were alone, Ed drew them back to the discussion of Marcus's move home prompted by the unexpected death of his father. "Everything going okay up in Logan?"

Marcus shrugged and focused on pulling apart his dinner roll. "It's weird, mostly. We finished clearing out the house last weekend. Arthur and Paul are helping me do some repairs and repainting before we put it on the market."

"You're not going to stay at your folks' place?"

"Too many memories." Marcus twirled the bread in his hands in sad distraction. "I still expect to see Dad come around the corner. It was okay until we moved Mom into the care center, even though she wasn't exactly her old self, especially these past six months. I could pretend, with her there. Like she was having an off day and she'd be in the kitchen grumbling about how much she hated cooking until Dad goosed her out of her mood." He shrugged, as if maybe the sadness would slough away with the gestures. "I'm going to live with Arthur and Paul and work at the mill, as a logger. Same as I did out of high school."

Ed shook his head in disbelief. "Dude, I couldn't. Ever. Not for a short afternoon."

Marcus reached for a second roll and gestured at Ed with it. "Your turn. Tell me how you're doing. How's the PT going? Pain manageable?"

Ed rubbed his neck. "It's not worse."

"Is it still keeping you from working?" Marcus pursed his lips. "Sorry. I didn't mean to be so blunt."

Tomás regarded Ed with concern. "I didn't realize you were hurting. *I'm* sorry for not noticing."

Ed twirled the knife idly on top of his place mat. "Yeah. It's keeping me from working much at all. I had to quit coaching because I couldn't be reliably counted on to come to practice, let alone the games. I'm at home, mostly. Probably permanently. It's going to be me and a whole lot of disability payments, forever."

Marcus frowned. "What about stem cell therapy? Is it too expensive?"

"It doesn't really apply, as far as I understand it. Well, not yet anyway. The biggest change they've made is giving me some steroid injections, which are great for pain, but they make me moody and come with big-time side effects. They could do another surgery, but every time they go in there they risk making it worse instead of better." Ed shrugged, doing his best to appear as if he'd made peace with this. "Do I like it? No. But it beats being dead."

Tomás worried Ed's remark would strike too close to home for Marcus, but he only scratched his beard, appearing thoughtful, not offended. "Maybe I'm too caught up in my own experiences right now, so take this with a deer lick's worth of salt. But I'm a big advocate of demanding more than simply being alive as a return on investment. It might be a while before you can find the thing that keeps you from hurting yourself but still matters. Your bliss, as Joseph Campbell always said. I think keeping the searchlights on is worth it, if they help you find the thing that makes your life hum."

Their waiter arrived with salads, disrupting the moment, and by unspoken agreement, they ended that conversation—and Marcus turned to Tomás. "Tell me about your family. About their situation, about what you've done and what you haven't done. Give me all the information you can, so I know how to help best."

Tomás glanced around, uneasy about doing this in a public place, but they were in a deserted section of the restaurant, and no one was paying them any attention. He cleared his throat and dove in. "My parents first came to the US in 1983. I never got the full story as to why—I think there was some kind of trouble with a drug cartel. They lived in Chilapa, both of them working pretty good jobs. Mom was a bank teller, and dad was an accountant or something like that. But I guess someone Dad knew joined the cartel and tried to pressure him to join also. Basically it got to the point they had to leave the country. I don't know if they were really in danger or if they were simply afraid. They don't talk about it much. I mean, they might have had romantic ideas about the US too. They were barely twenty. But whatever the reason, they went to Arizona and picked fruit and vegetables." He rubbed his jaw, remembering his mother telling the stories, always bits and fragments, and never much detail. "I know it was hard work, and when a company man told them they could make more work at a meat packing plant in Iowa, they left. But then that plant closed, and they moved to Minneapolis. I was six at the time. I was born in Arizona, but I only remember Minnesota."

Marcus nodded, listening. When Tomás drifted into quiet, he said, "Talk to me about your sister and how you've ended up working so many jobs."

God, where to start. "Alisa fell into the wrong crowd early. Junior high, I think. She left high school to run off with a boyfriend—tenth grade. She came back pregnant and penniless when I was a sophomore, which was when I got a job on the weekends to help out. But Alisa ran off before the end of that year, leaving Sabrina. Mom had to quit work to care for the baby, so I changed my school schedule to take an extra job. When Dad got injured, I had to finish school through an alternative system so I could work more." He flattened his lips. "Then Alisa came home with not one but two babies. She eventually got an apartment and took the kids, but they live more at our place than their own home. And lately we've thought she's drinking and using again.

"And how have immigration enforcement agencies and DHS been involved?"

"We did our best to take the kids from Alisa when she got dark, but once a neighbor called DHS before we could get them out. We ended up taking them anyway because we were the nearest kin, but having us in the system started raising flags. Someone somewhere reported that my parents aren't legal immigrants. They haven't actually come to confront my parents yet, but one of the social workers who liked us tipped us off, let us know it was a danger."

"So no one has taken custody from Alisa?"

"Not formally. She's good at cleaning her act up enough to pass inspection. And meanwhile the kids keep going back and forth because the judge in her case believes in keeping kids with parents."

"You know you could argue your case against her," Marcus pointed out.

"Yes—and risk exposing my parents." Tomás ran a hand through his hair. "I'd apply to be their guardians myself, but the state won't give me any money, or not much, and I can't do it without my mom as a babysitter. And my parents as support. But right now I'm supporting *all* of them—my parents, the kids, my sister—and yet I can only claim myself on my taxes."

Ed frowned. "Why can't you claim them if you're clearly supporting them?"

Marcus snorted. "Because his parents are illegal and therefore don't exist in the eyes of the government. The kids are his sister's deduction if she keeps them more than half the year under her custody, and since his sister doesn't live with them, he can't claim her." He shook his head. "It's a rough situation, that's for sure. And I hate to tell you, Tomás, though I'm sure you're not surprised to hear, you're not the only person with a story like this. In fact, I know plenty much worse."

The waiter appeared with their orders, but Tomás wasn't hungry anymore. As soon as the waiter was out of earshot, he turned to Marcus. "Do you really know someone who could help us? Is there *any* way my parents could become citizens?"

"Oh, there are ways, but most of them are going to be a hard sell in this political environment. It's going to come down to who you know who can vouch for you."

Tomás wanted to be sick, because he didn't know *anyone* with influence, but Ed lifted his chin. "I'll get Laurie's godfather Oliver on board. He's probably good for covering these costs Marcus mentioned too." When Tomás began to object, Ed overrode him. "Don't fight us on bringing in the big guns. This is your family. It's too important."

"It's important to every family in this situation. But the law isn't the law, not the way people think. It's malleable, interpretable. So much of how these things go down depends on who speaks for you, how much they know, and yes, sometimes who they know. If

Oliver Thompson suggests another lawyer for this, take his advice. He's ten thousand times more influential and connected than me." Marcus turned to Tomás, in full lawyer mode. "The magic bullet is proving your parents need to be here. Probably that's going to be about the kids—and you're going to hate this part, but it's going to involve throwing your sister under the bus, most likely."

Tomás recoiled. "I can't do that. She makes me furious yes, but she's still family. I can't betray her."

"You might have to if you want to keep your parents here. There's a mild case to be made for amnesty because of the cartel, though by this time the evidence may be weak at best. Your easiest route is to argue it's in the best interest of the children—legal US citizens— to have your parents remain. Which means arguing your sister isn't fit to be their parent. It would go smoother if you could get her to voluntarily surrender rights. *And* it means getting the most experienced immigration lawyer you can get your hands on. That part I can help you with."

He put a business card on the table, but Tomás couldn't touch it. *Alisa.* Oh, he hated her, but he didn't hate her this much.

Marcus put a hand on his shoulder, his expression sad. "Take the card. You might well find yourself quickly deciding which is worse, denouncing your sister or having to travel fifteen hundred miles to see your parents. And to be blunt, if Alisa is pulling this kind of stuff, the kids would absolutely be a lot better out of her care."

Tomás didn't have much to say after that, and Ed and Marcus politely steered the conversation away again, allowing him to marinate in his thoughts for the rest of the meal.

He considered what Marcus said all the way home and late into the night as he lay unsleeping on his bed, staring at the ceiling. Not about choosing his parents over his sister—he couldn't go there. But he did think a lot about demanding more from life than simply being alive. Following his bliss.

Tomás certainly wasn't following his bliss. He was too busy, too focused on keeping his family in one piece. But he did want bliss. He didn't let himself think about that normally, but it was getting more and more difficult not to. Especially since all his thoughts of bliss were tied up in one thing and one person. And it was impossible to pretend it didn't hurt to watch his sister fuck them all over so hard Tomás didn't have the time or energy for a simple date.

CHAPTER TEN

A S THE MINNESOTA winter rolled on, Spenser did get more dates. Of course, with Tomás's schedule, these events happened weekly at best, though often they went every two weeks. They saw each other nearly daily still, and those meetings were full of smiles and stolen kisses once Duon returned to his room. Several of their official dates had happened between Tomás's work shifts, which had picked up in intensity. There seemed to be something going on, something bothering him, but when Spenser asked if he was okay, "Sorry, I have something I'm saving up for," was all Tomás would say.

They didn't have another night alone, though, because the two times they had dates when Tomás didn't have to go to bed early or rush off to another job, Laurie and Ed were busy and couldn't take Duon. Spenser would have been down for turning on a box fan in the hallway and making love to Tomás quietly, but he couldn't quite get the courage up to mention this as an option, in case Tomás felt they shouldn't have hanky-panky with Duon present. So they were, once more, resigned to heavy petting in the dark corner of the kitchen.

Not that the petting was bad. Though to be honest, any touching at all was wonderful to Spenser.

Thanks to therapy, he'd acknowledged long ago that his relationship to touch was unusual due to his disjointed upbringing. His mother hadn't been cruel, only absent, though when she was around she did hug them and promise them ridiculous things even Spenser had known couldn't ever happen. *Next summer we'll go to Disney World. Maybe next month we can go to that water park.* They were lucky if they went to a city park, and it only happened if Spenser agreed to babysit the younger ones while his mother napped on a blanket. But he'd had physical contact with his sisters all the time—helping them out of the gap in the fence to the huge drainpipe they loved to dance in, getting them dressed, bathing them, snuggling on the couch watching TV and movies from the library. Most of his youth was fuzzy in his mind, but he remembered that touching.

Just as he then remembered the lack of it when he'd moved to foster care. Several of his foster moms had tried to hug him, but accepting strangers felt like a betrayal. He couldn't shake the feeling that if he let himself join another family, *his* family's reunion could never happen. In hindsight he suspected this was why he failed to remain at a foster family even before they knew he was gay, but he hadn't figured it out in time to find himself a real home, not until Clara and Betsy. There'd been no touching at the shelter, nothing welcome—only shoves, flicks against his arm, scuffles in the hallway. No, no one really touched Spenser until one night after he'd aged out of the system, alone in his first apartment, he spent the night prowling the streets to find someone to bring home to it.

By the time he messed up his life so much he landed in the Avenue's program with Clara and Betsy, it had been over a decade since anyone had hugged him. He resisted them at first out of habit, but Betsy in particular had a way of wearing him down. They taught him to accept, appreciate, and most precious of all, *expect* familial touch. Brushes of shoulders, touches of hands, fussing with hair, and hugs. Lots and lots of hugs.

Tomás, however, was something new. His casual touches had thrilled Spenser since they'd become close through working with Duon, but now that they were dating, Tomás touched Spenser all the time in a way no one else had. Not his sisters, who had needed him. Not Clara and Betsy, who parented him. Not the men he'd taken home to his apartment, who wanted to fuck him or be fucked. It was clear Tomás wanted to sleep with him. But it was equally apparent this wasn't *all* he wanted. For the first time in his life, someone touched Spenser not out of need or pity or guidance but *want*. Patient, unwavering desire.

This knowledge undid Spenser more than the kisses

Tomás trailed down his cheeks, more than the burn of his whiskers as he pressed his lips into the curve of Spenser's neck. Those were lovely too. But what made him want to purr was the way Tomás looked at him as he drew back, stroking his cheek one last time as he whispered good night, making it casually clear he would wait forever for Spenser, if he had to.

Nothing was more precious to Spenser in the world than those looks, those caresses.

They didn't only meet in Spenser's kitchen, however. Where they met the most often and for the longest period of time were during Spenser's dance lessons twice a week, which Laurie had gently badgered him into taking in the studio after hours. Laurie still led the lessons, but more often than not Tomás was present too, sometimes helping, sometimes observing. Laurie taught Spenser tap as well as general dance concepts, focusing on balance and body awareness in addition to some basic steps.

"Your body is your instrument. Don't control it. Dwell in it. Feel it. Don't be upset with what it can't do or feel ashamed because you don't understand it yet. You will."

Laurie said this every lesson, but the night the two of them were alone in the studio, Spenser wasn't in the mood to pretend he could dance. Tomás had taken Duon home early to help him with some homework, and Spenser knew by the time he got home, Tomás would be in bed. He resented having this lesson at all, and wasn't in the mood to hear fantasies about how he could master the skill.

"I don't particularly like my body. I never have." Spenser rubbed his arm as he fixed his gaze on the floor. "I don't want to dwell in it."

"Do you know why you dislike your body so much? Do you not think you're handsome? Because Tomás in particular would take issue with that comment."

Spenser shrugged. "I don't think I'm ugly, but no, I don't turn heads at a club. I never have. I don't care about that, though. I wish I weren't so awkward and clumsy, so self-conscious."

Laurie put his hands on Spenser's shoulders, briefly as a reassuring touch, but then he pivoted Spenser toward the wall of mirrors. When Spenser flinched and glanced away from his reflection, Laurie gently turned his face back. "You avoid the image of yourself a great deal, I've noticed. In fact, you make more mistakes when you're watching the mirror."

He did? Spenser shrugged. "I'm always making mistakes. It upsets me. Doesn't it everyone?"

"Not quite like it does you. You're a perfectionist, which is normal enough. But where you allow yourself growth in teaching and in your caring for Duon, you don't in dance. In your perception of your body." Laurie let go of Spenser and moved to face him, so that Spenser saw his reflection beside the real-life Laurie.

Laurie was beautiful. Poised. Handsome in a lean,

feminine way. Beside him Spenser would look like a half-starved troll if he smiled and stood as proudly as he could. Spenser glowered at himself. "It's easy for you to say that. You've done so much. Been everywhere. Even when you're not dancing, you're graceful and put together. I haven't done anything. I couldn't be anything like you, not if I practiced for the rest of my life. I'm not that way, and I can't be. I don't speak up, I don't dazzle or draw people's attention. I'm not good for—" He cut himself off before he could blurt out anything else.

Laurie huffed through his nose. "Put together? I'm sure I can appear so. A lifetime of rigorous training will do that to a person. Plus appearing flawless has always been my shield. I would never presume to name my hell worse than anyone else's, but I promise you until recently I was lonely, lost, and miserable beneath my veneer. I didn't look in the mirror and see the man you see in me." He nodded at Spenser's reflection. "The thing Ed has taught me most is that the best cure for self-hate is to dare to believe in the vision of someone who sees something more than you are, more than you believe you can be. I look at you, Spenser, and I see compassion. Quiet, abiding compassion and love. You love so much sometimes it hurts. I find those qualities beautiful and powerful, and whether you're dancing or taking care of Duon or talking with Tomás, when you forget to guard yourself and let it shine, you are more beautiful than anyone who has ever stood on a stage."

He put a hand on Spenser's shoulder. "You don't have to dance perfectly. You don't have to *be* perfect, or outlandish. You don't have to ride in on a horse to be a hero. You don't have to stand in the spotlight to be a star. If you save one person, if you shine light for one soul—why is it less than saving two, or three, or four? You *know* you have done this for Duon. For the children in your classroom. For Tomás, who still works too hard but has a spring in his step now, yearning for the moment when he can spend more time with you. *That* is who I want to see dance. *That* is what you bring to the floor. To everyone in your life. To *life*. Show me *that* dancer, Spenser."

Spenser was dizzy, unsure of how to respond. He felt winded, blindsided—but Laurie led him through the steps again and again, until he couldn't think anymore, could only follow. He let go, he supposed, but mostly he was so overwhelmed he danced on autopilot, until Laurie declared the lesson over. Laurie's words echoed in Spenser's head as he drove to his apartment, rang in his ears as he walked through the crisp late-winter air and down the hall to his apartment.

Quiet, abiding compassion.

You love so much sometimes it hurts.

You are more beautiful than anyone who has ever stood on a stage.

It wasn't him, Spenser knew. But he couldn't chase the words away because they were who he wanted to be. Old ghosts whispered memories, things he wanted to leave behind. They were all live now, dancing around his head, piercing his heart.

When Spenser entered the apartment, he saw that as he had predicted, Tomás had already left. Duon remained at the kitchen table, however, bent over his homework. He glanced up when Spenser entered, began to give his standard, "Yo, Spense," greeting, then stopped as he got a good look at his guardian's face. "Hey, man. You okay?"

Spenser did what he could to push the melancholy down, but it was like trying to stuff an octopus in a bag. He sank into the chair opposite Duon and rubbed his temples with a sigh. "Laurie got under my skin. Not that he was mean or anything. He stirred things up, is all."

Duon snorted. "He does that." He shifted in his chair, putting his pen down. "He was trying to find your inner dancer? Show you how to make your own spotlight?"

Spenser frowned, replaying the lecture in his head. "No. He told me—" Emotion caught him unawares, and he batted it away. "He told me I'm compassionate, that it's beautiful, and I shouldn't feel like shining for one person isn't as grand as…" He wiped a thumb deftly across his eyes to stop his tears, and he laughed to cover them. "Sorry."

Duon grew serious. "But you *are* compassionate. You're good at it. The best. If I have a shit day at school, I think about how I'll go home and you'll be smiling with dinner on the table, asking me about my day. And it was shit, but then I feel like it's all right. You're good with that. You don't just make a safe space. You *are* one."

Spenser wiped his eyes again, but it was useless now. Tears sliding down his cheeks, he took the back of Duon's hand, gently, and held it as he closed his other over Duon's palm. He gave a watery smile. "Thank you for listening, Duon. Thank you for being here with me, for being my family. And for frequently being smarter and more put together than the man who's supposed to be taking care of you."

Duon grinned shyly, but with more than a bit of pride. "We cool. We're here for each other, yeah? You and me. And Tomás."

Spenser squeezed Duon's hand, realizing he was Betsy now, the one offering that precious touch. "It's an honor to be allowed to care for you. To have you in my family."

Now it was Duon who wiped away tears. But he smiled too, and squeezed Spenser's hand. Then, as if overcome with emotion, Duon stood and took Spenser into his arms. Shutting his eyes and taking a deep breath, Spenser hugged him back.

When they bid each other good night and went to their respective bedrooms, Spenser didn't sleep. He lay awake, staring at his ceiling, thinking of what Laurie had said, and Duon. He imagined the whole world as a stage, full of people vying for the center and the bright beam of light. He stopped thinking of how he could endure the spotlight and instead let himself materialize in the shadows, in the wings, opening his arms and beaming light onto those who had quit trying, who had exited the fray and were worn and weary, needing a breath of hope.

That is the dance I want to dance.

TOMÁS WAS DOING okay.

His life had felt like a million balls in the air since as long as he could remember, and he wanted more out of it, sure, but overall he was fine. His family was healthy. He had Spenser and Duon and Laurie and Ed and the studio. Did he want more time to date Spenser so he felt he could legitimately call the man his boyfriend, maybe find time to do more than kiss and fondle him? Yes. Would he like to take the kids to the park or his mother shopping or sit and have a beer with his dad? Yes. Would it be great to go with Ed and Laurie and everyone to the Minnesota United for All Families meetings to help lobby legislators to make sure the marriage equality amendment passed the statehouse? Obviously, yes. Would he like to not worry every time he saw an unfamiliar car in his building's parking lot, thinking they were DHS or INS? Hell *yes.*

Tomás wanted so, so many things. But he wanted none of them enough to sacrifice his sister for them. Even if she was annoying and borderline dangerous.

Even if he did lie awake at night wondering where the line was, what he'd cross to decide he had the right to make the decision for her. He couldn't square it in a way that let him choose them over her. Couldn't be sure not acting was as simple as choosing her over them, either. But he wasn't ready to go there. Not yet.

So he floated on, but as March wore into April, he began to get tired. So tired he missed steps in dance class and was almost late for his shifts at Starbucks. So tired he sat down for a break at the nursing home and fell asleep without meaning to, and snored away all but the last fifteen minutes of his shift.

The nurse who found him covered for him, but Ed confronted him at Starbucks the next day, coming in as he was almost done with work and lingering until Tomás was ready to go. Ed joined him as he headed for the door, but once they were in the parking lot, Ed pulled him aside.

"I need to talk to you about a couple of things, and it's hard to pin you down lately. You're more than burning the candle at both ends. You're out of wick and living on the fumes of your own determination."

"I fell asleep for a few minutes, no big. A few floors didn't get cleaned, toilet paper not changed." It wasn't until Ed blinked at him in confusion that Tomás realized Ed wasn't talking about, couldn't know about, his falling asleep at the nursing home. He tried to recover. "I'm overworked, yes. This isn't news."

He went for his car door, but Ed stopped him with

a hand on his shoulder. "The other thing I need to talk to you about is the lawyer we found for you."

Tomás's stomach rolled. He opened his mouth to tell Ed he was good, thanks but no thanks, but nothing came out. He felt dizzy, and he leaned on the car to support himself.

Ed moved to block the sun, crowding Tomás in a way that was comforting, not threatening. "Hey. It's okay."

It wasn't close to okay. "I gotta get to the studio. It's my turn at the desk."

"Laurie's got the desk. He knew I was going to find you." He jerked his thumb at his car, which was parked a few stalls over. "Come on. Let's go for a ride."

Tomás held up his hands. "I don't want to go see the lawyer, or Marcus, or anybody. Not right now." *Not ever.*

"I know. We're going to drive, is all. Talk a little of this out. Push some of this off your shoulders. All right?"

Tomás didn't really want to go with Ed, but it was easier to let his body be moved along, to sit shotgun in Ed's Charger and be driven randomly around the streets of St. Paul, listening to Britney Spears. Listening to Ed talk.

"Meeting with the lawyer doesn't set anything in stone. It gives you more information. Vicky's willing to talk with you too. Explain the situation with the kids, if there's anything you're worried about there."

"I can't use my sister for this. That's a nonstarter no matter how you slice it."

"I get this is complicated, and it's a heavy thing to have on your shoulders. That's why we're trying to help. Because it's more than your sister. It's not trading her for your parents. The kids are part of this too. And *you*, bucko. There are a lot of lives your sister's choices affect, and one of those lives is yours. You have a right to a different path. Speaking up for it for yourself, for your family, hell, for Spenser and Duon—that's not being selfish. You aren't responsible for her choices."

"Family's all I've ever had. We've always been everything for each other. You don't understand what you ask when you suggest I should betray that."

"Isn't it a betrayal to let her drag you all down?"

"*She's my sister.*"

"And you're my friend." Ed's voice was sharp, the soft edges gone. They were at a stoplight, and he turned the full force of his conviction on Tomás. "I know we haven't known each other long, not compared to you and your sister. But you're more than the teacher Laurie relies on the most. More than the official studio translator. More than the guy who stole my place as Duon's favorite. Your sister is your family, but *you are ours*. We have the same right to fight for you."

The light turned green, but Tomás didn't get a respite. Ed kept talking as he angled onto the road leading toward Starbucks. "You're getting the day off today. Laurie's covering your classes. I'm giving you the name of a lawyer, and you can either call him or toss the card in your glove box and joyride around the Twin Cities. You can go home and nap. You can chase your sister and give her what for. You can sit in your car and be pissed off at me for making you do this. But you're going to slow down. You're going to do one damn thing for yourself and yourself alone."

They were at the parking lot now. Ed handed Tomás a card, and Tomás tucked it into his hand without looking at it. "I have to pick up Duon."

"I've got that job. Duon already knows—sent him a text." Ed made shooing motions at him. "Go on. Go take a break."

Tomás left the car and got into his own. He drove around aimlessly, feeling anxious and more than a little lost. What was he supposed to do with himself now? He couldn't go home. His mother would ask him what was wrong, and anyway, the kids would be there, running around at full steam. He'd watch them and think about how he had the phone number of a man who would help him betray their mother. He could go to Halcyon and burn off some frustration at the gym, but Vicky might find him and have the conversation Ed had threatened him with. So he kept driving.

He hadn't meant to end up at Spenser's school, or at least he hadn't consciously decided to go there. Once he arrived, though, he glanced at the dashboard clock and the lineup of yellow buses and parents in cars and thought that this seemed to be about the time school got out.

And there was Spenser's car.

Tomás parked on the side street near the teacher's parking lot, turning on the radio and trying to look like a parent, not a hot mess someone might mistake for a child predator. He acknowledged he was a rather unkempt, Latin man of significant stature in a car, implying he couldn't afford private school for his theoretical children. He stepped on the voice that whispered he should leave, send Spenser a text, and ask him to dinner. He imagined his actual nieces and nephew, pretended to be the not-so-wealthy lovable uncle who was pinch-hitting for his sister.

His sister.

For a moment, Tomás couldn't breathe.

He got out of the car, did a lap around the street, staying away from the pickup area now swarming with children and teachers helping get them on the bus and into their parents' loving arms. He saw one of them clock him, then excuse herself from the fray and cross over, a polite but distant smile on her face. "Hello there. Can I help you?"

Tomás scrambled to appear normal, calm. "I'm fine, thank you. I'm waiting for a friend of mine. A teacher. Spenser Harris."

The woman hesitated, this response clearly not in any of the narratives she was expecting. "Would you like me to tell him you're waiting for him?"

Did he? Tomás was fairly sure he should give this

up and leave, but he couldn't. "I don't want to trouble him. I'm happy to wait."

She left him then, but of course it wasn't long before Spenser himself came outside, frowning as he hurried up to Tomás in concern. "Tomás? Why are you—has something happened?"

He hadn't seen it coming, but it was then that Tomás broke. He gave up trying to mask his anxiety or push it down, or dress it up or any other of the million tactics he'd developed to escape it. He simply let out a long, ragged breath. "I'm sorry. I didn't mean to bother you."

Spenser's expression transformed into empathy and concern, and it wasn't until Tomás felt the force of it that he realized this was what he'd come for. This was what he needed. Spenser took his hand, squeezing it. "I need to finish up inside before I can leave. Come in with me, and wait in my room?"

Tomás let Spenser lead him into the school—by his hand until they were clear of a copse of bushes, then by standing beside him and shepherding him gently through the halls. Tomás noted the crucifix on the walls, the prayer board by the chapel door, the flyer noting a time for a marriage protection rally hanging on the wall of the main office, where Spenser carefully introduced Tomás as his friend.

It hit Tomás then—Spenser wasn't out, not at work. *Couldn't* be out. He tried not to let his gaze linger on the flyer, but in so many ways it was all he could see. Every time Spenser went into the office to ask for photocopies or a stapler refill, he had to look at the damn thing. God knew—*ha*—what else he had to endure here about first the amendment, now the efforts to block impending legislation to make marriage equality the law of the land.

No way was Spenser going to marriage equality rallies. He could call his representatives, and that was about it.

So Tomás did his best to look like Spenser's friend, not the guy who wanted more than anything to go back to this guy's apartment and lose himself in the man's arms, bed, life. He smiled politely and shook hands with teachers who made Spenser pause and introduce Tomás. In a way it all was good medicine, centering Tomás and taking his mind off the spiral that had brought him here.

Then Spenser led Tomás into a classroom and shut the door. Alone with Spenser, Tomás knew an entirely different kind of tension.

The kindergarten decor—brightly colored alphabet and number lines, bulletin boards featuring shapes and colors and inquiries about the weather—kept Tomás's desire in check. It was a comfortable, welcoming space, with a reading nook and an art corner and a line of cubbies marked with laminated nameplates in a cheerful font. Spenser fit into it better than Tomás would have predicted, well-scrubbed and welcoming in his khakis, checkered dress shirt, and tan boat shoes.

Tomás had no difficulty imagining Spenser sitting on the tuffet reading to children in a semicircle or crouching and speaking in a soft voice to a troubled child.

Right now Tomás was the troubled individual, and though Spenser had to look up slightly rather than crouch down, he was all gentleness and concern. "What happened? What has you so upset?"

Tomás didn't know where to begin, didn't know what detail to offer first. Wasn't sure what he should and shouldn't say. He tried to glance away, to see if avoiding Spenser's gaze would give him some clarity, but he fixed on the teasing hint of his collarbone. He felt ridiculous for being here, for putting this on their barely begun relationship. "I'm sorry. I shouldn't have come here. I don't know what I was thinking."

Spenser led him to a chair and pushed on his shoulders until he sat in it. The chair was designed for six-year-olds, which meant Tomás's knees came up to his chin. Spenser sat on the edge of the worktable opposite and regarded him with worry. "There's no problem with you coming here. I'm glad you did, if something has you upset."

Tomás remembered the sign in the office. "I know you're not out here, that you can't be. I didn't mean to put you at risk."

"I'm not out, no, but there isn't anyone operating under the illusion I'll bring a nice young lady as my date to the employee picnic, either." Spenser nudged Tomás's ankle with his foot. "Don't worry about that, seriously. Why did you seem so upset outside? Why do you look upset now?"

He couldn't get out of this confession now. Tomás ran a hand over his face and stared into the tight-knit fibers of the industrial-grade carpet. "It's complicated and involved to explain." When Spenser let the silence stretch out, Tomás filled it without meaning to. "It's about my family. I have a decision to make, and I don't want to make it." He met Spenser's gaze. "And if I tell you any more, you have to promise me you'll keep my confidence. No more of this mandatory reporting stuff."

He expected Spenser to dismiss the idea, but no, Spenser's expression remained serious. "Give me the general gist of the topic, and I'll let you know whether or not I can offer you that assurance."

Moment of truth. Tomás drew a breath. "I need to tell you a story involving an undocumented immigrant."

Spenser's whole body relaxed, and though he didn't smile, his posture was easier now. "I'm not required by law to report undocumented immigrants. But if this undocumented immigrant threatens the health and safety of a minor, whether or not the minor is a US citizen, I'm obligated to report the matter." He leaned forward, touching Tomás's leg. "Are...you the undocumented immigrant?"

Tomás shook his head. "No. But both my parents are." He felt cold admitting it out loud, despite what

Spenser had assured him. "My sister is a citizen as well, but she's a terrible parent and has already been reported to DHS. Multiple times. Someone is threatening to report my parents too, possibly my sister's worker. So I keep acting as Alisa's backup. I've been named as guardian a few times, and I get a tiny monthly stipend that covers one or two meals' worth of food at best. But usually I don't get anything at all. Alisa knows we're over a barrel and leaves the kids with us all the time while she runs off." He hesitated, realizing he'd wandered into the health-and-safety-of-a-minor territory. "DHS knows all this. They watch us like hawks. And any second they're going to swoop in, take my sister's kids, and bring in the ICE to haul my parents back to Mexico."

He paused for breath, and Spenser's grip on his leg tightened. "Tomás—I'm so sorry. That must be terrible for you."

Tomás laughed darkly. "Oh, that's not the issue. What's got me now is Ed and Laurie found me a lawyer to help with the immigration aspect who thinks the best way to save my parents and the kids is to turn on my sister." He exhaled, the last of his fight escaping. "I can't. I can't take it anymore."

With his hand still on Tomás's thigh, Spenser leaned forward and pressed a kiss on Tomás's forehead. "Let me get you home."

Tomás tensed. "That's the problem. I don't want to go—"

Spenser laid a finger against his lips. "I meant to my

home. Let me make you dinner." He traced the outline of Tomás's lips and dragged the pad of his thumb across the stubble of his chin. "Let me take care of you."

It was what Tomás wanted more than anything, to be taken care of. To be with Spenser and forget the rest of the world, if only for a little while. But the claws of doubt and despair wouldn't let him go so easily, and they tried to tear this apart too. "You deserve better than this. I'm too busy to date. I'm never around. I'm all bottled up."

Spenser leaned in close, kissing the point of Tomás's jaw just below his ear. "Let me get you home and uncork you."

Part of Tomás wanted to cry, to weep in relief and collapse in surrender in this man's arms. But he laughed instead, his despair transforming in the magic of Spenser's embrace. Shutting his eyes, Tomás turned his face so his lips could meet Spenser's own.

A noise in the hall made Spenser leap back, reminding them both of where they were. Before Tomás could apologize again, though, Spenser took his hand and pulled him to his feet.

"Come on. Let's go home."

This time Tomás didn't misunderstand Spenser. He did admit to himself, however, this was why he'd come to Spenser, the dream he was chasing: that the man smiling at him and urging him to his car could be his safe space.

That Spenser could be his home.

CHAPTER ELEVEN

SPENSER WASN'T ENTIRELY sure he knew how to ease Tomás's burden, but he did know he would do his damnedest to try.

Tomás tensed as they approached Spenser's door, which of course was directly across the hall from his own. Spenser could hear José and Renata's voices drifting through the panel, along with the sounds and smell of a meal being prepared. He herded Tomás into his apartment with a quiet whisper. Once he shut the door, however, he spied one of Duon's hoodies over the back of a chair and acknowledged a snafu in his plan. "Who's picking up Duon tonight?"

"Ed said he'd take care of it." Tomás paced in agitation, listless beside the table. "They're going to see my car and wonder why I didn't come in."

It took Spenser a second to realize Tomás meant his parents. Spenser did his best to think on his feet. "Why don't you go wash up, and then we can make dinner together. I'll tell your parents you're having dinner with me."

Tomás hesitated, then nodded and disappeared into the living room, heading for the bathroom. Spenser grabbed his phone from his schoolbag, texting Ed frantically as he walked toward the door.

You have Duon? I have Tomás. He's upset. I'm going to keep him here at my place and calm him down.

The reply came before Spenser made it all the way in the hall. *We've got Duon. He can have a night getting spoiled with his uncles. You kids have fun.*

Spenser typed a quick *thanks*, then tucked his phone into his pocket as he knocked on the door to Tomás's place.

Renata answered the door. She had on an apron, and her face and hair were damp with the steam from her cooking. She smiled as she saw Spenser, speaking slowly and carefully in English. "Hello, Spenser. How can I help you?"

Spenser thought of what Tomás had confessed, that at any moment this kind woman could be removed from his life forever. He took a breath and put himself back on track. "Hello, Renata. I wanted to tell you Tomás is with me, in my apartment. I'm making him dinner."

If she knew something was wrong, she didn't say anything. She only put her hands on either side of his face, drew him down, and kissed each of his cheeks. "Have a good dinner." Releasing him, she reached for the door, smiling as she pushed it closed.

Spenser's cheeks were still flushed as he returned to

his own place, but Tomás wasn't in the room, so he took refuge in fussing in the fridge and the pantry as he attempted to invent something for dinner. He'd planned leftovers for Duon and himself, but now he fished a package of Italian sausage out of the freezer, set it to defrost in the microwave as he pulled out a box of pasta, a jar of sauce, and a bag of salad. When Tomás came into the kitchen, Spenser nodded at the potential spread with a rueful smile. "It's not going to be much of a dinner, I'm afraid."

Tomás came up behind him, crowding Spenser with his body. Spenser thought Tomás was going to put his chin on his shoulder, but he only lingered close. Close enough for his scent to overpower Spenser. "Spaghetti is always good."

Spaghetti was always easy, which was why Spenser made it often. "I've never been a great cook."

"I enjoy your cooking. Your apartment always smells like a church potluck. And I love church potlucks."

Spenser put a pot below the faucet and began to fill it. "My adoptive mother, Clara, was practically a gourmet chef. I never knew what I was eating half the time. When I got out on my own, I ate takeout a lot, until my cooperating teacher taught me about hot dishes. How to cut recipes in half or make enough to freeze for lunches."

Tomás leaned on the counter, but when the pasta pot was full of water, he carried it to the stove before

Spenser could. They worked in tandem, cooking together, Tomás frying the sausage while Spenser cut vegetables for a salad, all the while casually discussing Spenser's past.

Tomás's fingers brushed Spenser's and stole a slice of freshly sliced cucumber. "How many places did you live? I mean, how many different families and shelters?"

Spenser paused his knife as he did the math. "Seven. Eight, counting my mother. But if you go by houses, adding her gives us another six. And three more school districts."

"That's so much change. Do you remember all of it? I mean, for most of what I remember of my life, I was always with my parents in this place across the hall, and it all blurs together."

Spenser had to think about his answer, which he decided was answer in itself. "I remember, vaguely, but I don't think about it much. The past is a box I keep tucked away in the back of my mind." He sprinkled the sliced cucumber over the salad. "I'm not full of trauma, though, if that's what you're thinking. My life wasn't an after-school special. It's just my life. A little chaotic, a little lonely."

"Are you lonely now? I mean, I never saw you go out much, before we..." Tomás rolled his eyes at himself. "Sorry, I'm fucking this up."

His self-consciousness was endearing. "No, I don't get out much, but I do get out. I'm busy with my job, is all. And now with Duon. I'm a quiet person." He shook the tip of his knife playfully at Tomás while he grabbed a tomato. "Besides, you're the last person who can pull off throwing shade at me for not getting out much, Mr. Workaholic."

Tomás grunted and stabbed at the sausage with his spatula. "Touché. But it's not by choice. I'm a people person. I prefer a job where I can interact."

"Have you ever been able to go hang out? Meet friends at a bar? Socialize without scheduling it?"

He paused, considering, then grimaced and shook his head. "Not really, no. But it's like I said. There's no room for it. I make all the money in the family. I'm responsible for everyone."

Tomás didn't say it in a complaining way, but the heaviness of his burden broke Spenser's heart. He wanted to take the man into his arms, kiss him, and lead him to the bedroom and make him forget about everything. Before he could come up with a consoling reply, Tomás stole another cucumber from the salad, sighing with regret before he put it in his mouth. "I really have to remember to leave a bottle of Tajín over here someday."

Spenser frowned. "A bottle of what?"

Tomás's grin made Spenser's belly flutter. "It's a spice, I guess you'd say. Condiment." He made shaking motions over an invisible cucumber slice in his other palm. "You put it on cucumbers, watermelon, every-thing. The kids have been known to sneak the bottle and eat it in front of the television."

Spenser couldn't imagine a spice he'd do that to. "What in the world is in this stuff?"

"Huh, you know, I never thought about it. Lime, for sure. A little cayenne. Sugar too. Salt." He grinned again, resuming his stirring of the meat. "And magic."

Anything that made Tomás smile like that was something Spenser wanted to have on hand. He made a note to ask Renata where she bought it.

But even without Tajín, they made their own magic. They cooked together. Ate together. Almost burned the garlic bread because they flirted with each other at the cupboard too long instead of setting the table and remembering to set a timer. When the meal was done, they did dishes while MPR chatted in the background, as they complained they'd eaten too much while picking at the last of the bread until Spenser put it away. It was a soft, companionable evening, and from the way they touched each other's arms, shoulders, backs, Spenser knew they were headed to something more than a good-night kiss at the door.

But as Tomás drained the dishwater and Spenser hung up his towel, the room grew quiet enough that the voice from the radio punctuated their bubble.

Despite the failed November vote to define marriage as be-tween one man and one woman, opposition groups are renewing their vows to block the statehouse's efforts to move forward with a marriage equality bill. Several local demonstrations have been planned throughout the state, as well as a rally at the statehouse in St. Paul later this month.

Tomás glanced at Spenser, his expression sober, wary. "I saw a flyer about the rally, I think, in the office at your school. Do they put pressure on you regarding the equality issue?"

Spenser hesitated, then nodded. "It's a difficult position to be in. As I said, I think they all know and are content to ignore my orientation. But the principal is insisting we all participate in what he calls *awareness* on the issue. I'm mostly hoping it all goes away."

"But you do want marriage equality, right?"

"Of course I do. In Minnesota, in the United States, in the whole world." Spenser wrapped his arms around himself. "But I want to keep my job too. And honestly, I'm pessimistic about the whole thing. The vote failing was a wonderful surprise, but I can't see them actually passing equality. Or, if they do, the Supreme Court is going to show up and end everything. I'd rather not get my hopes up."

Tomás opened his mouth, then shut it with a sigh. "I don't know. I do hope still. For marriage equality. For immigration reform. I keep thinking, if they only see us. See Ed and Laurie and you and me and Duon, and my parents, and…everyone. When it's real people, not policy, it's different. It has to be. People can't hate as easily when they see you."

Spenser didn't know how to respond. Not without admitting, no, it wasn't any different when they knew who you were. Or rather, it was different in the wrong way. He wasn't actively cynical, but he didn't have the hope Tomás did. He wanted it, though. Wanted the flame burning bright inside the man before him. The conviction, naive or not, that the world might turn out okay. That people wouldn't look you right in the eye and despise you for being who you were. He wanted, like Tomás, to have a belief in a better tomorrow. In a better world. In people, believing they would do the right thing.

Or maybe, Spenser acknowledged, he simply want-ed the man who felt so passionately to feel passionate about him.

Spenser uncrossed his arms and closed the distance between them. Ran his hands up Tomás's arms. "I want to take you to my bed, Tomás. And I don't want anything to interrupt us. Not even if your mother shows up with empanadas stuffed with nectar from the gods."

Laughing, Tomás wrapped his arms around Spenser and drew him close. "I suspect she's decided we've courted long enough." He ran his nose along Spenser's forehead and down his cheek. "Except I kept trying to tell her I was always interested in more than sleeping with you."

Spenser nuzzled him back, his whole body awake to the electric potential awaiting it. "It was my hot dish. It brings all the boys to my yard."

Tomás drew Spenser's earlobe briefly into his mouth. "It was the way you danced the night of the election. When you stopped feeling self-conscious, when you let go and enjoyed yourself. With me."

Spenser's startle was as much from what Tomás said as it was the way his stubble tickled Spenser's skin. He attempted to come up with a rejoinder, but all he could do was grip him tight and whisper, "Tomás."

"I'm right here."

Tomás led him across the apartment, into Spenser's bedroom. Closed the door. Kept his smoldering gaze on Spenser as he peeled off his shirt, unbuckled his pants, and took Spenser into his arms.

OH, BUT TOMÁS liked the way Spenser's expression went dark and unfocused when Tomás stepped out of his pants. Or rather, his focus was concentrated on Tomás and Tomás alone. Hungry. Aching. Tomás had no intention to deny him. But when he reached for Spenser's waistband, tugging on the panels of his shirt, Spenser stiffened and pushed at Tomás's hands, abruptly self-conscious.

"I don't—I didn't realize. But of course you'd have a great body. You're a dancer." His gaze drifted over the planes of Tomás's chest, his fingers following. "You're hard everywhere." He withdrew his touch and rounded his shoulders as he backed into the door. "I'm…not."

"I'm eager to get to know your body better," Tomás assured him. "Just as it is."

"It's pasty and doughy." His hands skimmed over Tomás's pectorals, his expression turning hungry. "God, but you're like a *sculpture*."

Tomás pressed in close, smiling as he learned his close proximity caused Spenser to tremble and inspired him to touch Tomás more boldly. He didn't attempt to untuck Spenser's shirt again, but he did knead him slowly, deliberately through his clothing. *If you're dough, darling, I'll work you until you're elastic in my hands.*

Tomás trailed soft kisses to Spenser's ear, along his neck, worked his buttons loose one by one. By the time Tomás slid his shirt panels aside, Spenser didn't have enough breath to object, and when he fumbled to push him away, all he managed was to lace his fingers in Tomás's hair as he kissed his way down his throat.

"You're so beautiful." Tomás ran his tongue along the edge of Spenser's clavicle, blood humming as the gesture made Spenser gasp and clutch him tighter. "So sexy."

"I'm not," Spenser whispered.

"You're terribly sexy." On impulse, he repeated it in Spanish. *"Eres terriblemente sexy. Tan increíblemente sexy."*

Spenser shuddered, his knees giving out as he flattened his back into the door. "Oh God—what...what did you say to me?"

Smiling into Spenser's skin, Tomás kissed his way across his lover's chest, murmuring tender endearments his mother would blush to hear in her native tongue.

He remained in Spanish until Spenser was goo in his hands, until he was so far gone he didn't notice Tomás had unbuttoned his trousers and had worked them over his hips. When they fell away, Tomás cupped Spenser's erection through his briefs and repeated it all, this time in English.

"You're the sexiest man I've ever known, darling. The way you move. So quiet, but so graceful. You say you don't dance, but you do. Your smiles would soothe the heart of a devil. But the slope of your neck would tempt an angel. You tempt me every day, lover. You make me want to get on my knees." He was on his knees now, and he nuzzled the bulge before him as he continued his litany. "I want to take you in my mouth. Make love to you. Make you gasp my name, cry out as I taste you. I want to lick every inch of your skin, until my tongue is alive with your salt." He nudged the elastic band down so Spenser's cock could spring free. "Come into my mouth, Spenser. Let me take you home."

The guttural sound Spenser made thrilled Tomás, but it was nothing on the rush he felt when Spenser tugged his hair, pulled his head back, and aimed his cock at Tomás's face. Tomás helped him out, guiding him closer. Then Spenser was inside him, and he forgot everything else.

Softness and heat. The pressure on his knees, the tension of the grip on his hair, the desperate thrusts of Spenser moving in and out of his mouth. Everything about it was perfect. It had been a long time since Tomás had slept with anyone, yes, but this was more than sex. This was Spenser. This was the man he'd danced around for months. The man he'd danced *with*.

This was the man, he realized, he had oh so many hopes for. The man he wanted to be *his* future. *His* family.

The realization shook him, making him feel vulnerable, more open than he'd meant. But it felt so good to hope. To dream of not only this night but endless more chances to make love. To confess his joys and his sorrows.

I need this. I deserve this.

I have this.

He would have swallowed Spenser down, but as Tomás felt his lover's climax building, Spenser pulled away and sank down the door, gasping. He held Tomás's face in his hands, kissing him with his whole body trembling.

"Come to bed with me."

They rose together, kissing as they discarded the last of their clothes and stumbled together toward the mattress.

"Tell me what you want." Tomás nipped at Spenser's bottom lip, hands moving over his lover's body. "Tell me what you want, so I can give it to you."

Spenser's self-consciousness was gone now, smothered under his desire. "I want to be under you. To feel you move with me." They'd bumped into the end table, and Spenser fumbled with a drawer, producing a bottle of lube. "I want to come with you."

Tomás kissed Spenser long and slow, easing him onto the mattress. Pressed their bodies together, naked and damp with sweat. Captured Spenser's hands and held them over his head, pinning them down as he opened the lube in the other.

Spenser jumped when Tomás captured him, but as the friction of his touch warmed the lube, as Tomás brought their cocks together, drawing them slick and tight in the heat of his hand, Spenser shut his eyes and pushed into him. When his mouth opened on a sigh, Tomás leaned forward and took possession of it, swallowing the cries as he ground them out of his lover.

He hadn't meant for this grinding to be their whole opening act. Tomás had laid Spenser out with a multi-layered seduction in mind, intending to drive him into a mindless frenzy before giving them both their release. As soon as Tomás slid his body against Spenser, however, all his plans evaporated. *Everything* evaporated. His plans, his fears, his soul-crushing responsibilities. The world condensed and concentrated in the man beneath him.

Spenser.

He was so perfect, lying there. Unleashed, he didn't reveal a tiger or a sex kitten—in the throes of passion, Spenser became soft and open, fragile in a way Tomás hadn't expected to witness. This was what his walls, his reserve protected. A tenderness and vulnerability shaking Tomás to his core. It drove him to shield Spenser with his body as he spun his lover out further, as Tomás delved deeper into this sweet, wondrous experience that was Spenser unbound.

He wanted to love this man until they both exploded into light.

He wanted to protect this man so nothing ever made him put up those walls again.

He wanted to *be* those walls for Spenser.

They came together, gasping and pushing and clawing their way to release. Spenser cried out, then melted into the mattress as if he had no bones. Tomás, shaking, fell into Spenser, sheltering him with his body and burying his face in his lover's neck as he fought to regain his breath. As he shut his eyes and drank in the moment, never wanting it to end.

When Tomás woke in the morning, they were spooned together, Spenser snuggled in front of him and hugging a pillow. Tomás roused him with kisses on his shoulder, and Spenser smiled and rolled over sleepily in Tomás's arms.

He brushed a lock of hair from Tomás's face, still soft and vulnerable. "I want to do this again."

Tomás wanted to do it right now. All of it. The dinner, the sex, the snuggling. He caught Spenser's fingers, kissed them lightly, then drew each one into his mouth. He liked the way Spenser's breath hitched, the way his erection stirred along Tomás's leg. He took hold of it, coaxing him to full attention.

Spenser thrust into his hand, but though his gaze became feral, unfocused, he didn't shut his eyes. He threaded his fingers through Tomás's hair. "Your turn," he whispered. "Tell me what *you* want."

Tomás wasn't in the mood to speak. He reached for the lube, warmed a dollop in his hand, then massaged Spenser's cock. His balls. His taint, the circle of his entrance.

Spenser clutched his shoulders, slid his knee up Tomás's hip, giving him better access. Gasped as Tomás pushed inside, stared back as Tomás loosened him. When Tomás added a second finger, Spenser shut his eyes, tipped his head back, and slid his knee higher.

Tomás rolled Spenser onto his back, tucking his lover's trembling leg over his shoulder as his cock nudged the inside of Spenser's thigh. He stared down, riding the rush of power and determination to protect this man as Spenser melted for him, surrendering his body, yielding his tight heat unti he gave way.

Tomás pressed deep enough to make Spenser cry out, then growled into his neck and thrust along the path leading to the place he most wanted to be. "I want to be inside you. I want to come inside you."

Spenser clawed at his back, drawing his other knee higher, opening himself for Tomás as he fought for breath. "Yes. Please, Tomás. Do it, please." He sucked and bit at Tomás's neck. "I haven't... It's been so long."

Tomás did his best to cling to sense, but Spenser

was too close, too sexy-sweet. He tried to hold back, to only tease his cock at Spenser's entrance, but it was too easy to push inside. Too easy to give into the desperate sounds Spenser made as Tomás began to fuck him, hard and slow. Tomás would not rush this. He would be good to this man. So good. So perfect.

As perfect as he was.

"Fuck me, Tomás." Spenser slid his leg over Tomás's arm, thrusting himself onto more of Tomás's cock. "Oh, God, fuck me, *please.*"

Tomás did. He held Spenser's waist, pulled back, and slammed home. The raw heat hit him—he growled, gripped tighter, and ground his hips. This time he wasn't undone by Spenser's release to passion. This time he reveled in it, determined to show he and he alone was the one who could treat the gift of this man with the care he deserved. He took his time, pushing deep and keeping himself there until Spenser begged him to move. Read his body until he knew exactly how to please it, how to give Spenser a safe space to release. Held Spenser in place, letting his head fall over the edge of the bed so he could stretch himself out as he chased his bliss, so Tomás could see his beautiful, slender throat while he fucked into him.

There was no more world for them, not for what felt like a lifetime. Only their bodies, the smell, sound, and feel of sex. Tomás felt like he could stay this way for the rest of his life, moving in and out of Spenser's body.

Spenser's fingernails dug into Tomás's arms. "*Please.*" He lifted his head enough to stare at Tomás, fucked out, passion drunk, lost. "Please—more. Please…please harder. Rougher." His fingers relaxed, stroking in silent plea along Tomás's skin. "Fuck me so hard I explode."

The whispered, tender request for something so raw snapped the last of Tomás's control. He pulled out, drew Spenser to him, and kissed him with the full brunt of that intensity. Turned him around, pushed him to the mattress, knelt behind him and entered him again, keeping Spenser's head angled so he could kiss him as he gave his lover the fucking he had asked for. Gave him hard and rough. Gave him pleasure so focused Spenser could do nothing but surrender to it, dissolve in it.

Gave him all of his love, his promise to protect and keep him.

My Spenser. Mine.

He came inside Spenser first, biting his neck as Spenser whimpered and shuddered and followed suit, shooting against the sheets. But as they collapsed onto the bed, Tomás drew Spenser closer, hands still moving over him.

"I could fuck you all day," he whispered. *I could love you for a lifetime.*

Spenser ran fingers over Tomás's arm as if the gesture took all the strength he had. "Don't you have to work?"

Tomás did. A shift at Starbucks starting at noon. He would make almost one hundred dollars, money he needed. Money his family needed. Yet for the first time since he'd told his mother he'd get a job to help out, as he did the math on where the shift's money would go, how much it would sting not to have it…he couldn't talk himself into the sacrifice. Because he'd found his bliss. The thing Marcus had said he should search for. The spark that made life *living*.

Loving Spenser. Being with, taking care of Spenser.

Tomás shut his eyes and held Spenser tighter to him. "I'm calling in sick. I'm staying with you."

And that's exactly what he did.

CHAPTER TWELVE

THE NEXT FEW weeks were a wonderful blur for Tomás.

Sure, after his weekend of hooky he went back to working way too much, but he also saw a whole lot more of Spenser. Metaphorically and literally. He tried to be discreet with his affections, but every time he saw the man he wanted to take him somewhere quiet and remove all his clothes, and as much as he could, that was exactly what he did. Spenser made noise at first about not being able to have sex while Duon was around, but all Tomás had to do was lock the bedroom door and press his erection into Spenser's back, and it was all over. Often Tomás came over for "breakfast," coaxing Spenser into making out against the closet door of his bedroom. Usually with Tomás whispering naughty Spanish into his ear.

"What did you say?" Spenser fought for breath as Tomás pounded behind him. "What did you tell me to do?"

"I told you to hold still while I make love to you."

Tomás ground his hips, sliding a hand around their bodies to stroke Spenser's cock. "I'm going to make you sticky with me, lover. Fill you up and fuck you out. You won't be able to walk, I'll fuck you so hard."

Spenser shut his eyes and pushed against him, spreading his legs wider than Tomás was forcing him open. "Yes. Oh God, yes."

Tomás had never engaged in dirty talk before. But he'd never been in a relationship like the one he had with Spenser. Light. Happy. Fun. Even when they barely saw each other for days, they made time to kiss and nuzzle one another, to ask each other how things were going.

And they danced.

Spenser still insisted he wasn't any good, but he came to his tap lessons every week, sometimes with Laurie, sometimes with Tomás, and sometimes in a group with the three of them and Duon. Sometimes Ed was along. Spenser was getting quite good, and they were all trying to convince him to work up an act for the summer show.

"It's not anything huge," Laurie assured him. "Friends and family, and donors of Halcyon Center."

"I'm not ready for that yet," Spenser kept saying, but Tomás thought he was beginning to soften on the issue.

He and Duon were locked and loaded for the performance, though. They each had their own pointe shoes now, and the three of them—Duon, Laurie, and

Tomás—had worked out a routine together. "Men en pointe," Duon said every time they strapped into their shoes, and he spoke the words with pride.

"These pointe lessons are good for him," Tomás remarked one afternoon as they waited for Duon to arrive. "Have you noticed how much more confident his ballet overall has become since he started? Hell, how confident he is in general?"

Laurie nodded, smiling with quiet self-satisfaction. "It was the same way for me, which is why I didn't hesitate to teach him once he showed interest. Pointe to me, when I discovered it, felt a bit like ballet drag, but I don't believe Duon would describe it in those terms. It's more of a pure discipline, as if pointe closes a circle for him. Shows him who he is as a dancer. The right dance can do that."

The right dance and the right partner, Tomás thought, heart lifting as the door to the studio opened and Spenser entered with Duon.

Tomás's mother knew they were officially a couple now, and it was clear she and his father couldn't be more pleased. She invited Spenser and Duon over for dinner almost every other night, and when they couldn't make it, she sent them care packages of food "for later." She also began shopping for Spenser on her thrift store runs, a move which perplexed Spenser and delighted Tomás.

Duon had also figured out they were an item, and he seemed to be the only one happier than Renata. He joked about "my two dads" and asked when they were going to ask him to be the ring bearer at their wedding. It was also clear he wasn't making a joke but trying to egg them on.

"You two are good together." Duon pointed this out at every opportunity, but one day he added, "You should take it to the next level."

Tomás, who was driving Duon to a Saturday rehearsal at the time, raised an eyebrow. "What next level is that?"

Duon gestured vaguely at the air above the dashboard. "You know. Move in. You practically live with us as it is."

Tomás couldn't say he hadn't wished for such a scenario too. But in addition to it being too soon, there were complications. "I have to live where I can be there for my nieces and nephew. And I don't know what that does to Spenser's suitable other placement for you."

"Then marry him. They gonna pass the law any second now. Then you can get married right here. Move into a nice house in the burbs." Duon made a face out the window at Oakdale. "Maybe not this uppity one. But somewhere nice. With a yard. You could get a dog."

Which was to say *Duon* could get a dog. And a yard. And two dads. "You do understand you'd have three young siblings as well. And grandparents."

"It can be a big house. Your mom can cook. She

loves it. Your dad can do the yard and stuff. I'll help clean. I'm good at it. Ask Spense. He'll tell you how good I am."

It was a pretty picture that Duon painted, for himself and for everyone. "I don't know if Spenser's school would like it."

"Whatever, man. I'm sick of this shit. We gotta worry about nonsense every time we turn around. My social worker. Your sister. Spenser's job. The stupid government and their rules about who can get married. It's horseshit. You love Spenser. He loves you. We make a good team. It'd be a kickass life, in a house in the suburbs. All of us in there. It's fucked up there's all this shit in the way."

Tomás couldn't disagree, not even with Duon's cavalier assessment of Tomás's feelings for Spenser. But the shit *was* all in the way. And it bummed him out to admit he didn't know how they were supposed to clear the path. The more he thought about it, the more Tomás wanted that life, the house Duon described. The more he wanted Spenser at the heart of it all. But he couldn't have him, once again, because of complications and obligations he'd had no hand in creating.

At the top of the list of the people making the complications was Tomás's sister.

Alisa had never had a problem with him being gay per se, but then he'd never been in a relationship before, not to the degree that she came home to pick up the kids and saw her brother flirting with another man.

She was fine when he'd first introduced them, a casual pass on her way out the door. But one night when she saw Spenser reading with Jasmin and Ashton on his lap, the kids staring starry-eyed at Spenser and ignoring their mother, she pulled Tomás aside.

She'd been drinking, not enough to cause alarm but enough to make her punchy. "I don't like this white faggot spending all this time with my kids."

The slur caught Tomás unawares, making him stammer his reply. "You...what? What did you say?"

Alisa gestured vaguely at the bedroom where Spenser was. "You heard me. It's fine if you need to fuck him. I'm no bigot. But you can't have him around my kids. It's dangerous. And gross."

Where the fuck was all this coming from? The blows kept knocking Tomás for loops, and he couldn't find his ground. "But you're okay with *this* faggot around them? I can't believe you'd actually say this to me. You know what I do for this family. You know how much I work. You know what I do to keep Mom and Dad here. To keep *your kids* here."

She waved her hands at him, flashing her cheap jewelry at him. "You think you're such a saint. You don't know what I do. You don't know."

Tomás studied his sister more closely and got a better look at her pupils. "You're not just drunk. You're on something."

She went on as if he hadn't spoken, aiming her acrylic nails at his face. "*You don't know.* You don't know how hard it is for me. To be without my kids. To know you all hate me. Blame me for all your problems." She pulled a nasty face. "Saint Tomás. Sacrificing for everyone. You think you're so great. Think there should be a saint candle for *you* burning on the kitchen counter. Think you're better than me. Maybe you are. Maybe you're not. But I know what *is* true. I can tell you not to let that cocksucker around my kids."

Their mother appeared, pushing them apart as she addressed them in rapid-fire Spanish, telling them to calm down, to behave. Tomás didn't want to. He wanted to punch Alisa in the face. Wanted to tell her to get out. Wanted to show her the fat file from the Department of Human Services, the letters and emails and notices they got every damn week. Wanted to show her his pay stubs, the hours he'd worked. Wanted to rub her nose in Spenser's awards and praise for his teaching. Wanted to demand to know how she dared call him names and imply he was bad for children when she was the one who came to pick them up drunk and high.

But he didn't. He let his mom and dad separate them, talk her down quietly, and put her to bed in their room so they could sleep on the sofa again. He told them not to bother, that they should go to his bed because he was going home with Spenser.

He made love to Spenser in the dark quiet of his room, but it all felt desperate somehow. He lay awake long into the night, marinating in his anger. The truth was, his sister could get her way, if she wanted it. She could make him keep Spenser away, because if she pitched a fit, the whole scheme would fall. His parents would get deported. The kids would go to foster care. She had them over a barrel, and there wasn't anything they could do about it.

But of course that wasn't true. Not if Tomás got over his guilt and pulled out his own barrel. The one with an immigration lawyer inside.

He called first thing in the morning before his rage mellowed out and made an appointment for the next week. Of course within a day or two he regretted making the call at all. He tried to forget about it until it was time to meet the lawyer, but he couldn't. He ping-ponged between fury and guilt, and there was no safe ground.

If Spenser had heard Alisa yelling, he never said anything about it. He had his own troubles with his school, where his principal beat the drum harder every day, insisting Spenser attend one of the anti-equality rallies. "I'm afraid I'm going to have to attend one," he confessed early one Saturday morning as the two of them lay together in Spenser's bed, enjoying a moment before Tomás had to go off to work.

Tomás hugged him closer, kissing his temple. He wanted to say no, Spenser shouldn't, but who was he to tell him how to handle his job? "I can go with you, if I'm not at work. Or send my mom."

Spenser threaded his fingers through the hair on

Tomás's chest. "I keep wondering if I shouldn't get a different job. If I work at a public school, they can't fire me. I'm pretty sure, anyway."

"We need equal protection laws. National ones."

Spenser laughed. "Yes. Unfortunately I think we're as likely to get them as we are immigration reform, unless we get the country to vote in Democrats across the board in 2014 and 2016."

"Maybe they will."

Spenser snuggled in closer, wrapping his body tighter around Tomás. "This is my favorite part of you. You always have hope. I never do. I think the world is a terrible, dark place full of awful, selfish people. I don't trust them to do anything for me, ever."

And yet that was all Spenser did, do things for other people, usually strangers.

By the time Tomás got to his appointment with the lawyer, he was still torn between guilt and anger, but what he had cemented was his resolve. Right or wrong, he was going to do this. His parents were less convinced, but Alisa's displays were becoming more and more alarming, and even Renata's bright outlook couldn't illuminate a path where their current situation would continue to work. He went to the law office in a new shirt and khakis—new to him, anyway, his mother's latest thrift store find.

The lawyer was kind, shaking his hand and smiling genially as he encouraged Tomás to have a seat in his office. When Tomás assured the man he had some money saved for a retainer, the lawyer waved him down. "It's taken care of. I'm working this pro bono as a favor to Oliver Thompson."

Tomás blinked at him. "I don't understand what you mean."

"I'm not charging you. No worries on payment. You have influential friends." He winked. "If you thank anyone, thank Laurence Parker. It sounds like this was his doing."

The lawyer went over the things Tomás had expected from the meeting: forms, documentation on himself and his parents. He said to expect phone calls from several different clerks, and he gave the names so Tomás could pass this information on to his parents. He gave him an additional card as well, explaining this was a lawyer they were consulting with who specialized in immigration law. "We work with her often on these kinds of cases. She and her staff all speak Spanish, so your parents will be able to converse with their entire office in their native language."

It was hours and hours of that kind of thing, questions and interviews and explanations, and when Tomás left, his head was spinning. He knew he needed to thank Laurie, and he would when he went to work in a few hours, but first he needed to talk to his parents. He went home, and he told them everything.

"They're building a case against Alisa. They plan to take custody and argue the two of you are integral to their well-being. I guess they can use this to keep you in the country. You might have to leave, briefly, while they process your application for citizenship, but they're trying to get that waived too. They're going to come and talk to you, some clerks and a lawyer who speak Spanish. You can tell them everything, and you need to be honest. They can't build a case without the facts."

Renata dried her eyes and whispered a prayer while José frowned at Tomás. "But this sounds expensive. How will we pay?"

Tomás felt dizzy simply thinking about it. "It's free. He's doing it all as a favor to my boss's godfather."

José kept shaking his head. "But this isn't right. You said it would be many thousands of dollars. We have some saved, enough for the retainer. Give them the money. Tell them we can pay."

It took Tomás almost an hour to get his father to understand what pro bono meant, and even then he was sure José would be calling the number on the card as soon as he was out of earshot. Tomás left for the studio in a daze, but when he parked, he realized he was about to go in to Laurie and face him, to thank him, and he couldn't move. He sat there for ten minutes, trying to psych himself out of the car, when the passenger door opened and Ed got in.

"Hey there. You okay? For a second there I thought you were having a seizure."

Tomás forced his mouth to work. "I met with the lawyer. They're doing the case for free."

Ed smiled, something easing in him. "Oh, good. I'd hoped they would. Laurie hinted they might."

Tomás fought to breathe, and when he spoke, his throat was thick. "It's not right."

Ed frowned at him. "Why? What do you mean? Laurie doesn't mind, and honestly Oliver loves to—"

"*It's not right.*" Guilt returned now, but for a different reason. "Do you have any idea how many people need this kind of help but don't have someone who can pull a favor for them? Even if they have the money, they don't begin to know where to go." He wiped at his eyes, but the tears, once spilled over, wouldn't stop now. "It's not right. It's *not right.*"

Ed put a hand on his shoulder, rubbing small, soothing circles through Tomás's jacket. "You're right. It's not. But that doesn't mean you can't accept the help."

Tomás couldn't stop crying, the dam broken now. "Three jobs. I've worked three jobs for four years, sometimes four jobs, once five. I only have a car because my dad fixes it. We've been crammed into that apartment my whole life, always wondering if today was the day we'd lose our family. And now, just like this, it's done? Or on the road to being done?" He thought of his savings, the thousands of dollars which, if this lawyer were to be believed, was now money saved. He laugh-cried, snorting snot out his nose, then fished around for the spare napkins in his glove compartment.

Ed found them first and passed them over. Then he caught Tomás's arm, squeezed it, and held on until Tomás looked him in the eye. "I'm so sorry this is happening to you and your family. But I'm so glad we're able to help you. You're a good man. A good son. And your parents are good people. Your nieces and nephew are good kids. You deserve this."

"A lot of good people deserve this," Tomás whispered into his napkin.

"You're right. But you're the people we can help right now." Ed squeezed his arm again. "Come on inside. At least you'll be able to blow your nose into an actual tissue."

Tomás tried to laugh, but he still felt overwhelmed. When he entered the studio, the first person he saw was Laurie, and his emotions bubbled over almost immediately.

Laurie looked concerned, but after a whispered word from his husband, he led Tomás into his office with an arm around his shoulders.

"Thank you." Tomás did his best to keep himself level, to not fall apart while he spoke, but it didn't work. "Even if this doesn't work, I owe you and your godfather for the rest of my life."

Laurie pulled him into an embrace, holding him tight. "You don't owe me anything. You're my friend. I'm glad Oliver was able to help you pull some strings."

Tomás understood Laurie would never know. That he couldn't, rich white man that he was, had always been. "If you ever need anything from me, if I can ever do anything at all for you, name it and it's yours."

Laurie waggled his eyebrows. "How about you quit your weekend job and maybe dial back a little at Starbucks so I don't watch you dance and worry you're about to pass out?"

Tomás laughed, more mirth than sob this time. "Yeah. I think I can do that for you."

IT MOVED SPENSER to see how much the meetings with the immigration lawyers affected Tomás and his family. Nothing exactly was happening, only interviews and law clerks taking notes, but the forward momentum clearly meant the world to the Jimenez household. Even Alisa's children seemed happier, probably because there was less stress around them. Alisa herself was off on another one of her benders, almost as if she'd heard the news that her family needed her to perform as poorly as possible while so many people were watching and documenting her behavior.

It was good to see his boyfriend's family so happy, obviously. Spenser and Duon spent more and more time at the Jimenez family table, Renata and José making it clear they already considered them part of the clan. Duon for his part ate it up.

Spenser enjoyed it too. Except sometimes it hit him too squarely in the chest.

He hadn't done so in a while, but spurred by the

Jimenez lovefest, Spenser looked up his sisters again, and after several bottles of beer late one Saturday night, he also searched for his mother. But though his searches didn't turn up anything, the simple act inspired him to drink more, until he was drunk, at which point he felt guilty for being drunk when he was supposed to be taking care of Duon. When Tomás came home from covering a late shift at Starbucks and dropped by to say hi, he got worried when he saw how troubled Spenser was, but Spenser refused to tell him why and let him think it was general upset over his school. Which, granted, there was more than enough unhappiness to warrant tears. But when he gripped his boyfriend tight and chased pleasure as he welcomed him into his body, it wasn't his job Spenser was trying to forget. It was his family.

The family he knew he would never have a happy reunion with, that a skyscraper full of lawyers couldn't rescue from so much as a garbage bin.

When he woke, once he had enough coffee and painkiller in him to make him human, Spenser called his adoptive mother.

She answered on the third ring, launching directly into her usual effusive greeting. "Spenser, what a delight. I haven't heard from you in months. How are you?"

He gripped the phone tighter. "I wondered if you had time to meet. Maybe for dinner."

"For you, sweetheart, I can meet anytime. How

about today? Are you free now? I could take you to this lovely brunch place I found."

This was what ended up happening, Clara picking Spenser up in front of his apartment building in her shiny black Mercedes, greeting him with a frail hug and a kiss on each cheek as he got into the car. She beamed at Spenser. "Look at you. Handsome as ever."

Spenser smoothed a hand over his hair. "Thank you. You're looking well yourself." She was, but she also appeared older. He felt guilty for putting off visiting her. He had nightmares of getting a phone call one day, hearing she was dead, or worse, calling her at a moment like this and finding out she'd been gone for eight weeks.

She was with him now, though, and as she drove him into the eastern suburbs, she babbled animatedly about several charities she was helping organize as well as the charming widow she was dating. "She married a man, the poor thing, though she knew she could only ever be attracted to women. Has three boys, all Republican like their father." She chuckled. "Oh, but she loves using me to scandalize the family."

"Do you ever think you'll go back to being a host home for Avenues? I know you stopped when Betsy became ill, but I wondered if you might start up again eventually."

"Oh, no, darling. Getting too old, and it truly was more Betsy's project than mine." She reached over and patted his leg. "I love you all, and you know full well you were always my favorite. But I'm focusing on helping them raise money now. They want to open a shelter in Brooklyn Park, and I'm trying to help them do it." She waved a hand. "Enough about me. What's going on with you? Tell me everything."

Spenser rubbed his cheek. "Well, to start, I suppose you could say I took your place in the host home program."

She gasped in delight, and he couldn't help a smile as he told her about Duon, which of course by extension led him to tell her about Tomás. And without giving away their secret, he told her about Tomás's family.

They were at the restaurant by then, on their second round from the buffet when his stories about Tomás and Duon wound down. Clara thanked the waitress as she refreshed her coffee, adding a cheeky wink as the young lady withdrew. Clara cradled the cup in her hands as she studied Spenser. "Now, tell me why you really wanted to see me."

Spenser fiddled with his knife on the tablecloth, wishing he'd had this conversation in the privacy of her car. "It's ridiculous. I shouldn't feel this way, but I can't help it."

"And how do you feel, sweetheart?"

He ran his thumb up and down the smooth, heavy utensil, gaze focused absently on the shiny surface. "Jealous. I'm jealous of Tomás and his family. Which is awful. They're going through hell, a nightmare I can barely understand, but all I can think about is how happy they are together, how much they love each other." His throat became thick, his eyes blurry, and he fiddled more nervously with the knife. "They say I'm one of them now, but I'm not. It isn't the same as having a family of my own."

Her thin, wrinkled hand closed over his, stilling his nervous twitch. "This has been your struggle ever since I've known you. And it's not something to feel guilty about or angry with yourself over. It's not fair that you don't have a family like Tomás does. You have every right to be upset. But at the same time, you can't let hurt keep you from embracing the loved ones you do have. The family we make is as valid as the family we're born to. Sometimes it's a thousand times better."

Spenser wiped at his eyes and turned his palm so she could squeeze his hand more completely. "I know. I keep trying, but I can't let it go. I've been to therapy for it, I've had conversations with myself to get through it, but it's a shadow I can't find my way around."

"Well that's your first mistake, thinking you'll ever be completely over it. All lives cast shadows. Pretending otherwise is how we end up accidentally living in darkness." She let go of his hand and leaned back in her booth, a sad, wistful expression on her face. "Maybe it's so hard for you because it wasn't your choice. Not that parting ways with my family was on my to-do list, mind you, but when they said it was Betsy or them, I chose Betsy, and I never regretted it. It was the same for her. We were sad, yes, but we'd removed ourselves.

I think part of you is still a little boy watching his sisters get stolen away from him."

Spenser couldn't argue with her. "It was easier when I was focused on work. With Duon around, I'm always seeing my story in him. And now in Tomás's nieces and nephew."

"Have you contacted your sisters? Perhaps you could start up relationships there."

"I tried looking them up, but it was too over-whelming. I'm afraid of what I'll find."

Clara tapped her finger on the table, then nodded as if coming to a decision. "Let me do some digging for you. I'll see if one of them would be safe to approach. I can be your buffer at a meeting if you like."

The idea sounded both wonderful and terrifying at the same time. "I don't want to put you out."

She rolled her eyes, but she grinned too. "Yes, it'll be tough squeezing it into my busy schedule. Don't worry about it. I'm happy to do this for you. *You* are *my* family, Spenser. I'll do anything for you, anytime." She shook a finger at him. "And no feeling guilty for not contacting me for so long. You're living your life. I keep tabs on you too, mister. If I thought you needed nudging, I'd have nudged."

Spenser smiled shyly, focusing on his plate. But then he reached for Clara's hand and clasped it tight. "Thank you, Clara."

She drew their joined hands to her mouth and kissed his knuckles. "You're welcome."

CHAPTER THIRTEEN

S PENSER KEPT CLARA'S words about family in mind as he had dinner with Duon and the Jimenez family that night. Tomás had to work late at Starbucks, so after Duon and Spenser helped Renata with the dishes, they had a quiet evening at home, watching random reality television and eating sliced cucumbers doused in Tajín. They had their own bottle at home now, and while Spenser appreciated it in conservative circumstances, Duon had embraced it wholeheartedly. When the cucumbers ran out, Duon raced Jasmin to collect the excess spice from the plate with dampened fingers.

During one of the commercials, Spenser turned to Duon.

"I want you to know I consider you family. You always have a place with me. I have every intention of keeping you through high school, but when you're out in the world, when you need something, you come to me, okay?"

Duon appeared moved but unsurprisingly hid it

behind bravado and a wry smile. "You been watching the Lifetime channel, Spense?"

Spenser ignored the tease and put a hand on the couch cushion beside Duon's leg. "I want you to remember that. I don't want you to ever feel you don't have somewhere to be. You always belong with me, even if it's been a long time since we've spoken. You're my family. Whether you like it or not."

Duon softened and, glanced down, abashed but subdued. "Sure, man. But I wasn't worried, really."

"I know. But I needed to say it." Spenser withdrew his hand. "It's hard for me sometimes, watching Tomás's family. I get jealous. So I went to see my adoptive mother today. She helped me get my head on straight about a few things. And I wanted to make sure I was doing right by you."

"You do right just fine, man. I swear." His face clouded. "But it's weird that you bring it up now, actually. Because I ran into my cousin the other day. His mom is in town. And I don't know if it was him being an asshole or what, but he said my aunt has been on my grandma's case and they were gonna try to get me back. Mom and Grandma. They found out I was with a gay man, and they all having fits."

Spenser lost his breath. "Have you told your social worker about this?"

Duon pulled a face. "Hell, no. I hate her."

"Did you tell Vicky?" When Duon glowered, Spenser held up his hands, which were shaking. "I'm trying to process, is all. You threw me for a loop, telling me that."

Duon studied Spenser more carefully. "You scared. Why?"

Spenser wasn't entirely sure. He tried to parse it out and edit it to what seemed appropriate to share with his charge. "The idea that someone could take you away because of my orientation is upsetting. It's the same thing with my job. I have tenure, which should mean greater job protections, but because I'm gay, any second they could fire me if I give them evidence. It doesn't have to be much, either. Someone sees me out with Tomás, or…anything."

"But Ed keeps saying how they're gonna pass that law for equality. So all you gotta do is hold on until then. Same for this bullshit with my family."

Spenser shook his head. "My school is a private, religious institution. They can do what they want."

Duon was clearly worried now too. "But my family can't do shit, though, because this is a state thing. Right?"

Spenser had no idea. He leaned into the cushion and pressed his fingers to his temple. "I'm going to call the host home coordinator. And your social worker, probably. I hope this is a tempest in a teapot, but I can't be sure."

When he made the phone calls on his break at school the next day, he was mollified somewhat. Both Ryan from Avenues and the social worker felt the family didn't have much ground to stand on, since Duon had been formally surrendered to his care. "I'd keep your nose clean, though. Don't bring guys home, and maybe stay away from gay clubs for a while."

Spenser was so taken aback he almost didn't know what to say. "Are you telling me I can be a gay parent only if I'm celibate and a shut-in? Or is a night out acceptable so long as I'm surrounded by straight buffers?"

"Of course not." She laughed nervously. "I'm only saying discretion would go a long way here. And it's a delicate line. Duon is still a child in the eyes of the law. You have more leeway as a suitable other placement than if you were a foster parent, but he's not your child. Not legally."

"What if he was legally my child?"

"Then his family would have no say at all."

Spenser let the gravity of the situation rock him a moment, and then he said, "Fine. How do I adopt him?"

"If you become a foster parent and adopt him through the system? You attend some classes, have another home study, this one more official and detailed. You get a foster care adoption license, which will close once the adoption is final. Of course, the family has the right to appeal, and some courts favor family over foster parents."

I am his family. Spenser wanted to bulldoze forward and tell her to get him the paperwork, but of course it

wasn't his decision alone. "I'll talk to Duon about it."
And Tomás.

"Wonderful. I hope you get back to me saying
that's what you want to do. In the meantime, I
wouldn't worry too much about the family's objections.
We have same-sex couples adopt all the time. In fact
the court might look more highly on you if you did
have a partner."

Spenser considered bringing up Tomás, but remembered his family and their struggles and decided
not to. "I'll let you know."

He thought about what it would mean to adopt
Duon all though the school day, and in fact he was so
distracted by it he missed his principal calling his name
until the man was practically standing in front of him.

"Oh, I'm sorry, Dr. Harvey. I'm afraid I'm a little
distracted. How can I help you?"

Harvey pressed his lips together before addressing
Spenser. "I didn't see you at the rally yesterday. I believe I made it clear I expected all staff to attend."

Spenser had forgotten all about the rally. He ran a
hand through his hair, trying to tease out an acceptable
response, but there wasn't one. And he realized he
didn't care. He met his principal's gaze. "I had a family
situation with the child in my guardianship."

This only took a bit of wind out of Harvey's sails.
"Then I expect to see a letter to the legislature on my
desk tomorrow morning, condemning the upcoming
vote against natural marriage."

Any other day, Spenser would have felt sick, would have done tap dancing that would have impressed Laurie to get around the demand. But not today. Not with Tomás's fears and Duon's family pressure and his own existential struggle with his past. Not with the social worker's well-meaning but insulting admonition in his ears.

Spenser set his jaw and looked his principal in the eye. "I won't be giving you a letter, no."

Harvey shook a finger at Spenser. "Watch yourself, Harris. You're on thin ice as it is. Don't think I haven't heard the rumors."

There it was, his worst fear. Funny how now that it was here before him, Spenser didn't give one fuck about it.

He glanced at his watch. "My contract time was up fifteen minutes ago, Dr. Harvey. If you have something you require of me regarding the education of St. Anthony's students, please let me know, and I'll be happy to comply. Otherwise, I must be on my way."

"Protecting the children of this school from sexual deviants is absolutely part of your job."

"My job is to educate. To teach my students letters and shapes and days of the week and how to sit still and stay in a line. To get along with one another, to not judge or to hate. To respect each other." When Harvey looked ready to bluster again, Spenser inclined his head and turned to leave. "I'll see you tomorrow."

He left, but his head spun and he felt like he would

vomit as he drove away. He didn't go home, only drove around aimlessly, the gravity of what he had just done ringing inside him. When he stopped the car, it was in front of Laurie's studio.

It was right in the middle of their busiest time of the day, the studio space full of students taking lessons. Laurie and Tomás led them, Laurie giving the instruction while Tomás assisted. Duon was in the class, dancing his heart out. Ballet, Spenser knew from the shoes and the movements.

He regretted coming inside, ashamed for invading a lesson with his feelings, and he would have left, but Laurie saw him, whispered something to Tomás, and then Tomás crossed over to him, concerned. "What's wrong?"

Spenser didn't know where to begin. Wasn't sure what he should share, or how. He drew a breath, then covered his mouth and averted his gaze from the students, choking on the words before he could get them out.

Tomás took his arm. "Come with me. I'll take you somewhere more private, and we can talk."

Spenser resisted, shaking his head. "You're working. I shouldn't have come."

"You're upset. I'm going to comfort you."

Spenser wiped his eyes, still trying to hide himself. "I don't know how to explain it. I don't want to talk about it. I just want..." He shut his eyes, drew a shaky breath, and went quiet.

This time when Tomás took his arm, Spenser didn't fight him. He let himself be led to the back of the studio, out into the alley—and then, to his surprise, to the building next door to the studio.

"Where are we going? Whose building is this?"

Tomás smiled over his shoulder. "Laurie and Ed's. They decided instead of buying a house for themselves they'd buy this place so they could expand the studio." He unlocked the door with a key and led Spenser into the darkness. "It's not up to code and will take a lot of work, but when it's done, it's going to be gorgeous."

He flicked a switch on the wall, and after a slight hesitation, a series of overhead fluorescents blinked greenish-yellow light into the room. It was a large and dusty space, originally a restaurant or bar of some kind, considering the kitchen they stood in. But through a large opening, Spenser saw a great expanse of wooden floor lit in gentle pools by the lights dangling above.

Tomás drew Spenser through the kitchen and onto the floor. He kissed Spenser's hand, pulled out his phone, and set it on a dusty shelf. As music began to play from its tiny speakers, he laced his fingers through Spenser's and smiled at him. "Dance with me, sweetheart."

Spenser drew away. "I can't dance right now. I'm too jumbled inside."

Tomás held him fast. "That's exactly why you need to dance." He jerked his head at the floor. "Come on. It's just you and me and this big, open space. You don't have to talk about what's upsetting you. You don't have to do anything but be with me."

Spenser attempted once more to get away, but Tomás was devious and made the tug part of their dance. It wasn't formal dancing like their classes together, but because Tomás had dancing in his blood, their give-and-take was punctuated with steps and pauses, and it seemed to follow the beat.

Damn it all, but it was what Spenser needed somehow. The resistance and the dancing both.

A new song came on, this one an eerie, upbeat, minor tune. A woman sang, over and over, that she was so sorry life was like this. The lyrics angered Spenser, because he didn't want apologies. Didn't want to give them, didn't want to receive them. He wanted action. He wanted justice. For himself, for Duon, for Tomás, for Ed and Laurie. He was furious with the world, and he didn't want to put that anger down because it felt like the only thing keeping him from sinking into despair.

He fought Tomás, dragging, trying to trip him. But Tomás was much better at dancing than he was, and he met every challenge. The more Spenser tried to derail them, the more deftly Tomás maneuvered Spenser into the dance.

Spenser didn't realize he was crying until Tomás spun him out and the room stayed blurry after his return to position. When he faltered, Tomás eased him into an embrace and pressed a kiss on his ear. "It's okay. Let everything out. It's you and me and the dance."

Spenser didn't want to let it out, didn't want to fall into the blackness of his fear, but Tomás and the dance wouldn't let him do anything else. It stole the fight from him until all he had were his tears and the ache in his soul. The music shifted, but the apology song echoed in Spenser's head.

I'm sorry. So sorry…

Tomás led him off the floor, pushed him to the wall, and kissed him. Slowly, sweetly, not an apology but a soothing gesture. An affectionate gesture.

A loving gesture.

Spenser began to cry again. "It's too much," he whispered. "Everything is happening, everything is wrong, and it's too much. I can't do it."

"Shh. You can. Because I'll do it with you."

Discretion would go a long way here.

Protecting the children of this school from sexual deviants is absolutely part of your job.

The court would look more highly on you if you did have a partner.

I'm sorry. So sorry…

Spenser buried his face in Tomás's neck and wrapped his arms around him, giving up. "I don't want to lose any of it. Not my job. Not Duon. Not you."

Tomás hugged him closer, crowding him into the wall, surrounding Spenser with his presence. "You're not going to lose me."

Spenser didn't know how to explain this wasn't what he meant—he hadn't gotten far enough into his fears to worry about that, because he was more afraid the world would make him choose *between* the things he loved. He felt the sob welling, but he didn't want to let it out. Not without more to hold on to.

Tomás nuzzled his face, his neck, kissing him slowly and sweetly, drawing the sadness out in soft wisps, drawing it into himself and exhaling it, cleansed and defeated. Spenser gave it over inch by inch, until there was nothing left but that which he had his hand closed fast around. When Tomás lifted his mouth from Spenser's and rested their foreheads together, Spenser released his confession in a whisper. His most vulnerable confession, his hollow, sorrowful ache.

"I finally found a family. And now it's going to be taken away from me."

Tomás kissed his temple. "No one is taking us away."

"Yes, they are. They're trying. Duon's family. The social worker. My school."

Tomás gripped Spenser's shoulders. "Listen to me. No one can take you away from me, or me you."

Spenser couldn't stop the tide now. He closed his fists over Tomás's chest, pressing into the fabric of his leotard. "I need to adopt Duon, or I might lose him. But it'll be harder without a partner. Except it's better if I don't, because if I did I'd lose my job for sure."

Tomás stopped the flood with a sweet, gentle kiss.

When he spoke, his voice was soft and rough with emotion. "I love you."

The words stilled Spenser, catching his breath. His fists unclenched, his fingers drifting to the skin of Tomás's neck. "I love you too. So much. And I love Duon. And your parents. Your whole family."

"Then why don't you join it? You and Duon both." Tomás stroked Spenser's cheek. Once. Twice. Three times. "Marry me."

Denials and questions rose automatically to Spenser's throat but didn't pass his lips. *It's too soon. We shouldn't. Are you asking me because of Duon? Because of your family?* The objections died away, though, melted by the expression on Tomás's face.

He wasn't playing around. He was serious. He wasn't asking because he was trying to solve Spenser's problems. They were simply an excuse to bring up what had clearly already been on his mind.

One snarl, sadly, could not be denied. "I'd lose my job. No question."

"We'll help you find another one." Tomás smiled wryly, stroking Spenser's face again. "I'm good at finding jobs."

Spenser let the resistance pull him a little longer. Then he sighed and let himself float away—into Tomás, the pit of fear and solitude melting away like snow on a sunny day. "Okay."

Tomás kneaded his arm and slid his hand to Spenser's hip. "No you don't. You have to say the words."

Oh, they were hard words. Harder than *I love you.* Harder than confessing his fear. This was the most dangerous moment of all, the one where Spenser let himself believe, where he surrendered to hope. But he wanted it so much. Ached for it. Burned for it.

It was right here before him. Waiting.

Spenser let out a breath, swallowed, and looked Tomás in the eye. "Yes. I'll marry you."

The world he knew shuddered, shattered, and crumbled as Tomás kissed him again and urged Spenser out of his clothes as he struggled to get his leotard, tights, and dance belt off his own body. But even before Tomás pressed their skin together, before their mouths met once more and they chased release as one—as Spenser watched his old sense of his life fall away, he saw before him something new. Something strange and bright and full of possibility, despite the looming shadows.

Hope. He saw hope. The most dangerous, wonderful, powerful drug of all.

He took it into his body along with Tomás and found the hollows and spaces he'd tried to fill in so long ago. Let it flood him with joy and wonder and dreams of a life with a family, a partner, a future full of love and laughter.

Let it fill the empty places inside him and make him whole.

I'M GOING TO marry Spenser.

It wasn't a question he'd expected to ask—not yet. And yet it had felt perfectly right. He *did* love Spenser. He *did* know, with bone-deep certainty, this was the guy for him. When Spenser had spoken about adopting Duon, the urge to be part of their union tugged at Tomás like an ache in his gut. It wasn't why he'd proposed, but it made him realize he wanted Spenser in his life. *He* wanted to be the one who filled that space for Spenser, who welcomed him into *his* family.

Still, he felt punch-drunk as he righted his leotard, kissed Spenser with a stupid grin, and led him back to the studio. Laurie halted the class to confront them. "What's wrong? What do you need?"

Tomás pulled Spenser to him, but before either of them could answer, he spied Duon lingering nervously in the background. "I think…we need to talk to Duon first."

Spenser nodded and addressed Laurie. "Can we use your office?"

"Of course you can use my office." Laurie studied them carefully. "Just tell me everything's okay."

"Not right now, no." Spenser squeezed Tomás's hand. "But I'm hoping it will be soon."

Duon looked ready to throw up when they led him into Laurie's office. Tomás realized he must think something horrible had happened in regards to him, that he was about to go back to his grandmother, to a shelter, or God knew what. He felt bad for putting him through that, but he didn't know how to breach this.

Spenser did. He took Duon's hand and sat him on the edge of Laurie's desk. "Sweetheart, we need to ask you something. Tell you, and ask you." He reached for Tomás's hand. "I wanted to ask if you would be open to being adopted by me. Formally. But now…" He bit his lip, staying a smile as he looked at Tomás. "*We* need to ask if you'd be open to being adopted by *us*."

Duon sat up straight, his apprehension sloughing away with the motion. "Are you telling me you two are engaged?"

Tomás put his arm around Spenser, heart pounding but soaring too. "Yeah. We are."

Duon hooted, leaping off the desk and waving his hands in the air and shouting in joy before wrapping his arms around them both as he jumped up and down. "*Cheah*, I want you to adopt me. Holy shit. *Holy fucking shit.*"

He was laughing, and so were Tomás and Spenser, and when Laurie came into the office to ask what was going on, Duon pulled him into the circle too.

"They getting married. They're adopting me and getting married. *We all getting married!*"

Laurie's eyes went wide, and he turned to Spenser and Tomás, but then he was laughing too, and hugging them, and they were a hot mess of tears and joy and love. Ed was in the other room, and when he heard them carrying on, he joined them, and it became a party of Tomás, his boyfriend—*fiancé*—his soon-to-be son, and his best friends. They moved into the main room, where Laurie put on some music, and they all began to dance. The students joined in, thrilled for one of their favorite teachers.

Spenser glanced at the stereo, then laughed. "This is the song you made me dance to at my school."

Laurie waggled his eyebrows. "But this version is mostly in English."

It was. The song, with its lyrics in a language he could understand, admonished Spenser to essentially relax and live. Pointed out he only got one life, so he shouldn't waste it. And that, above all, he should dance.

"Who sings this?" Spenser asked.

Laurie danced casually in place as he replied. "MI-KA is his stage name. He was born Michael Holbrook Penniman, Jr., Mica for short, but everyone got it wrong, so he changed it to a more phonetic spelling. He was born in Beirut, but his parents are American, his mother with Lebanese heritage. He attended a French boarding school for a time, but he was so bullied he stopped speaking. He was homeschooled until they moved to a school in England, where he discovered his love of music and received training. And now he's an international pop star."

Spenser's head spun as he processed the story. The man who sang so insistently to Emily to dance was singing mostly to himself.

Laurie leaned in closer, eyes twinkling as he spoke sotto voce. "And I should mention MIKA confirmed publicly this year he's gay. So he's an *out* international pop star who was once so pushed down by life he couldn't bear to speak." Laurie stepped into Ed's arms and took up a tango as he winked at Spenser. "Dance, Spenser, dance."

He did. They all did. In pairs, in groups, as a tribe. Laurie and Ed mostly danced with each other, showing off their considerable ballroom dance skills, but several times Tomás cut in, claiming first Laurie, then Ed. Duon followed suit, but he danced with Spenser too. It was a riot of dance, of joy.

It was everything.

When they finally left to go home, it was after several rounds of hugs and tears and Laurie's promise to throw them an engagement party. When Spenser confessed this would unquestionably mean the loss of his job the second his school learned he was gay and engaged, everyone vowed to help him find a new one. "You could always substitute until you found somewhere in the metro area you liked," Ed pointed out. But when Laurie said he'd talk to his godfather, Spenser shook his head.

"He's already done so much for Tomás. I don't want to impose on him for my problems too. Ed's right. I'll find something through substitute teaching, probably."

Laurie took Spenser's hand. "You don't understand. Oliver loves helping people. It's literally his job. He's never happier than when he connects people with other people. But what he loves most of all is helping people, especially when ridiculous laws and prejudice are keeping good people from happiness. He's a huge, bleeding heart with money and influence. And he's not going to be able to give you a job, only help you network with someone who has a job for you. Someone who won't make you chose between being true to yourself and connecting with kids."

This comment started off another round of hugs and tears, but eventually they headed home. Tomás fully intended to spend the night in their apartment and have dinner with them. He'd take them across the hall to share the news with his mother and father and nieces and nephew, yeah, but then he wanted to be with this part of his family. The one he was building for himself.

Maybe when the naturalization process was done and his parents were citizens, or at least when they were out of the woods, they could all move in together. Into a nice house with a yard. Rooms for the kids, his parents, and Spenser and Tomás. A big kitchen for his mom to cook in. A garage for his dad to putter in and have beers with the guys. A backyard to sit with Spenser in, for Tomás to mow and fuss over. Tomás could see it so clearly in his mind's eye. It would be so perfect.

He smiled to himself as he got out of the car, the image lingering. He pulled his phone out of his pocket, realizing he hadn't checked it in awhile, hoping for a little insight on whether or not his parents were home, if the kids were in bed yet. He did a double take as he saw several text notifications and four missed calls, and he thumbed through them, trying to figure out what was going on, what he had missed.

As he read, then listened, his joyful, buoyant mood crashed, destroying not only his happiness but his whole world.

Spenser hurried up to him, Duon on his heels. "What is it? What's wrong?"

It felt like someone else said the words, and from a million miles away. "My dad had a heart attack." The world fell away to darkness as he added, "ICE is at the hospital, saying they're going to deport him as soon as he's stable enough to transfer."

CHAPTER FOURTEEN

THE HOSPITAL WAS chaos.

Spenser followed Tomás through the winding corridors as they hurried to the ICCU, where Spenser and Duon waited in a lounge as Tomás went inside to see his father. As Tomás disappeared through the double doors, they caught a glimpse of the immigration officials. The sight left Spenser queasy, making him ache for Tomás and the rest of the Jimenez family. But all he could do was lead Duon to the waiting area and settle in to see what happened.

Duon was restless, tapping his feet and glancing at the door every time the slightest sound came from that direction. "Are they going to take José away, for real? Can they do that when he's sick?"

"I don't know," Spenser admitted. "But he's not a US citizen. So I imagine they can do whatever they like."

This answer didn't please Duon. "We need to call that lawyer. Or call Laurie and get his godfather on the case."

That was a good idea. Spenser did call Laurie, who said Tomás had already been in contact with them. He promised not only to call Oliver but to get to the hospital as soon as they could. "Let us know if you need anything. You or Tomás's family. Okay?"

Spenser agreed, and then it was the two of them again, agitated and helpless. When Tomás returned to the waiting area, they practically jumped him.

"He's going to be okay." Tomás rubbed his face, looking like he needed a stiff drink. Several of them. "They brought him out of emergency surgery just now. He's out of it, but they have a Spanish-speaking nurse in there, and she says everything is normal. Triple bypass. My *mom*, though, is in the ER. They had to give her a sedative because she was hysterical, worrying about my father and then the children and now the immigration officers. I got in there in time to stop them from calling DHS for the kids."

Spenser noted the conspicuous absence of the children. "Where *are* they?"

"Ed's taking them to his parents until I can take them home. Or maybe I'm staying there tonight. I honestly don't know what's going on. Laurie's playing politics in the hallway with the lawyers and DHS and immigration." Tomás let out a shuddering sigh, and when he spoke next, his voice broke. "All I know is I'm terrified that my parents are about to be taken away from me and I'll never get them back."

Spenser took Tomás in his arms, and Duon did

too, enveloping them both in a sideways hug until Tomás and Spenser loosened those arms and drew him into their circle. "We're going to get through this together."

But it was the three of them Laurie needed to reassure when he finally entered the lounge. He had a hot look about him, like he'd just stepped out of the ring and was ready for another round. "Nothing is decided yet, but I'll tell you, Oliver called in the right favor. That lawyer isn't messing around. I can't promise he can pull a rabbit out of his hat, but if anyone can, it's him."

"What can he do?" Tomás asked.

"I don't know, honestly," Laurie confessed. "But he kept bringing up the children, that your parents are the primary caretakers. And when I told them you two were engaged—I hope that was okay—the lawyer dug his heels in deeper, arguing the government was putting undue burden on Tomás for its own convenience."

"But why did immigration get involved?" Spenser couldn't understand that part no matter how he tried. "Why did they come after a heart attack, for the love of God?"

Tomás's expression was grim. "It happens all the time. The hospitals don't want to foot the bill, and the Affordable Care Act is making it harder for them to deal with uninsured patients. If they repatriate them to a Mexican hospital, it's cheaper. They're not after my mom, but it's not like she'll have a choice. They'll send him the second he's stable. Preferably when he's still unconscious. She'll have to follow to take care of him."

"The lawyer made it clear they'll get a whole lot of ugly attention if they do that." Laurie looked smug. "They got a call from Oliver too. He runs their annual fundraiser. He's not pleased."

Spenser's heart dared to lift again. "So they won't deport him?"

Tomás shook his head. "It's too late. U.S. Immigration and Customs Enforcement is up their nose now."

"Don't give up hope." Laurie took his hand. "We're in this together. Okay?"

They stayed at the hospital all night, the three of them and Laurie, and Ed, once he joined them from getting the kids settled at his parents' place. All of them called in sick to work and school—it was a terrible time of year for Spenser to do that, and his parting conversation with Harvey made things that much worse, but he couldn't leave Tomás and his family, not like this. He supported Tomás however he could—getting him coffee, making him eat breakfast, running back to the apartment to get him a change of clothes. He took Duon with him, stopping by Ed's parents' house to gift them one more child and thank them for their help.

Ed's parents were wonderful, but if he were honest, Spenser fell in love with their neighborhood more. They had a charming three-bedroom bungalow in Union Park, not too fancy and not too run-down. Some houses were perfectly maintained, some less so, but the whole street said *friendly* and *family*. There was a realness about the place, though. It didn't feel like a carefully manicured burb. It felt like a community full of people with strengths and weaknesses and quirks. It was, in Spenser's mind, perfect.

When Spenser confessed this to Ed's parents, they brightened and insisted on introducing him to the neighbors. While the kids played in the yard, Duon leading them in a game of hide-and-seek, Dick and Annette took Spenser next door and to the house across the street, where the neighbors welcomed him with smiles and offers to come inside and have a cup of coffee.

"He can't stay," Annette said before Spenser could decline. "His fiancé's family is at the hospital. We're watching the kids while the boys take care of the parents."

"Bless their hearts." The woman they were speaking to put a hand on her chest. "I'll have my church circle get some frozen meals ready. A good hot dish never goes amiss at moments such as these."

Dick nudged Spenser with his elbow. "Lizzy, Spenser here is a teacher, same as you were."

The women brightened. "You don't say. What grade?"

"Kindergarten." Spenser's heart sank, and he added, "Though I'm fairly sure I'll need to look for a new job for the fall."

"Oh, really? Well, I'll see if I can't get word on

open positions. I'm out of the game, but I still keep my ear to the ground." She winked at him. "I'll let the Maurers know if I find anything."

As they finished the tour, Spenser noticed a for-sale sign peeking out through the weeds of a house three doors down from Dick and Annette's place. When his focus lingered on it, Dick came and stood beside him to gaze with him.

"That's the Davis place. Went up for sale last month." He shook his head. "Old Mrs. Davis passed away in September, but the kids were such a mess they didn't get the estate settled until now. Been empty since she went into the care center last spring. Asking the moon for the place, more than they'd get if it was in good shape. It'll take the better part of a year to sell."

Spenser couldn't look away from the house. Yes, it was rough, but…well, it spoke to him. The lawn was weeds, but he could imagine it cut short, flowerpots lining the stairs, once they were repaired and painted. The house resembled a barn because of the way the roof sloped, but it wasn't overly big. Despite the peeling paint and general disrepair, Spenser could feel the strength of the place, could sense the solidity of the bones beneath the surface. It would look lovely painted a sunny yellow with mint-green trim. And light-brown shingles. And some shutters put beside the windows. Maybe those would be slate blue. Or robin's-egg blue.

Annette, who had appeared beside them, gave Spenser a long look, then a wry smile. "Would you care to see the inside?"

Spenser's heart skipped a beat. "It's open?"

"Oh, heavens no. But we have the key. I imagine the kids forgot about that. I keep meaning to catch the real estate agent to give it to her, but you know how it goes."

She went to the house to fetch it, and then…then Spenser went inside and fell in love.

It was *very* run-down, yes. Not only paint and wallpaper peeling, but in places the plaster and lath were exposed from water damage and who knew what else. The hardwood floors were damaged as well, their polish long gone, marks, scratches, and stains marring their surface. The stair treads were worn into divots, the edges splintered or broken. The dining room ceiling sagged alarmingly. The kitchen was ghastly, completely out of date, tiny, and utterly without windows.

But the woodwork, even damaged, took Spenser's breath away. The newel post, the lintels of doors and frames of every window were all carved with intricate roses and flowers. The built-in hutch in the dining room had leaded glass with not a single pane broken. Many of the outside windows were cracked or unable to open, but they were large and framed by breathtaking woodworking. The possibility in the place was huge. And for all the downsides, there were so many unique features. A butler's pantry. A narrow back stairway. A former servant's bedroom that begged to be made into an office. And a walk-up attic that could so easily become a fifth bedroom or a master suite.

"It was the grandest house on the block, back in the day." Annette stroked a doorway sadly. "It was a showplace when I was young. Even when the Davises first bought it. But they had six boys who wrecked the place, and Harold Davis developed a drinking habit that broke the family. Margaret did what she could with the house, but her spirit left her long ago, bless her. We all took care of her as best we could, but she was sour toward the end. Such a shame to see a family fall apart before your eyes. And such a fine house to go to ruin. I feared they'd have to condemn it, but the inspectors said no, it only needs some tender loving care."

"What does the backyard look like?" Spenser asked.

Dick winced. "A mess, I'm afraid. But you're welcome to see."

It was indeed a mess. But it was also achingly perfect. Long and wide, with a shed and collapsed garage in the back and what had obviously once been a garden. A shattered concrete patio had a crumbling brick grill beside it. Spenser had no trouble imagining a seven-foot fence around the property, herbs and flowers growing along its carefully manicured lines, a modern deck covering the wreckage of concrete. The lawn was neatly kept and full of children laughing and chasing a dog. Two dogs, both shelter adoptees. The garden grew tall and proud, tended by Renata, who admonished the children in Spanish to behave between affectionate smiles. Tomás and his father stood over a car peeking out from the repaired garage, and Duon lay in a hammock strung on posts beneath the great oak tree on the side, watching something on his phone and laughing at it.

Annette smiled at Spenser, a glint in her eye. "Looking to buy a house, are you?"

Spenser sighed. "Not when I'm about to lose my job, no. And not when I don't know if I'm going to be able to keep the family I want to put in it."

She patted his arm and gave it a gentle squeeze. "Well, like I said. The house won't be going anywhere. And we'll keep doing whatever we can to make sure we can say the same for your family."

When Spenser finally went back to the hospital, his heart was lighter. Things improved further when he met Tomás coming out of the ICCU, grinning because apparently the lawyer really did have teeth. The hospital had reconsidered the repatriation, and the ICE was drowning in documentation about how Renata and José Jimenez were essential to the caretaking of their grandchildren.

"The lawyer says there's no way anything will happen right now," Tomás said. "We can go home tonight. Laurie gave me the week off work, and Starbucks gave me until Friday. Ed's parents will babysit all week if need be."

Spenser took his hand and kissed his cheek. "That's wonderful. I'm so glad."

"We're not out of the woods yet. We're going to

have a hearing in June. But it's better than yesterday, when I thought I was about to lose them." He drew Spenser close, hugging him tight before kissing his cheek. "Come on. Let's go home."

Home. As Tomás drove them with MPR playing in the background, Spenser mused on the word. *Home.* The concept had been a spear for so much of his life. His homes were always borrowed, reminders that he had none of his own, that he never would. Even now he couldn't shake the ache of loss at having the one he'd known, however broken it had been, ripped from his hands. He thought of his hope and terror of Clara's promise to try to track down his blood family. Thought of the rush of longing he'd had in the Davis house, even with all its flaws. Maybe because of the flaws. Oh, but he ached to have a place like that he could put right. A house that deserved better. He could make it better. He could heal it, then fill it with his family. *His* family. The one he made with Tomás.

They had pulled into the parking lot and were about to turn off the car when the newscast cut through the silence.

Today the Minnesota House of Representatives voted seventy-five to fifty-nine to pass HF1054, which will officially sign marriage equality into law within the state. The Senate is scheduled to take up a vote early next week, where it is expected to pass, and Governor Dayton promises to sign the bill into law as soon as it arrives at his desk. This comes on the heels of growing anticipation of the US Supreme Court's impending ruling in the case of United States vs. Windsor, which could strike down the Defense of Marriage Act.

Spenser and Tomás looked at one another, not saying a word. The space inside the car was charged with emotion, with joy and fear. *So much dangerous hope.* Spenser couldn't help but think of the Davis house again. Of being legally married to Tomás. Of being legally the parent of Duon. Of the Jimenez family legally remaining in the United States.

Then he thought of how easily it all could be taken away, and tears he hadn't known had been brewing spilled over.

"It's not right." He swallowed the thickness in his throat. "It's not right that all our happiness is in other people's hands. That people who don't know us, who don't know your family or Duon or me will decide whether or not we get to be together. All my life, people have taken my family away. I hate how I have to call it a victory when people *stop* doing things to tear us apart. I hate that I have to dare to hope to have what everyone else takes for granted."

Tomás took his hand. He didn't cry, but when he spoke, his voice was rough, almost broken. "They will never take me away. I will never go away. I am your family, Spenser Harris. Forever. No matter what any law says, now or in the future."

Spenser's reply was barely a whisper. "But I want *all* of them in my family."

A tear rolled down Tomás's cheek as he reached

across the seat to wipe away Spenser's own. "Me too, baby. Me too."

ON MAY 13, 2013, Minnesota signed marriage equality into law.

Though new same-sex marriages weren't possible until August, the same time marriages from other states would also be legally recognized in Minnesota, Laurie and Ed threw a spontaneous party at the studio, in the not-yet-remodeled space next door. The place where Tomás had proposed to Spenser. In the span of a few hours, it was turned into a shabby-chic paradise, with twinkling lights, a makeshift bar, spotlights, and of course, ample dance floor space.

Tomás had helped set up for the party, but once it began, Laurie dragged him away from the tables and insisted he get out and have fun. "You're off the clock tonight. Dance with your fiancé and your son-to-be. Oh, and there's Oliver. I'll introduce you to him and his husband."

The casualness with which Laurie said this rattled Tomás. Meet the man who had done so much to change his life? He didn't know what he would say, and when the white-haired, bespeckled, smiling white man took his hand, Tomás was barely able to stammer out that it was a pleasure to meet him.

Oliver Thompson ignored Tomás's nerves, winking and shaking his hand as if they'd gone to an expensive college together. "Such a joy to finally meet you. I hope your father is recovering well?"

Tomás nodded, scrambling to marshal his composure. "He is, sir. Thank you." The word freed him, and Tomás let the rest of it tumble out. "Thank you for all you've done for my parents. We owe you so much. Thank you from me, and from every member of my family."

"You're entirely welcome. But you owe me nothing. And call me Oliver, not sir."

Tomás could not call this man by his given name, no. "You stopped them from deporting my father. If this works, if the lawyer you brought us can get them citizenship, you have saved my family. It will mean I can take the job I want, not have three jobs just to be able to get us by. It will mean I don't have to wake up every morning worrying I'll come home that night and find them gone. It will mean I won't have to worry about my nieces and nephew. It will mean my life, sir. I do owe you. So much."

Oliver shook his head, his expression serious. "This is the problem with the world today. Hell, the problem with it since we started forming societies. Every emphasis is on ourselves or abstract ideals. Perfect economies. Perfect behavior and perfect societies. *Idealism.*" He wrinkled his nose in derision. "What does any of that matter, when there are real people right in front of us in need? Usually telling us exactly what they require. Food. Shelter. Help climbing out of addiction and debt. Legal aid. You say I owe you, and I say I'm grateful for you, for being someone I can help. Thank you for allowing me to take a swipe at the injustice and selfishness in the world, for introducing me to good people I could help to stay here so they can do more good things."

"But *you* did all that. Without you, my parents would already be gone, and there would be no hope for them ever coming back. It's like a fairy tale. No one ever gets help like that. *No one.*"

Oliver waved this away almost in annoyance. "I didn't do anything extraordinary. I played politics. I pulled strings and called in favors. And you wisely took advantage of what I offered. Don't feel guilty for doing so." He gestured across the room at Vicky, who was talking animatedly with a gentleman in a tie who looked as if he desperately longed to get out of the conversation. "She has a difficult time with that lesson. She longs for the ideal. For the world where good wins and people do the right thing. Her idealism serves her well in that it keeps her at her desk, digging for another miracle, but she worships the perfect vision so much she can decline help because she fears it's not pure enough. She doesn't care for the strings. She's loosened up in the past couple of years, but it's still hard for her." Oliver turned back to Tomás. "You, and Spenser too—you know differently. You know you have to take what you can when it's offered."

"Yes, but *why* do you offer? Why do you help so

much?"

Oliver's cool facade cracked. "Because while I've had money all my life, I know what loss is. I know what injustice tastes like." He glanced around, then as if making a decision, lowered his voice and plowed ahead, all his pompous rich-man tone gone. "When I was nineteen, I went to a party that got raided. We were on Fire Island, a year before the Stonewall riots. They treated us all terribly, calling us every ugly name they could think of, hauling us out like cattle. But they knew who among us came from money and who did not. I was arrested and taken away in relative quiet, my father summoned to pay my fees and more under the table to keep the charges at public drunkenness and a few other misdemeanors, none of which included the crime of sodomy. My lover, however, was a shy, quiet young man of no money from Brooklyn. In addition to being subjected to brutality and humiliation by the arresting officers, he was ruined, publicly, personally, and emotionally. Shortly after the riots at the Stonewall Inn, he shot himself."

Tomás didn't know what to say. All he could manage was, "I'm so sorry."

"It was a dark time. But while I'd rather no one would have had to endure such treatment, I'm grateful for the lesson it taught me. Money and influence mattered, and I had both. I vowed that in the same way my father had used it for me, I would use it for others." Oliver laughed, rolling his eyes. "Oh, at first I was a fool. Ran around showing my bleeding heart to everyone, naively thinking it would be enough to turn the tides. Eventually I learned I needed to be a cuckoo in the nest. I went back to school, knuckled down, took my place beside my father in the family business. Made myself a great big pile of money and built myself the thickest net of influence and connection I could. I never married a woman, but by the time I met Christopher and introduced him as my partner, no one blinked. They don't, when you have money and your finger in every pie." He raised his glass to Tomás. "I can't go back to Fire Island and stop the injustice my friend and others endured. But every time I help someone like you and your family, I take away some of their pain. Every bit of joy I put back in the world fights the ugliness leading to that night. And so no, Mr. Jimenez. You owe me nothing. Thank you for showing me another place to light a candle."

Tomás smiled, clinking his glass to Oliver's. "Call me Tomás, Oliver."

Oliver winked. "Cheers, Tomás." He drank, then made shooing motions at him. "Now go find your man and dance. I need to collect my husband and do the same."

They did dance. Laurie, Ed, and all their friends and family filled the floor, hands up and hips moving to the beat all night long. Several times Laurie and Ed stole the show with their ballroom dancing, and Duon garnered quite a crowd with his bold moves, drawing

Tomás in to dance with him. At one point Duon disappeared and came back with their toe shoes, Laurie's too, and the three of them ended up giving an impromptu recital en pointe. But they couldn't get Spenser to show off his budding tap moves. He did, though, dance often with Tomás, cutting loose whenever a MIKA song came on.

"I asked Laurie to play several songs," Spenser confessed when they were dancing to "Celebrate," the third of the artist's songs to play inside of ninety minutes. "I like MIKA."

"I like you." Tomás spun Spenser out, then into his embrace, where he pressed a long kiss on his lips. "I love you, in fact."

"I love you too." Spenser touched Tomás's cheek. "Maybe the Supreme Court will decide in our favor. Maybe when we get married, it'll be really married."

Tomás kissed him again. "We *will* be really married. No matter what."

Ed's parents had come to the party too, with the kids. Tomás took them home with him, and they bounced on the backseat all the way because they'd found out they got to sleep over at Spenser's apartment in the living room in their sleeping bags. It took forever to get them to sleep, but Tomás felt good going to bed knowing they were all under the same roof, that they were all safe, at least for now.

After a call to the hospital to check on his parents, Tomás made love to Spenser quietly, one ear tuned the whole time for the kids. While Spenser fell asleep almost immediately after, Tomás lay awake, thinking about what Oliver had said about pulling levers on the world. Using what you had. Seeing the world as it was, unblinking, and making it a better place.

He didn't think he had it in him to bully hospitals and marshal lawyers, even with all the money and connection in the world. But he absolutely was committed to his parents, to Spenser, to Duon and the kids. Was that enough candle lighting?

He thought of Richard, the organizer of the car wraps. Of Ed and Laurie and their decision to expand the studio, not buy a house. Of Spenser, taking in Duon, who he didn't know, without blinking. Of Ryan of Avenues. Of Marcus, helping Tomás and his family begin this journey to citizenship. Of Vicky, idealism and all.

So many candles. So many ways to pierce the darkness.

I'm going to keep trying to light candles, Tomás vowed. *Until the day I die, I'm going to do all I can to bring light and love into the world.* He didn't know how, just yet. But with so many wonderful examples around him, surely he could find a way.

CHAPTER FIFTEEN

J OSÉ SPENT A little over a week in the hospital after
his surgery, but when he came home, he was still
clearly quite ill. Renata fussed over him, whispering
admonishments in Spanish—Spenser assumed they
were admonishments from her tone—but she also
kissed him constantly on the forehead and prayed over
him several times a day. Spenser had grown accustomed to the saint candles in the Jimenez household,
but now there was an actual altar. Beside the photo of
St. Frances Xavier Cabrini was a sea-green card with a
drawing of a man holding a cross. A medal was pinned
to it.

"Saint John of God," Tomás explained. "Patron
saint of heart disease. Dad has another card at his
bedside and a medal on a necklace. He keeps arranging
it over his incision, over the bandages."

Spenser could hardly blame him. "I did some research, trying to find ways to modify some of the
dishes your father loves to be heart healthier but familiar. It's rough, but I'm still digging. I mean, there's

plenty of Latin-*like* dishes. But there's not a super-great substitute for lard that still tastes the same as lard."

Tomás kissed him. "Thank you. That's so sweet."

Tomás's sister had come to the hospital, but not to the apartment. Spenser hadn't spoken with her, but he'd seen her arrive, standing off to the side with her hand over her mouth until Tomás approached her and pulled her into another room. Spenser had wanted to ask Tomás if everything was okay with Alisa, but the look on his fiancé's face when he returned had told him that wasn't the moment. Now it felt like the matter was better off left alone.

Spenser and Duon spent a lot of time in the Jimenez apartment, helping out with cooking, cleaning, laundry, and childcare. Tomás was back to his frenetic working schedule, and while Duon and Tomás were at the studio, Spenser hurried home to help Renata as best he could. The language barrier was often a challenge, but they powered through, laughing when their inability to communicate led them to stick-figure drawings and pantomime. But he loved helping her, loved especially cooking with her. Loved learning that she believed her secret to the perfect tortillas was to pray over them. Spenser wasn't religious at all, but he prayed alongside her and with José over his Saint John of God card. Spenser didn't need to know Spanish to fall in love with his future in-laws. The thought that the hearing at the end of June might take them from his life made him ill.

His principal stopped dogging him to attend rallies, since marriage equality was now a settled issue, but it was clear Harvey had his eye on Spenser, looking for an excuse to fire him. Meanwhile, Spenser ached every time a parent told him they'd requested him for their child in the fall, or a child hugged his legs and said they'd miss him all summer. He kept putting off turning in his resignation letter, still dreaming of a way to have his family and his job too.

His adoption of Duon, at least, was smoother sailing. During the hearing, Spenser squeezed Tomás's hand so tight he left fingerprint bruises as the lawyers and social workers presented their cases to the judge. Duon's aunt and grandmother sat on the other side of the courtroom, never making so much as eye contact with Spenser or Tomás. When their lawyer spoke for them, describing how hard Duon's grandmother worked, how she defied the odds to provide a good home for her grandchildren with almost no support, Spenser had a pang of doubt, and it cut deep.

Dorothy. Somehow in all this he had missed that Duon's grandmother's name was Dorothy.

Her name was an anchor, and as her lawyers argued her case, Spenser felt uneasy. Oh, he still wanted Duon to stay with him, but for the first time since the day Duon had appeared on his doorstep, Spenser understood that taking Duon in meant taking him *away*. As Dorothy's representatives wound down and Duon's social workers, guardian ad litem, and the lawyer Oliver

Thompson had procured for Spenser produced an endless line of witnesses and experts to testify, Spenser couldn't deny that even if Dorothy changed her mind and surrendered Duon voluntarily one more time, this action was removing Duon from the very family connection Spenser couldn't stop pining for.

So many people spoke up for Duon, for Spenser, for Tomás. Duon's teachers, previous social workers, Vicky, Ed, Laurie, Oliver himself—everyone appeared to give their testimony. There were psychologists who had nothing to do with Duon's case who confirmed a same-sex household was no risk to a child and was in fact as good as any heterosexual household. Spenser's lawyer also offered up Clara, who lavished praise on Spenser, as did Ryan from Avenues when he was called to testify. As the lawyer and social workers had predicted, the judge declared there were no grounds to halt the adoption. Their side of the courtroom burst into cheers, tears, and rounds of hugs.

Spenser cheered too, but he couldn't stop one last glance across the courtroom, where Dorothy Graves's stony expression cut through him like a knife.

Clara came up to Spenser, distracting him from his doubt by hugging him tight and whispering in his ear. "Your mother wants to see you."

Spenser drew back, more than a little rattled. It would have been jarring any day, but today of all days, it nearly knocked him over. "My…mom?"

Clara squeezed his hands in hers. "We've had lunch

several times now. I don't want to give away anything we talked about because you have the right to hear her story from her, but I will tell you as your other mother, I believe you should meet her. I think it will help you, especially now. It will be healing for you both."

Not knowing what else to do, Spenser agreed, and he was so caught up in the whirlwind of the adoption that he let Clara arrange a meeting the next day, a Saturday morning coffee. But it and his revelation about Dorothy nagged him all through their celebratory dinner at the Jimenez family table, and that night he lay awake in Tomás's arms, trembling with nerves.

"I shouldn't have said yes. I saw her when I was nineteen and she got out of prison, and it was awful. I can't remember why anymore, if it was her who made it unpleasant, or me, or both of us. All I know is I didn't want to do it again. What if this is a mistake? What if that happens again?"

"You can still cancel," Tomás pointed out.

"But I don't want to. Especially after seeing Dorothy. I feel like I *have* to see my mother now."

"You don't have to do anything you don't want to do. And don't feel guilty about Duon's grandmother. The judge examined the evidence and ruled in our favor. We're what's best for Duon."

"Yes, but we had Oliver Thompson's lawyers." Spenser couldn't bring himself to wonder it out loud, but he couldn't stop thinking…had it made a difference that he was white? Would the courts prefer a white parent over a Black one?

Probably, he admitted to himself, and the thought made him sick. And yet if the judge appeared before him right now and asked if Spenser wanted her to rule fairly, even if that meant he'd lose Duon…he wouldn't want fair. Not unless Duon chose otherwise. Spenser wouldn't fight him, but it would break him in half.

Spenser shut his eyes and buried his face in Tomás's neck. "I hate this. I hate feeling like this. Hope and terror. It's all I ever know. Hope things might actually be getting better. Terror I might have been a fool for letting myself hope. I'm going to worry until they give us the adoption papers that they'll still try to take Duon from us. I'll worry even after. Every time I turn on MPR on Supreme Court days, I hold my breath in case they rule on the DOMA case. Every time I pray with Renata I blink back tears because I'm afraid I won't get to do that much longer. Every part of my life is tossed into the wind, and I don't know how to pin any of it down. Or to trust it's firmly in my hands."

Tomás pulled Spenser's hand away from his body and unlaced the fist clenched tight. He threaded their fingers together, drawing the knuckles up to his lips for a kiss. "There's no guarantee in life of anything. Every second is precious. Every breath is a miracle. Every connection is a gift, each drop of joy a treasure. If you spend your whole life with your breath held for a moment of true safety, you'll never exhale. All you can do is live as best you can. As hard as you can."

He rocked their joined hands back and forth, a soothing gesture. "Every time I dance, every time I leap into the air, I risk maiming myself. If I land incorrectly, if I slip or if I simply turn at the wrong time, I could cripple myself for life, if I'm unlucky enough. The more advanced the dancer, the greater the risk of injury. You've seen my ugly feet. Look at Laurie's sometime. Hell, look at Ed. Runs KT Tape along his neck and dances, though the wrong head snap could paralyze him. But we dance, Spenser. We dance and enjoy our lives despite the pain and potential for destruction because it's our way of spitting in the face of the futility and hopelessness of it all. Of *dancing* in the face of despair. The only promise of life is death. Nothing else is guaranteed. Not love, not fame, not simple courtesy. Only that one day, no matter what we do, there will be darkness and end. But the time between the spark and the curtain's close is ours to shape."

He released Spenser's hand, drew their bodies so close they were practically one, and whispered into Spenser's ear. "Your dance is beautiful. No matter what happens to you, to us, to the world—no one can take that from you."

They made love, slow and sweet, Tomás wringing an orgasm out of Spenser so complete he slept without dreaming, waking to the faint stream of sun through his curtains and the polite interruption of his alarm, telling him it was time to get up, shower, and get dressed. And go meet his mother.

Clara had set up the meeting at the coffeehouse next door to Laurie's studio. She met Spenser outside, hugging him in the parking lot. "She's inside, waiting. She's nervous. And excited."

Spenser didn't know what he was. Both of those, and several emotions that felt like tornadoes with a thousand teeth. He hugged himself, pressing his forearms against his riotous stomach. "I hope this doesn't turn out to be a terrible idea."

"If it does, I'll be over on that park bench. If you need me, you come out and get me."

Spenser drew her to him in a fierce embrace. "I love you so much, Clara. I don't know what I'd do without you."

"Hush, none of that." She patted him on the back. "Go on. The worst part will be walking in the door."

It was. The coffeehouse wasn't large, but the walk to and through the front door was the longest walk of Spenser's life. Then he rounded the corner—and there she was.

Christina Harris. Spenser's mom.

She seemed different than the last time he'd seen her. Better. Much, much better. By rights she should have appeared older, and in a way she did, but she had a brightness about her now. A sparkle. A terror too, her body rigid and trembling as she pushed away from the table, standing as if she meant to come meet him, stopping abruptly as she second-guessed herself. But unlike the last time Spenser had seen her, she was *healthy.* Her hair was shinier. Her skin had more wrinkles, but her cheeks were fuller. Eyes sharper. Clothes neater. Not fancy, but…neater. It was the first time in Spenser's memory he'd seen her take care with her appearance.

She looked like him. He was male and she female, but he saw echoes of the face that looked back at him when he gazed into his own mirror.

Mine. This woman, for better or for worse, is mine.

He closed the distance between them but stopped at his side of the table, where a cup of tea waited, bag still steeping in the water. She had the same before her. He smiled at her tentatively, keeping his hands to himself. "Hi, Mom."

She smiled back, nervous, but not tentative at all. "Hello, sweetheart. Look at you. You look so good."

"You do too." When the conversation stalled, he gestured to the table, their seats, the mugs of tea. "Do you want to sit and talk awhile?"

"I'd love to."

They sat. Spenser noticed they gripped their mugs the same way. Saw her bite her lip briefly, absently, in the same way Tomás teased him he liked to do.

She cleared her throat. "I hear you're getting married and adopting a child too. Congratulations. That's so wonderful."

"Thank you." He couldn't help himself from adding, "You know I'm marrying a man, right?"

"Yes. I knew you were gay. Gina told me, when we

met last year."

Spenser's face clouded at the mention of his middle sister. "Whatever she told you about me couldn't have been good."

"No, unfortunately. But I've been working on her, and Hannah too. I couldn't get them to vote against the amendment last fall. But they didn't vote for it. They promised me they wouldn't."

Spenser blinked. "You…lobbied them?"

"Of course I did." She cut her glance away. "I've done you wrong all my life. The least I could do was try to stop something that would harm you more."

Spenser stared at her, ears ringing. She'd lobbied his sisters for him. To stop something that would harm him.

His chin trembled, and before he could prepare himself to hold them back, silent tears fell down his face.

Christina's eyes welled up too, but whereas Spenser couldn't look away from her, she could not seem to bring herself to look at him. "I'm grateful you came to see me today because I wanted to apologize to you in person for what I've done. Technically it's one of my Steps, one long overdue, but I'd want to do this even if I weren't in AA."

She lifted her eyes then, her tears flowing freely, though she held her voice steady. "I'm sorry, Spenser. I'm so sorry for what I did to you. To our family. I'm sorry I wasn't the mother you or the girls deserved. I didn't mean to be what I turned out to be, but I was, and I hurt you, and I'm sorry. I'm sorry you grew up alone. I'm sorry you had to live so many places, with people who didn't want you. I'm glad you met Clara, but I'm sorry you had to. I'm sorry I wasn't part of your life. I would love to be a part of your life now, even a small part—but if you're not ready for that, or if you never are, that's okay too. Right now what I want you to hear is that I love you, I've always loved you, and I'm sorry for failing you."

Spenser had been frozen in place while his mother spoke, almost out-of-body, but when she finished, he became aware of himself and the world around him. Of his breathing. Of the salt of the tears on his lips. The stuffiness of his nose. The bittersweet scent of blackberry tea, of the coffee and baked goods behind the counter. The soft music playing, the scrape of chairs and whirr of the coffee grinder and the *whoosh* of the espresso machine. The muted quality of the light landing in faint, patchy squares on their table and the floor.

It was his turn to talk now. His turn in the dance. Except he didn't move across the floor, but rather along a wire. The same thin wire he'd been on for months, ever since the day he'd found Duon in front of his apartment door. Tomás was wrong. He couldn't dance on this. He could barely move without falling. And now he was supposed to reply to his mother. The woman he had hated and loved his whole life. Who he had yearned for as much as he had tried so hard not to think of her. The woman who had left the greatest ache in him, the one he knew now he could never fill.

Not without her in his life to take up the space.

He drew in a shuddering breath, feeling the wire beneath his feet shake. The world was trembling, a terrible quake of his life. He choked back a sob, but it escaped anyway. He could not stay on this wire. He could not keep this up, not for another minute. He was going to fall. Right here, in a coffeehouse full of people.

Christina sobbed too, and as if she couldn't stand it any longer, rose and came around the table to him.

Spenser let her engulf him, let the scent of her surround him, a memory so powerful it brushed him off the wire as if he were nothing but a speck of dust, sending him into the void…and directly into her arms. He wept. People were no doubt staring at them, whispering, but Spenser ignored them all. His mother—one of many, not always the best but forever the first, this one the mother of his birth, the one who had been taken from him—crouched before him, swaying him back and forth as if he were a tiny child.

"It's all right, sweetheart." She kissed his hair, pulling him tighter into her arms. "It's all right."

It was. Spenser knew enough to understand he and his mother had a great deal of work to do before they could have the kind of relationship they both dreamed of, that there were so many ways it could fall apart before then and be worse than it had ever been. But in that moment, it was good.

In that moment, in his mother's arms, Spenser Harris danced.

TOMÁS WAS GLAD the meeting had gone so well for Spenser and his mom. He listened with a smile on his face as his fiancé retold the story of the reunion, and the hope he saw in Spenser's eyes gave him hope too. Unfortunately there weren't enough good wishes in the world to bolster him for his scheduled meeting with Alisa.

He hadn't had a chance to give her a warning of what the lawyers were planning to do before she appeared in the hospital. In his defense, he hadn't been able to find her. The lawyer pointed out it was probably better this way, because the intensity of José's situation permeated more than words ever could. While this was likely true, it didn't make Tomás feel any better. It was ironic that he'd spent so much time convincing Spenser it was okay to use the lawyers to secure Duon's safety, but now that it was his family and his sister, logic felt hollow, cold, and impersonal. Nasty was how it felt, honestly. Tomás couldn't decide who he resented more, his sister, the lawyers, or the ICE workers. Though there were plenty of days where the person he hated the most was himself.

The lawyers were right though, because Alisa didn't simply agree to meet with Tomás to discuss custody, she actually showed up for the appointment. She was fifteen minutes late, but in Alisa time that was practically early. She arrived at the law office wearing a sundress too cool for the day's temperature, though it was clean and mostly professional, which Tomás knew was Alisa's way of making an effort. It moved him, so much so that when he caught her shivering, he shrugged out of his sport coat and passed it to her.

She accepted it with a small, awkward smile of thanks. "Should've brought a sweater. Didn't have time to get to the laundry, though."

Thomas resisted the urge to remind her she could have brought her laundry by the apartment. He wasn't sure that was appropriate right now. He barely understood what was. "Thank you for coming."

"How could I not?" She had the jacket on, but she still rubbed her arms, as if there wasn't enough heat in the world to warm her. Her gaze looked hollow, and for the first time in a long time Tomás thought she might not be on anything. "I can't let the ICE take Mama and Papa. I don't want to lose my babies, but I can't let our parents go."

Her words punched Tomás in the gut. He glanced at the lawyers, unsure of what he should say, but they were busy chatting with each other. Laughing at a story in a way that told Tomás they weren't discussing the Jimenez family. It was jarring, but he told himself for them this was another day at work. It made him want to always have a job where his greatest worry was getting a coffee order wrong or not having enough people to cover a shift. He never wanted to feel blasé about breaking up one part of a family to save another.

Fuck it.

Tomás turned to his sister and took her hand. "You don't have to lose the kids. Yes, you need to give them up to our parents for now, but you can still see them. We don't want to shut you out. We only want what's best for the family. That includes you."

When tears began to leak down her face, he let go of her long enough to swipe a box of tissues from a decorative stand behind their table. She accepted one and blew her nose, but the tears kept coming. "I've made such a mess of my life. I never wanted it to come to this. I keep trying to do right, but I don't know how."

So many emotions warred in Tomás. He had seen her like this before, wanting to do better. He'd watched her try and then fall. Part of him wanted to guard his heart, to push her away. He thought maybe it would be the smart thing to do. But he couldn't be smart, if that's what it came down to.

He squeezed her hand, leaning in close to cradle her head as he spoke softly into her ear. "Keep trying, Alisa. Because I won't stop believing in you."

She blew her nose again. "You get so angry with me."

"Because I want better for you. I love you. You're my sister. I'm going to want you in my life no matter how many mistakes you make."

She collapsed onto his shoulder, sobbing silently, her shoulders shaking, her voice barely a whisper. "I'm the worst mama in the world if I give up my babies."

Tomás hugged her close. "No. Giving them up this way, today? It makes you the best mama in the world. And then you're going to get clean, get your life on track, so you can be in their lives again as that great mom. Spenser and Mom and Dad and I will all help you."

She clung to him, her body easing as he rocked her back and forth. "I'm sorry I said such bad things about Spenser. About you. For leaving so much work for you. For causing so much trouble. Can you ever forgive me?"

Tomás shut his eyes and let the last of his resentment sail over the top of the conference table. "It's already done."

CHAPTER SIXTEEN

O N THE LAST day of school, Spenser resigned.

It was a strangely anticlimatic moment, since it mainly involved submitting a letter to the principal and the head of the school board. He stood at the inter-office mail boxes for ten minutes, but once it was done, he felt sad but relieved. He'd gone round and round on whether or not he wanted to resign, to see if the school would decide to overlook the fact that he was getting married to a man, but in the end he decided preempting them and going quietly would be the better way to go, not only for the sake of his resume, but for his own peace of mind and that of his family.

Nothing else much happened on that front. A few teachers expressed their regret, and several parents tried to get him to reconsider, but overall Spenser's departure from his job was quiet and uneventful. He would have thought Harvey would gloat or at least glare in triumph, but he simmered with the same disdain as ever. Spenser wondered what triumph would look like for Harvey, if it could exist at all. What would the moment be that would make Harvey gloat, or smile in victory? Was such a moment possible? Clare had always told him hate was a cancer, and in that moment, Spenser understood what she meant. Hate could never have an endgame celebration. In Spenser's absence, Harvey would simply find someone or something else to despise.

The school issue was now settled, and the Jimenez family's immigration issues were as in hand as they could be this point. His adoption of Duon was proceeding without incident and with no further challenges to their parentage. But weeks later, Spenser still couldn't get Dorothy Graves out of his thoughts.

Eventually he spoke to Vicky about it. "I can't decide if I'm projecting my own family issues onto Duon or if this is legitimately something I should try to rectify. The social worker says it might be best to wait until after the adoption, but I can't help feeling as if I'm betraying him. Or maybe I feel as if I'm betraying her." He shook his head. "I don't know. I honestly can't make sense of that anymore."

Vicky nodded, patiently letting him talk until he'd laid all his emotions on the table. "It's not an easy situation. I always would rather see families stay together. I think it's good your instinct is to keep Duon connected to his. If it helps, I know he wants to be with you and Tomás. I think if she had a better understanding that your orientation doesn't make you a threat, Dorothy would welcome your help with what for her is an unstable and unfair situation. Maybe she will in time." She sighed. "But I have to agree with the social worker. Meeting her right now isn't the best plan. It might make you feel better, but it wouldn't be good for her or Duon. You need to let her grieve, to process this in her own way. Trust the social workers to know when would be the right time. That's their job, after all." She squeezed his hand. "I'll help you too."

It sobered Spenser, made him ashamed to acknowledge this *had* been about him and his guilt, more than altruism for Dorothy. Except he did feel for her still. It was such a difficult thing, to accept giving her space was the right way to honor her. "I want to *do* something. I don't care for the way the hearing had to make her sound like a bad choice. I wish it didn't have to be that way."

"Why don't you write her a letter? Don't send it yet, but give it to the social worker, or to me. Or share it with Tomás. Work your feelings out on paper. Write as many letters as you want. Then one day, when the time is right, you can use parts of them to actually write to Dorothy, to anyone in Duon's family you like. Invite them to join *your* family the way Clara invited your mother back into yours."

Spenser wiped tears away with his fingers. "I don't know if I'm good enough a parent to be like Clara."

"You're already a good parent. And you're going to become even better." She winked at him and released his hand. "Go write your letters."

Spenser did. He got up every morning and wrote Dorothy Graves a letter. One morning he wrote his mother a letter too. He wrote his sisters letters. He wrote Tomás, and Vicky, and Ed and Laurie. He wrote Duon. He wrote Clara, and the social workers, and even the ICE workers long, heartfelt letters he never sent, missives expressing the feelings he didn't know how to share. He was fairly sure it would take him months before he had enough of it out to compose an actual letter he could give to Duon's grandmother, but every day he wrote, he felt better.

But the best day was the one when he wrote to himself. The one that, late one night, he shared with Tomás, and as his fiancé read from the laptop screen, Spenser curled into the crook of his arm and read along.

Dear Spenser Harris,

I'm writing this letter to the eight-year-old Spenser. If I could, I would send this letter to you on the day the social workers came to take you away, delivered to you on the night you spent in an emergency foster placement, all alone. I would appear in the middle of the night and hand this to you, with a flashlight so you could read it under the covers instead of crying yourself to sleep.

Little Spenser, I want you to know that everything will be all right. I know adults say this all the time, and you don't want to believe it, but I'm actually in a position to tell you and know it will become truth. Things are dark now, and they're going to be hard for a while, but they will be all right eventually. I promise.

It will take you a long time to find a home you feel safe and loved in, but you will find it. And you won't only find one. You'll find two, then three, and then more than you can count. You will get married, Little Spenser. And yes, it will be to a man, even though you can't believe that's possible right now. You'll get married to a wonderful man who wants to take care of you and love you and live a life with you.

You'll have children too. One for sure, a sweet, beautiful boy who loves to dance and who will teach you how to dance too. You hopefully will have three more children, the nieces and nephew of your husband. Maybe you'll have more children, because you're going to be a foster parent. That's right. Someday you'll be able to take in families who need help just like you did. And if I can arrange it, you'll have a great big house so if four children need a home at once, you can give it to them.

You'll have wonderful in-laws, a father-in-law who can fix anything and a mother-in-law who teaches you the secret to perfect tortillas is to pray over them. And you won't mind doing it even though you don't believe in God—you believe in Renata, and that's enough.

You'll have friends. Lots of them, but your best ones will be your husband's employer and his husband. They will also teach you to dance.

So many people will teach you to dance, Little Spenser. You'll be afraid to do it, because a lot of people will tell you that you can't, and you'll be at the front of the line of those people. But you can dance, Spenser Harris. You can dance all day long. You can look like a fool or look like an angel, and it doesn't matter, so long as you dance. Because sometimes dancing is all we have—and no one can take it from us.

Life is hard. Your life will sometimes be exceptionally difficult. But it will also be good and wonderful. You're smart and you're perfect as you are, and you will rise above all your struggles and become an amazing, strong, loving adult. You won't ever be the fanciest man on the block. But you will always be the man who has the biggest heart and the most love around him. You can't see it yet, but it's coming.

Your life will be amazing, Little Spenser. All you have to do is open your heart and let yourself enjoy the dance.

When he finished reading, Tomás closed the laptop and set it aside, pulling Spenser tighter against his body as he kissed his forehead, his cheek, his lips. "It's beautiful, Spenser. As beautiful as you."

Spenser kissed him back, stroking his face. "I love you, Tomás. Whatever happens, I love you, and I always will."

"I love you too."

Tomás kissed him again, deeper this time, shifting in the bed to cover Spenser with his body. He pushed their clothes aside, and Spenser helped him, until they were naked and twined together, dancing with one another.

TOMÁS WAS NOT prepared for how long and grueling his parents' immigration hearings would be.

The worst part was it was clear that without Oliver Thompson's thumb on the judicial scale, the proceedings would have been more drawn-out, and they would have occurred with Tomás's parents in Mexico. As it was, their "fast-track" case was heard over three two-hour hearings throughout the month of June. Whereas the string of witnesses and testimonials the lawyers had trotted out for Duon had been designed to deliver a neutron bomb, Renata and José's lawyers were putting in six times the effort just to have a prayer of getting the outcome they desired. The lawyer constantly warned them not to think anything was settled. "Anything could happen. It's going to depend on the judge and how hard the ICE feels like pushing their side of the case. We have to hope we push harder."

Push they did. The lawyer presented reams and reams of depositions and testimony citing not only Renata and José's good standing as members of the community but arguments about why they were crucial to the well-being of the children. Alisa—trembling but bold—took the stand and testified she'd terminated her rights to the children and made it clear her wish was for her parents to act in her stead while she sought drug treatment and other programs to turn her life around. The lawyers laid Tomás's tax returns for the past six years on the table, pointing out it would be impossible for him to have custody of the children and continue earning enough to care for them without the help of his parents. They did the dance of the seven veils around the issue of his upcoming marriage and adoption, arguing that was different because Duon was being adopted by Spenser, that this was quite an assumption to say Tomás and Spenser must assume care of three children in addition to their own simply because the ICE would prefer to deport their caregivers or send them into the foster care system. They brought up José's health, noting he'd have no way to support himself in Mexico and that sending him back would be a death sentence. They trotted out pictures of houses shot up with gang bullets in the town Renata and José were originally from, pointing out this was the place they'd be going back to and giving as much evidence as they could that the cartel they'd fled from would still seek retribution. They showed pictures of a roofless wreck of a house Tomás had never seen, was shocked to find out was the home his parents had lived in before they went to Arizona, a home squatting on land that did not belong to the Jimenez family. Every angle they could work, the lawyers did.

Every night, Tomás went home, curled into a ball, and wept.

Spenser was beside him every moment of the ordeal, and he, Duon, and Laurie and Ed did their best to comfort Tomás, but there was no true comfort that could come until the hearing was finished. When the arguments were over and the final hearing was set for June 26, Tomás marked the date in red on his calendar, staring at it every morning as he numbly approached his personal doomsday.

He did his best to distract himself. The May recital was long over, but Duon coaxed him to try out for the summer talent show at Halcyon, and they spent hours perfecting a pointe routine with Laurie to keep him from thinking about whether or not he was counting down to his last days with his parents. He also, along with everyone else, threw up his hands in frustration with every passing day that the Supreme Court failed to rule on DOMA.

"Can they get away without saying anything at all?" Laurie asked one day as they all sat around in the studio, glaring at a radio that had once again failed to mention the Windsor DOMA case in their list of decisions for the day.

"They can do all sorts of things." Spenser waved a hand at the radio. "They can kick it back to the lower courts. They can uphold it. They can ask Congress to adjust it."

"And they can simply strike it down," Ed pointed out.

God, but Tomás needed them to do that. He thought about it late at night, his emotions so high he couldn't sleep and had to pace the apartment. Some-times they were so much he had to go to the roof, to stand there with the night wind whipping around him, trying in vain to steal his pain.

The night before the hearing he went to the roof with intent to remain there all night long, but he only had a few minutes to himself before the access door opened and Spenser and Duon emerged to join him.

"We couldn't sleep either." Spenser came over to him and hugged his side. "We didn't want you to be alone."

Tomás hugged him back, taking Duon under his other arm when he hovered close, looking like he was trying to find a way in. Tomás cherished this part of his family even as he sent up fervent, constant prayers he didn't lose the other half. He'd spent the evening with his parents, had been tempted to stay up with them all night, but they were as tense as he was, and his mother insisted his father get sleep.

"I don't know what I'll do if they send them away," he whispered, voice breaking.

"We'll move to Texas or Arizona," Spenser said. "Get passports. We'll visit them as often as we can."

"Both those states are hot as hell and bigoted as fuck. And even if they struck down DOMA, we wouldn't be married there."

"Maybe they'll rule for marriage equality someday, and we would be. And not everyone there is a bigot. We'll find a good place. We'll make it work."

"You're just getting back with your mom. We can't leave Minnesota." He let out a shuddering sigh. "I don't *want* to leave Minnesota."

"I can fly to her. She can fly to me." Spenser took hold of Tomás's arms and looked him in the eye. "We will make this work, do you hear me? No matter what. You are my family. You and Duon and your parents and your nieces and nephew. *We will make this work.* No matter if the government says your parents can be citizens or not. No matter if they say we're married or not. No matter what, Tomás Jimenez. Do you hear me? *No matter what.* We're going to dance, like you said. *Together.*"

Tomás nodded, swallowing the thickness in his throat as best he could. Then he looked around, frowning. "Where did Duon go?"

"I don't know. He was here a second ago, I thought."

Just as Tomás was about to go look for him, the door opened again, and Duon came through it— followed by Renata, José, and the kids. "I went to get something and heard them talking. We might as well all be awake together." He held up his Bluetooth speaker over his head. "And I figured we might as well make it a party."

They did. On the rooftop of the apartment building Tomás had lived in almost his entire life, they played music, held hands, hugged each other, laughed, cried, and danced. Duon played DJ, taking requests, hunting things down when Renata and José came up with songs he didn't have. But when a MIKA song began to play, Duon took Spenser's and Tomás's hands and led them into the center of the rooftop.

"This is our song. We gonna dance the sh—*heck* out of this," he amended, glancing at the kids.

Tomás had heard this particular song before because Duon and Spenser played it all the damn time. He hadn't thought of it as *his* song before. But as the three of them laughed, held hands, and boogied down that night, the words wrapped tight around Tomás, and it did indeed become his song. They were young and strong. They were where they belonged, didn't need anyone to tell them who or where they should be. And they would be there no matter what happened. They were free. They would go on, even if they had to move forward bloody against the tide.

But they would do it as a *family*. The three of them, the five of them, the eight of them, the nine of them. Because they would be together. Always, for as long as their lives would let them.

They never slept, though the kids did curl up on a blanket Renata fetched for them. Duon played "their" song over and over, and the three of them shouted the lyrics into the night.

At four in the morning they went back downstairs, where Renata made a great feast, cooking what seemed to be everything in the house. No one looked at the suitcases packed beside the door, which would be placed in the trunk of the car, in case. No one thought about what would happen if they needed to be used. In that moment, they lived and laughed together. They told stories. They teased each other. They made dreams and promises they weren't sure they'd be able to keep.

When the time came to drive to the courthouse, they went in silence. Spenser took Duon and the kids, and Tomás drove his parents, doing them proud by not crying, by being as strong as he possibly could. In the courtroom, they sat together on a long bench, all eight of them, holding hands. Behind them sat Laurie and Ed, Ed's parents, Vicky, Oliver, his husband. Their friends and neighbors filled the room. They sat together, chests tight and souls aching, waiting to see which way the winds of fate would send them. When Alisa arrived, they brought her over too, and all of them joined hands in their seats.

The judge began to speak. Tomás held his breath, not sure what words he should be listening for. Not sure what the judge was saying.

Not until he heard *temporary green cards*, until he heard Laurie and Spenser's intake of breath, Oliver's guttural *yes* murmured behind him. Not until his mother and father began to cry, to hug each other, and him.

They were staying.

They were allowed to stay.

His family wasn't going away, and no one could threaten them with that anymore. Not ever again.

The bailiff ushered them into the hall as they became too loud, and they were only into the first round of slobbery, joyful hugs when Laurie yelped. Everyone turned to him, where he stood staring at his phone, his hand over his mouth. He looked up, his face full of shock—and wonder.

"The Supreme Court decided Windsor." He turned his phone around, hand shaking so hard he nearly dropped it. "They struck it down. 5-4. *They struck it down. DOMA is dead.*"

There was a single heartbeat of the world where they all looked at one another, eyes wide, hearts falling open. Disbelief, wonder, emotion too much for any of them to contain.

They had won. Not one thing, not two.

They had won everything.

Their joy was a force now, a tide carrying them out of the courthouse and into the street, where they hugged and laughed and cried and danced each other and even a few total strangers around, moving to music more powerful than any song. The music of their hearts. Of hope. The sound of a perfect moment, where despite the darkness, despite weariness, despair, and death, hope didn't simply survive.

On that day, *it thrived.*

CHAPTER SEVENTEEN

June 26, 2015
St. Paul, Minnesota, Union Park District

IT WAS A bright, beautiful day when the US Supreme Court decided in favor of full marriage equality.

Spenser was making breakfast with Renata and the girls, and Tomás was in the backyard with Duon, José, and Ashton, when the verdict came over the radio. Running from the house into the fresh-cut grass, Spenser and Renata shouted at the boys in the garage, but they'd had the radio on too and came to meet them. After crying and hugging each other for several minutes, they ran down the street to Annette and Dick, where they hugged and cried again.

By five o'clock that evening, Spenser and Tomás's house was teeming with friends and family and smelling like barbecue, tamales, and the best refried beans in the state of Minnesota, and probably the nation, Spenser was sure of it. Tomás and Spenser took turns giving tours of the house, proudly showing off the remodeling the family had done themselves. "Once we refinished the floors and fixed the walls, everything was easy," Spenser told his teaching partner and her husband, both who had come over with their two kids to celebrate the good news. "We finished the attic last week, and as soon as Tomás and I can move our stuff up there, we have a bedroom free for another host home guest."

"Hopefully the extra space will mean Duon stops acting like we're going to kick him out of the house just because he's graduated," Tomás volunteered from the doorway of the bedroom Spenser had stopped in. "Honey, Oliver wants to make a toast in the backyard, as soon as you're finished."

They cut the tour short, Spenser promising to finish later. But before Spenser and Tomás could get outside, the doorbell rang. "It's probably my mom and sisters." Spenser squeezed Tomás's hand. "I hope."

"Your mom told you they were coming, and she won't let them change their minds now." Tomás bussed his cheek. "It'll be fine. Don't be nervous."

"It's just that I haven't seen Gina in so long." Spenser sighed and squared his shoulders. "Okay. Let's do this."

But when they opened the front door, it wasn't Spenser's mother who stood there, or any of his sisters. It was Dorothy Graves.

She was taller than Spenser remembered. Tall and broad and stately, her bearing as regal and severe as she'd been in the courtroom years ago. She wore a coral-pink floral dress, and she held a saran-wrapped plate in her hands.

"Mrs. Graves." Spenser stood straighter, letting go of Tomás to extend his hand to her. "It's a pleasure to see you. Won't you come in?"

She didn't accept his hand, and she peered through the open doorway to the chaos of the backyard with sharp eyes. "I see I've come at a poor time. I apologize. But I wanted to thank you for the letter you sent me, and I wanted to give Duon this." She held out the tray to Tomás, giving him a stern look that said *you will take this.* "They're molasses crinkles, Duon's favorite cookie from when he was little."

Tomás accepted the tray. "Thank you so much. I'm sure he'll be thrilled to have these. But please, won't you come in? This is a family gathering, and we'd be happy to have you."

Spenser knew she would refuse before she shook her head. It was too much too fast. After all, the social worker had waited nearly two years to send the letter it had taken him four months to write. "Perhaps you can come over some other time. Or perhaps we can arrange for Duon to visit. I could fetch him now, if you like."

"I can't leave the children alone too long. They get into trouble. But if he wants to come by and visit sometime, tell him he's welcome." She lifted her chin and looked Spenser hard in the eye. "You take care of him, do you hear me?"

"I will, Mrs. Graves." Spenser inclined his head in

what became a small bow. "I will."

When Dorothy left, Tomás and Spenser went into the backyard hand in hand. Oliver stood in the center of their circle of family, smiling, visibly moved. When the crowd settled in and took up their glasses, Oliver raised his own glass and began to speak.

"This day has been decades in the making. From the riots at the Stonewall Inn to the fall of DOMA two years ago on this same date. From the dark days when discrimination and censure were so common nearly no one would lift a finger to help a queer man or woman when they were down. When we didn't even know words like *non-binary gender identity*. When we were beaten and discarded without so much as a ripple of interest from society. When we didn't dare to dream of marriage. To be sure, there is much work yet to be done. Without question there will be backlash and attempts to tear our victory from our hands."

His eyes glistened and his voice broke. "But right now, on this day, we will celebrate. Because today we are *seen*. Today we are validated. Today, with a rap of a gavel, many of the people in this gathering are legally united not only in the eyes of Minnesota and an increasingly wide number of states, but by the entire United States of America. Today the fight of ages, the dream I was laughed at for dreaming only twenty years ago, is *reality*. Celebrate *that*. Celebrate this moment. *This life*." He lifted his glass high, his voice bright and strong now. "To us."

"To us," the gathering echoed, and clinked their glasses to their neighbors, drinking down their victory.

Duon hopped up on the picnic table, holding his soda bottle high. "All right now. *Everybody dance.*"

Music played, belting at a level that would have upset the neighbors had they not already been in Spenser and Tomás's yard. Spenser put his hands up, laughing as he moved his body, uncaring how good or bad he was or who saw him. Not today. Not ever again.

His husband put his arm around him, turning him around and into his arms with a beaming grin. "Dance with me, sweetheart?"

Spenser put his arms around his husband's neck, his husband in all fifty of the United States of America. "Always."

Author's Note

When I revisited *Dance With Me* to release the second edition, I was stunned to see how much the world had changed in the three years since it was first published. Particularly in regards to marriage equality, the story I wrote had become a historical, a novel written for another time. As I realized how much would have changed for the characters in that novel as well, I had the urge to write the space between then and now, because it would have been nothing short of a wild ride.

As stories are wont to do, telling that tale drew the focus of other narrative threads until they became the novel you have just finished reading. In the same way the story's arc of marriage equality is real, so is the struggle for undocumented immigrants and for teens in foster care, particularly queer teens. I assure you not only are all the trials related in *Enjoy the Dance* real issues, they sadly rarely have the happy ending I was able to author for them here.

Happily you, dear reader, are in a position to help change that.

To start, by purchasing this book you've made a donation to Avenues for Homeless Youth, an organization mentioned in this book (and in many others) which also happens to exist in real life, and Youth Standing Strong, a similar organization in my hometown. I make a monthly contribution to both these organizations, and your purchase means I can make my donation that much larger. You will also be contributing directly to a real-life Duon, whose savings account will increase with every royalty check I receive from this book.

But you can do so much more. Precious few of us are Oliver Thompson, but we still have a great deal of power. One simple but resonant action you can take is to vote. This book is being published in a US Presidential election year, but no matter where you are in the world, no matter what year it is, you can remember that the characters in this novel are all representations of real-life people all around you, and you can use your vote to help them. In local, state, and national elections, in your province or village, in whatever jurisdiction you reside. Learn the positions the candidates have on LGBT rights, on immigration, on the support for youth in foster care—then vote for the people you believe will effect change.

You can also help in direct ways. You can donate to Avenues for Homeless Youth or YSS or whatever similar organization exists near you. You can volunteer for these organizations too, and if it's right for you and your family, you can be a host home or you can apply to be a foster family and say you want your priority to be LGBT teens, particularly teens of color. You can rally for undocumented immigrants, particularly children. You can seek out local resources for that population and give them the help they need, or if no such support exists, you can create it.

I keep a list of organizations needing your help on my website. If you know of some I haven't listed, send the information to assist@heidicullinan.com. Additionally, if you want to learn more about LGBT homeless youth and how you can help, please check out Ryan Berg's *No House to Call My Home,* available everywhere books are sold.

About the Author

Heidi Cullinan has always enjoyed a good love story, provided it has a happy ending. Proud to be from the first Midwestern state with full marriage equality, Heidi is a vocal advocate for LGBT rights. She writes positive-outcome romances for LGBT characters struggling against insurmountable odds because she believes there's no such thing as too much happy ever after. When Heidi isn't writing, she enjoys cooking, reading, playing with her cats, and watching television with her family. Find out more about Heidi at heidicullinan.com.

Want to make sure you never miss any books by Heidi Cullinan? Sign up for the release-announcement-only newsletter.

Did you know several of the characters in this book exist in other books?

Ed and Laurie appear in Book 1 of the Dancing series, *Dance With Me*. They also cameo in *Lonely Hearts* and *Short Stay* in the Love Lessons series.

Were you worried about poor **Marcus** and his broken heart? Read *Let It Snow*, book one of the Minnesota Christmas series, to find out how another Twin Cities resident leads him into love.

THE DANCING SERIES
Dance With Me (also available in French)
Enjoy the Dance
Burn the Floor (coming soon)

Sometimes life requires a partner.

Ed Maurer has bounced back, more or less, from the neck injury that permanently benched his semipro football career. He hates his soul-killing office job, but he loves volunteering at a local community center. The only fly in his ointment is the dance instructor, Laurie Parker, who can't seem to stay out of his way.

Laurie was once one of the most celebrated ballet dancers in the world, but now he volunteers at Halcyon Center to avoid his society mother's machinations. It would be a perfect escape, except for the oaf of a football player cutting him glares from across the room.

When Laurie has a ballroom dancing emergency and Ed stands in as his partner, their perceptions of each other turn upside down. Dancing leads to friendship, being friends leads to becoming lovers, but most important of all, their partnership shows them how to heal the pain of their pasts. Because with every turn across the floor, Ed and Laurie realize the only escape from their personal demons is to keep dancing—together.

Other Books by Heidi Cullinan

LOVE LESSONS SERIES

Love Lessons (also available in German)
Fever Pitch (also available in German)
Lonely Hearts (also available in German)
Short Stay
Rebel Heart (coming 2017)

THE ROOSEVELT SERIES

Carry the Ocean
Shelter the Sea (coming 2017)
Unleash the Earth (coming soon)

CLOCKWORK LOVE SERIES

Clockwork Heart
Clockwork Pirate (coming soon)
Clockwork Princess (coming soon)

SPECIAL DELIVERY SERIES

Special Delivery (also available in German)
Double Blind (also available in German)
Tough Love

MINNESOTA CHRISTMAS SERIES

Let It Snow
Sleigh Ride
Winter Wonderland

TUCKER SPRINGS SERIES
Second Hand (written with Marie Sexton)
(available in French)
Dirty Laundry (available in French)
(more titles in this series by other authors)

SINGLE TITLES
Nowhere Ranch (available in Italian)
The Devil Will Do
Hero
Miles and the Magic Flute
Family Man (written with Marie Sexton)
A Private Gentleman

NONFICTION
Your A Game: Winning Promo for Genre Fiction
(written with Damon Suede)